1/08 ✓

WIT

[LADY

FIRST]

[LADY FIRST]

Relentless Aaron

ST. MARTIN'S GRIFFIN ❧ NEW YORK

LADY FIRST. Copyright © 2007 by Relentless Aaron. All rights reserved. Printed in the United States of America.
No part of this book may be used or reproduced in any manner whatsoever without written permission except in the case of brief quotations embodied in critical articles or reviews. For information, address St. Martin's Press, 175 Fifth Avenue, New York, N.Y. 10010.

www.stmartins.com

Library of Congress Cataloging-in-Publication Data

Relentless Aaron.
    Lady first / Relentless Aaron.—1st ed.
        p.   cm.
    ISBN-13: 978-0-312-35936-2
    ISBN-10: 0-312-35936-5
    1. African Americans—Fiction.   2. Stamford (Conn.)—
Fiction.   I. Title.
    PS3618.E57277L33 2007
    813'.6—dc22

                                            2007024547

First Edition: November 2007

10 9 8 7 6 5 4 3 2 1

*Dedicated to my brethren at
Fort Dix and every lockup
throughout the world.
Pursue your greatness regardless of
your circumstances.*

ACKNOWLEDGMENTS

I'd like to acknowledge all the many authors and publishers who have embraced me and encouraged me from day one. And to all those others who have nothing but ill will toward me, I thank you as well. Maybe one day you'll change your thinking, and you'll devote all that good energy toward writing a relevant, entertaining, and informative book or two, or ten.

In the meantime, to all you readers and supporters who have fueled my rise to greatness: thank you for being savvy and for securing my positioning with your hard-earned dollars. Your dollars are but votes that have put me in the world's biggest publications, as well as winning me awards to acknowledge my value in a very cluttered industry. Thank you, because it wasn't just my talent, but also your level of awareness.

Very Truly Yours,
Relentless

[LADY FIRST]

[PROLOGUE]

EIGHT YEARS AGO I hooked up with this older woman. She was an attractive, talented, and (once upon a time) a famous actress. She was also loaded, and lived on an estate in a rich area of Connecticut. But along with the wealth, the good food, and the raunchy sex came a world of drama. And now that I look back at things I'm thinking that it was all a twisted mess I could've avoided. Thing is, if I had to do it all over again . . . Absolutely.

[O N E]

I WAS RAISED in South Stamford, Connecticut. Far enough away from downtown Stamford that we couldn't hear the continuous construction of buildings, yet close enough to see it grow before our very own eyes. Watching tall glass buildings rise downtown was something like watching a flower grow. You see it sprout one day, and before you know it, *Wow!* The damned thing is in full bloom. But no matter how wonderfully my city is growing, something about it has always seemed so unobtainable. And so out of reach to someone with little means.

My side of town is the pits. Dull as the desert. It's the kind of place that doesn't encourage big dreams, only the priority of getting by or getting over. My pop is in sanitation; at least that's what *he* calls it. I say he's been a goddamned garbage man for as long as I can remember. Mom was always home taking care of me and my brother, Troy. By the time we were old enough to talk back, to curse, or to sneak and peek at girlie magazines, Mom started taking care of the neighbors' kids. When she wasn't doing that she was doing hair, running a raggedy at-home beauty salon. But all that shit did was chase me and Troy out of the house. The smell of chemicals and soiled baby diapers is a mix that should be labeled as toxic by somebody, somewhere, somehow.

Our neighborhood couldn't be called a neighborhood like the ones with newspaper boys, ice cream trucks, and folks walkin' their dogs. Newspaper boys would get robbed if they were to come down Dakota Street. So would the ice cream truck, which was why the vendor always parked his shit blocks away where a cop could be expected to drive by. And we had our share of dogs. But they weren't considered pets. Just like the stray cats, the rats that scurried around the alleys, and the mice and roaches that called our house their home, dogs were just as much a nuisance as the rodents and insects.

A lot of times me and Troy would find something to do, for lack of community programs. We'd go by the park and join in with other kids from around our way, playing dodge ball, wiffle ball, or hide-and-seek. When that got played out, we tried the big boys' games like basketball, spades, or smoking. Lucky for me the smoking thing never stuck. That first try was a shock to my lungs and the coughing that went with it was the kind that hurt, not like a response to an itch in my throat, but some real hurting cough.

Besides those limited activities, there were a big variety of girls around us all the time, like we were popular or some shit. But that never mattered. Jody, Faydra, and Patti were the "it girls" on our block, but I think Troy and I had our overdose of female odors to the point of nausea on account of that funk that hung in the air whenever Mom had more than six or seven females in our living room for any extended period of time. Fish, feet, and fur. Euchh!

Being turned off by girls pushed us into other endeavors. We quickly learned that there wasn't much you could do without money, so we got odd jobs. That's what started to separate us. Troy was lucky. He got a job at the local Kentucky Fried Chicken. First they had him sweeping. Then he was cleaning tables. One day I knew he'd be working cash register, maybe do me a hook-up here and there.

I could never figure out why they picked Troy over me. Like we're not cut from the same cloth. The chicken spot was the only big business within ten blocks in either direction of Dakota Street. Other than that, Mr. Jay's was our corner grocery store. The Right Look was the beauty salon next door, and there was a small tavern next to that. Everything else was a hustle. Collecting soda cans and newspapers to cash in at the recycling plant. Shoveling snow in the winters. Raking leaves or sweeping sidewalks in the off seasons. I had it hard until I ventured to take a bus downtown. It seemed the more I soldiered into downtown Stamford, the more I caught wind of opportunities. I got turned down for dozens of jobs. But the one I did get, I kept.

Waldbaum's took me in like a son. I was thirteen when they let me hustle, carrying groceries to cars and retrieving carts, making sure the parking lot was kept clean. But by the time my voice began to change and pubic hairs began to weed up around my skinny twig, the store manager gave me a job inside. From running between cashiers and packing brown shopping bags, I was then promoted to stock boy. I had my own uniform now. It wasn't shit but a green apron; to me it was someone accepting Spencer Lewis as part of a team.

I began to make a name for myself at Waldbaum's. All day long someone was calling "Spencer" over the store's P.A. system. And like a jackrabbit—or jackass—I'd show up within the blink of an eye. No matter if it was to retrieve a price for an unmarked item, or if it was to replace the item a customer selected that was damaged, it was Spencer to the rescue. Whether or not it was a superior attitude, I can't say. But I do know I had a heap of energy to work with.

It was after high school graduation that things became a little more serious than a hustle. A lot more critical than the few hundred dollars a week I was paid.

It was Troy's words that caught me off guard. He said, "Well, Spencer, I guess it's me on the south side and you uptown. I'll hold it down in the fast food department while you keep it nutritious with Waldbaum's."

The way he said that shit—how I was supposed to maintain my job for, what, *forever?*—that was pushing it. If we weren't drinking and celebrating my eighteenth birthday I'd have had a lot more to say. But the Bacardi had a heavy foot on my senses, and we were only talkin' shit besides. I just let it go.

However, the weeks and months passed, as did any hope of me going to college. For me, college was just as unobtainable as the glass structures in Stamford. Tuition, fees, room, and board—blah, blah, blah. I heard enough horror stories of dreams-gone-foul to wanna take a shortcut. Somehow. A shortcut.

It looked like everybody else was getting shortcuts. How

many big-name celebrities told the god's-honest-truth about dropping out of school to pursue their dreams? How many basketball players got multimillion-dollar contracts as soon as they left high school? Sure, I wasn't a baller or a rap star—not even close. But I figured since I had the almighty diploma, something many couldn't claim, I might've had a better shot at the big time than others who didn't have it. Maybe. So I stayed where I was.

I watched Jody, one of Dakota Street's "it girls," blossom as the years went by, and we even went to the school prom together.

What a waste of money, $500 for my tuxedo, a long limo, and a night at Tipton's Dance Club, all for what? To hear her tell me, "Don't expect anything tonight." Go on; just pop a guy's bubble! Couldn't she even let me hold on to some hope through the engagement, instead of stomping out my fantasy before the night began?

Even before I handed my invitation to the ladies at the reception table I wanted to take Miss Thang home. Jody, the bitch.

However, as they always said, where one door closes, another one opens.

I never planned to go back to work the next day, expecting to be bangin' Jody all night and until the cops came knockin' at our motel door. But being as how I was sober and so full of unspent energy, I went to work anyway.

I happened to be rotating the cheese in the dairy department, pulling the nearly outdated cheeses up front so that they'd be selected before all else. It was the same with the milk, the juice, and the meats as well.

I noticed a yellow-boned cutie down the way, picking

through loaves of bread. When one dropped and when she bent down to pick it up, an outrageous tear was born down the back of her skirt. She had one of those jobs that hugged her thighs enough to hide her behind. It was black with pink and blue flowers printed all over. She also had a soft white button-down sweater top that showed off her cheerleader's body. Nobody else was around to hear the rip or to see how the woman's ass was showing, but she was embarrassed just as if there were hordes of shoppers.

I hurried over to the woman's aid. I took off my apron and hooked it around her waist before she even knew what was happening.

"I can't go around like *this*," she said after melting out of her stupor.

"I could call you a cab . . . uh . . . maybe you could wait in the office till they come." She let out a frustrated growl, a sound a threatened cat might make. "Or . . . where do you stay at?"

"I'm at the Ramada."

"The Ramada?" I couldn't imagine why a girl—what was she, eighteen?—would be staying at the Ramada. Shouldn't she be away at school or something? Maybe showing off her body at a dance rehearsal or the beach?

Maybe she read my mind. She said, "I'm here with my dad. He's a CEO at First Insurance . . ."

I shook my head, saying no explanation was necessary— lying—and offered her a ride to the Ramada.

"If you wouldn't mind," she replied.

I ushered her through the back of the market and out to the employee parking area.

"Just a minute," I told her after I seated her in the used Volvo I bought months earlier. It was nothing to be flashy about, but it did the job. "I gotta let my boss know. Be right back."

Like a jackrabbit, I hurried in and informed the day manager. I got a grateful smile in return, and was back to the woman within record time.

"I'm Spencer," I said, offering my handshake.

"Roxy," she replied. "I . . ." She chuckled and spoke simultaneously. "I feel like a complete fool."

"Don't. Coulda happened to anybody," I said, trying to console her.

On the way to the hotel, Roxy explained how her father had her there in Stamford for the weekend. He'd be working. She'd be shopping while he was working. However, they intended on spending Saturday and Sunday as father and daughter, an occasion that Roxy thought should be more often than not.

"So that's how you do this? You stay in the hotel instead of with him?" I asked.

"A little agreement we have . . . to give each other space. But also . . . I don't quite get along with his girlfriend."

"Ah-ha!" I said, tryin' to put some energy into our acquaintance. "So the truth comes out."

Roxy smirked and directed me through the parking garage where she could slip through some glass doors into the hotel's underground entrance.

"Thanks a lot for the lift. You're a lifesaver." Her eyes matched her smile. Roxy hopped out and leaned in the window. "What about the apron?"

"Oh, that. You can . . ." I was gonna tell her to toss it, knowing that it wasn't a big deal. "Wanna bring it next time you shop?" I said, hoping for continuation. Roxy's face sought an answer.

"Wanna come up?"

"You sure?" Her father came to mind.

"Room three-one-five," she said and turned off for the entrance.

I didn't know how to feel. In one way I felt like this was an opportunity. In another, I was nervous as shit. Spencer the virgin at eighteen.

I parked and made the short journey to the third floor, half expecting the apron to be wedged around the doorknob or otherwise out in the hallway. But there was nothing close to my imagination.

Roxy and I made small talk. She spoke on her life and commuting between divorced parents. I spoke on Stamford and how we had more than one movie theater, night club, and shopping mall. One thing led to another and we were making the most of a conveniently isolated situation. Roxy was lonely and impulsive, and I was inexperienced and still horny from my prom-night letdown. I still had the condom in my wallet with Jody's name on it.

We submerged ourselves in foreplay. Me becoming familiar with a woman's body for the first time, her surrendering to my progressions with her innocent sighs and whimpers. Jesus, I didn't even know this girl's last name and I was pushing inside of her like my life depended on it. Like it was my birthday or something. When it was over there was guilt and shame fighting the silence in that hotel room. Meanwhile, Roxy's scratch marks on my back and a sperm-filled rubber were the only memories, outside of some incredible explosion, that I can recall about the day after the prom.

THEY SAID when it rains it pours, and when it did it was probably in relation to the summer months following my high school graduation.

I was bagging groceries, as I did my best, when I recognized a celebrity in the checkout line next to where I was working.

"Lemme switch with you, Stevie," I said to the coworker at the edge of the neighboring checkout line.

"No prob, dude. What's the hurry? Ain't no cuties over here."

"No biggie," I said. "Just tryin' to break up the monotony."

"I feel ya'," Stevie said, one of the coolest white boys I know.

I tried to figure out what TV show I'd seen the woman on, her Hollywood features just only hinting at age and her hair swept up in a motherly do. I didn't want to be so obvious so I avoided any extreme eye contact. Two customers were already asking for autographs. Phyllis? Lynn? Felicia? Yes! Felicia! She's that woman from—. My thoughts were interrupted. I had already packed up two of the woman's packages when she said, "Pardon me? Do you think you could help me carry the groceries to my car?" I was startled by the mere command of her voice. Her diction so precise and articulate.

"Oh, ah, sure. N-no problem," I replied, wanting to kick myself for being so nervous.

We have those state-of-the-art shopping carts at Waldbaum's and they couldn't get past the iron stations, poles really, that demarked the walkway out in front of the store from the parking lot. If not for those barriers, carriages would be all over the lot. As it was, some customers got creative and lifted shopping carts over the poles just for convenience. I never got that; how they'd bust their ass to labor the cart over the barriers for the wee bit of comfort . . . that cart-to-car ease. Some people just can't help being lazy. When I got outside the woman had me wait until she pulled the car up to the storefront. I couldn't help deciding whether to admire her good looks in that sundress or to think she was old enough to be my mother. I shook off the thoughts once the green Jaguar crawled to a stop at the curb. I immediately figured her to be caked-up from all of her years in entertainment. I thought of her husband as a lucky stiff.

"I've seen you around here before," she said as I loaded the groceries in her trunk. "They keep you mighty busy."

"Yes, ma'am, they do. It's been almost five years now." I found myself confiding in her as I would an aunt or a friend of my mother's.

"So what's next?" All manner of perfect diction thickening her voice.

"Next?" I asked, shutting the hood of the trunk.

"Surely you don't plan on working here for the rest of your life."

"Whoa! You sure we haven't spoken before? My brother and I were just . . . oh never mind. No . . . actually, I'm not sure yet where I wanna go or what I wanna do, but—you're right—I don't want to be *here* forever." She listened to me and sized me up, too.

"You think you could give me a call?" she asked as I did the gentlemanly bit, closing her in the car. "I could use . . . may I rephrase that? I believe you could prove to be a valuable contribution to my . . . to my routine."

"I guess I could call. Sure, that's not a big deal."

She jotted down her name and phone number on the inside of a matchbook. It was only in that idle moment that I realized she smoked. I peeped a cigarette butt in the well of an ashtray.

"Mrs. Stern," I read out loud. "Sure. I'll give you a call."

"You wouldn't lie to a lady, would you?"

"I wouldn't lie to myself, Mrs. Stern."

"Thank you. And, uh . . . I'll be sure to make it worth your while."

She put on some tinted glasses as a pro, breezing away from Waldbaum's like some kind of pipe dream. The way the woman winked at me was—how can I explain it?—promising.

[T W O]

THE CAPE OF Stamford was an area I'd never seen in my life. Eighteen years in Stamford and I missed *this*, these sprawling properties with custom landscapes and prime country homes. This was a community that at first seemed to be private, but in fact was just suburban and tranquil with here-and-there breathtaking views of the Long Island Sound. I couldn't imagine any of the homes having any less than five or six bedrooms.

Mrs. Stern didn't say much on the phone when I called, just that she had work that would be more rewarding than where I was presently employed. More important, she said she'd double whatever Waldbaum's was paying.

I pretended to be nonchalant about it, but in truth I couldn't wait to get off of the phone and mount my rocket—my secondhand Volvo—and blast off to wherever she was. It didn't matter if the woman lived on the moon; I'd be there in my usual lightning speed.

"Oh yeah," she said when she opened one of two

decorative doors that made the entrance to her home nothing but stately. "I almost forgot."

"Is it a bad time? I can always . . ."

"No, no, no, come on in. That's what I get for piling so much on my plate, really."

I stepped past the Mrs. into the entryway that led on to a dramatic, spacious living room. There were a lot of tall, ceiling-to-floor windows that gave the home a see-through effect. I wasn't sure that it was okay to walk on the carpet with its colorful flowers; it looked like it could've been handmade, maybe requiring special attention. But that concern diminished when the Mrs. said, "Take off your shoes. That's the rule around here." And without saying so, I could see why.

I followed her under a brilliant chandelier that was sparkling enough to be made of diamonds, yet massive enough to crush me if it ever fell. A moment more of stunning walls, floors, and ceilings brought me into a den with long and short jumbo, camel-colored leather couches. Some daylight filtered past a voluminous indoor tree, casting a modest effect about the mud-toned walls, the fireplace, and the short circular coffee table, its glass top accessorized with a small bronze statue of an opera singer. There was also a law book there at the center that must've been dipped in shellac. A candle sat on top of that.

"Have a seat," she said, indicating the long couch. She sat on the short one that faced me on an angle. She crossed her right leg over the chin of her left and cupped her hands on her skirted knee. "Were you able to get the day off?"

"Oh yeah. That was a cinch. I've done so much for that store; they couldn't turn me down for much of anything if I ask."

"Dependable, are you?"

"Very."

"Loyal?"

"Extremely."

"And yet, you'd leave at the drop of a dime."

"Well . . . I didn't say that, ma'am."

"Mrs. Stern. Please."

"Yes. Mrs. Stern. I'd have to give them some kind of notice, ya know? It's only right."

"No matter what the offer."

"I—I've gotta let my boss know, Mrs. Stern." I was trying to get comfortable with calling a black woman Mrs. Stern. It just didn't seem to fit. A Mrs. Williams, Mrs. Jones, or Mrs. Brown, okay. But Mrs. Stern took a lot to digest, obviously being a white family name. It was clear to me that she married into it.

"Relax, Spencer. I was merely testing you. Because what you'd do to your present employer you'd no doubt do to future employers. You understand."

"Oh." I smiled in relief, still stuck on the thought of being tested. "Nice place," I said, hoping to change the subject.

"Yes it is, isn't it? The curse of fame and fortune."

"I meant to ask you, weren't you Mrs.—"

"Young man, I'm warning you, if you're just another crazed fanatic you might as well leave here this moment."

"No-no, I . . ."

"Let me tell you something before this goes any further. I'm not a happy woman. Every time I step out of this house I'm under the public's microscope, telescope, and every other kind of scope. It's a burden. It's a hassle. And quite frankly, it can be a downright pain in the ass sometimes."

"But you were so popular. You still *are* popular. I saw those people's faces light up when you were shopping the other day, like you were . . ."

"I know, I know. Like I was their mother, I hear that all the time. All day, every day. Shit. Sometimes a woman wants to breathe."

I was a stone. Here was one of the greatest TV moms cursing right in front of me. It was like someone hollered, REALITY CHECK! "You wanna know the bottom line? I couldn't get an acting job if my life depended on it. The last three scripts I got were all mother or grandmother roles. Next to zero pay. Never a leading role. You are looking at the end of the rope for a black woman in Hollywood. They wanted me to do the Vegas thing, like Lena, like Diahann, like Pearl and Josephine did. But I was never a dancer or singer like those girls. I'm an actress. A dried-up, out-dated . . ."

Mrs. Stern seemed to deflate right there in front of me. Like a balloon that's been punctured, or like the exhaust of a steam engine at the end of its run.

"It's alright, Mrs. Stern. It's gonna be alright," I said, half wanting to hustle over to hug her. "You seem to be doing well for yourself. And you don't owe any excuses to anybody for your life or your decisions."

"Thank you," she said with the tissue to her eyes. I wanted to hear her proposal as much as I wanted to breathe clean air, but I could see and hear that she was going through some emotions at the moment.

"Is that Mister Stern?" I asked, looking at the portrait over the mantle.

"His name is David. Can you tell?"

"Just a guess," I replied. The man was bespeckled with a white mustache and was bald except for the half-moon of white hair circling his head from one temple to the other. "But like I said, you don't owe any excuses."

"But you're curious, aren't you? You want to know why a black woman such as myself . . ."

"A *beautiful* black woman, ma'am."

"Well, thank you, Spencer. That's sweet of you."

"If you're asking about my curiosity, I guess. I mean, you're attractive enough to have any man you want in the world. I mean, shoot, if I was twenty years older—"

"Oh, don't flatter me, Spencer. So full of compliments, you are. Well, the truth is that I needed security. Every woman does. You understand?"

"Sure," I lied. I snuck a peek back at David, then at the Mrs. I couldn't help wondering how those two made out in bed. The thought made my stomach queasy, too.

"I'm sorry to be so negligent. Can I get you something to drink? Do you drink?"

"Another test?"

She chuckled. It was that deep, hearty chuckle I remembered from the sitcom. Mrs. Stern rose up from the couch, her true shape showing against the fabric of her blouse as she did. I told myself that I was right. David Stern, the lucky stiff.

"How about some cider? Won't you join me?"

I followed her through a dimly lit hallway, its carpeting just as detailed as the last, wall hangings that would befit a Manhattan art gallery.

"So what's he do?"

"You mean his Royal Highness? He's a chief judge for the district court downtown. Too stubborn to retire and too old to do anything else."

I took her statement and tone of voice to be a stab of some kind, but I didn't venture to read any deeper into it.

"So, you seem to have that security you spoke on," I said, immediately sucked into the state-of-the-art kitchen, a mixture of pine-wooded cabinetry and stainless steel appliances. The kitchen seemed large enough for a small staff to operate, yet intimate enough for a simple home-cooked meal. "This house is like out of a fairy tale," I told her. But back home I'd say she was livin' large.

"Perhaps. But it's a lot for me to manage, which is why I called you over—"

I thought she'd never bring it up.

"I need a personal assistant. We call it a nurturing confidant."

I was silent.

"I need someone to handle the common things in life. The things I tend to forget from time to time. Even things like grocery shopping or light housekeeping . . ." I wandered why she didn't have a maid. "We have a cleaning lady who comes by three times a week—I'm not comfortable with any live-ins, you see . . ." I exhaled when I heard those words, elated that she didn't need me to clean windows and toilets anytime soon. "But . . . it's just a whole bunch of things, Spencer. Call me finicky . . . say I have whims, but . . . well, that's the job. Are you interested?"

The way she finished saying what she had to say had a frustrated tone to it. Like all of that was just bottled up inside of her until now, and I could take it or leave it. It didn't matter to her. Maybe she felt like she divulged too much of herself too soon. To tell the truth, it felt that way. But I liked her honesty. So I figured, let me be honest with her.

"How much are we talkin'?" I was almost afraid to ask.

She chuckled again and said, "I assure you, Spencer, I've got a deal that you won't refuse."

I was thinking that the saying went: I've got a deal you *can't* refuse. What the hell was she offering?

"Whew. Well, gee—I . . . can I sleep on it?"

"You can. Tomorrow. However, *today* I'd like to have you do a trial run for me."

"A trial run?"

"Correct." She reached under her blouse and took out a few bills that were snug beneath her bra. "How much do you make a week? Three hundred?" She was almost right, but I was too focused to argue. "Here's six. And this is only for today. Now . . . can you perform for me?"

"Uh-y-ah . . . shoot, Mrs. Stern, perform? I'll do a dance if you want." Why did I open my mouth?

THE MOMENT Mrs. Stern said "Come with me," I was her captive slave. "Now this wouldn't necessarily mean you'd be doing this kind of work for me, nor that you'd be doing it all of the time, I just want to see your, how should I say, work ethics." I ignored the devilish glimmer in her eye.

"You got it, ma'am. Your every wish is my command," I blurted, already spending the $600 in my pocket on a brake job, two new pairs of jeans, and the Nikes I saw in a *GQ* magazine.

"Let's start with my shoes," she said, taking the half-finished glass of cider from my hand. As I followed her up a long winding flight of steps, past a number of doorways, to the end of a hallway where the master bedroom was, I tried to put in proper perspective her smooth gait, her curves giving themselves to her soft bounce as she swayed ahead of me, some kind of femme-phenomenon. She slid a closet door open while I took a brief look around. Wrought-iron canopy bed. Some Arabian nights–like drawstring curtains that were heavy just to look at. Two matching candleholders, wrought iron like the bed, were positioned to each side of Mrs. Stern's framed picture—all of it up on the mantel above a six-foot-wide fireplace. There were accent lights set in the ceiling casting low-wattage glows on Egyptian artwork. The sand color of the walls and ceiling blended well with the stained-wood flooring.

"I want you to take these shoes out. We're gonna dust them down, brush them where necessary, and replace them in the order that they're in now. You must be careful with my Dolce & Gabbana's, the Valentino's as well."

I didn't have the slightest idea which of the dozens of shoes she was referring to, I just nodded in agreement. As I stepped past her I couldn't help taking in the jazzy, sweet fragrance. It was an essence that hung there in my senses for the entire shoe-moving project.

I counted forty-two pairs of shoes, some still in their original boxes and never worn. Some were sequined and others were the plainest stilettos that I'd ever seen. But I told myself that I had better get familiar with all this expensive stuff if I'd be working for this woman. Dolce & Gabbana. Pierre Cardin. Valentino. For a time I thought I was alone to complete the task, until I sensed Mrs. Stern's presence behind me. And then she spoke.

"This'll be good for you to familiarize yourself with my wardrobe . . . so this way, if I need you to grab a certain pair of shoes for me, you'll know exactly what I'm speaking of . . ."

Messages were skipping around in my head; *a wardrobe boy?* Getting her shoes? And I was *already* dusting them. But all of that was far outweighed by the $600 she offered me.

"All done," I said after an hour and a half of shoe orientation. "Now I see why you needed help. That was no small job." I said this with the idea of leaving. Washing up.

"Well, you did such a good job, Spencer. Now come with me to the master bath, would you?"

I tailed her through a short corridor, about to sneeze from the dust in my nostrils and on my clothes. Now we were facing a red sunken whirlpool tub.

"I'm big on taking bubble baths in the Jacuzzi, except the damned thing gets such a buildup sometimes."

"A buildup? I don't—"

"See the sides here? There's a faint ring that needs to come off. I like my Jacuzzi to glisten, ya know? Otherwise I just don't feel clean." She made a face. Grimy.

"I . . . see . . . what you mean. Would you like me to—?"

"Would you? I'd *so* appreciate it. The cleaning supplies are down under the sink. Don't use scouring powder, only Tilex, alright? Call me when you're done."

Her voice had a singsong tone to it. That whole life-is-grand aura. Again, her fragrance was left behind. I took a deep breath and attacked the job. At least I could say I'd been in a Jacuzzi for the first time, even if it *was* only to clean it. The Tilex made the job seem like a breeze. I almost felt guilty for frowning at the thought of cleaning the Jacuzzi and took the bleach fumes as a sort of admonishment for my misbehavior.

After twenty minutes of that I turned to find the Mrs. again, standing behind me as an overseer. Or was she enjoying this? No matter. I was just happy to be done with the work. It was only afternoon, and if I hurried I could drop the car off for the brake job—pick it up in the morning. Maybe I'd even stop by the Stamford Mall to buy my jeans, too.

"A quickie, huh?"

"Yeah, actually . . . your Jacuzzi, ma'am . . ." I took a bow. "Good as new. You should feel real good taking your bubble baths now."

"Indeed," she smiled.

I took a deep breath, a slight stretch with it. I said, "Now if there's nothing else . . ."

"Actually, there is . . . unless . . . you're *tired*," she said with her doubtful eyes. I'd seen those eyes on television once, not the least bit threatening now as they were then. But I respected her expression nonetheless.

"Oh . . . ah, well . . . ," I stammered, not wanting to let her down, but not wanting to commit either.

"Tell you what . . . hang with me a little while longer and . . ." She was inside of her bra again. "I'll toss in another two hundred. That's an eight-hundred-dollar day." There she went with the singsong voice again.

"Hey . . . whatever you say, ma'am."

She sucked her teeth. "The way you say that . . . Mrs. Stern. *Ma'am* makes me feel so old. It's haunting, really."

"I—"

"I asked for it, huh? Tell you what; seeing as how things appear to be going so well between you and me, why don't you call me Tia. That alright with you?"

I nodded, something I was already very used to doing.

"Alright then, Spencer. Mister Eight-hundred-dollar Man, *folley-me*. And bring your sneakers." What was she, Irish now?

I went along with Tia, observing more and more of her home as the seconds passed. High ceilings. A corridor here and there. Built-in closets and bookcases that were designed in fine carved wood. One room had pink marble floors and white stucco walls. Another room was muted with shades of burgundy, beige, and cream. House plants and trees were everywhere. Eventually we reached the formal dining room with its sliding glass doors that led out to a sun terrace, a courtyard, and a swimming pool. From the patio I could take in a panoramic view of the grounds with its manicured maze of box hedges, some kind of fruit trees, and two huge gardens where there wasn't grass. I sucked in air like it was precious and enriching, more so than any anywhere else I'd ever been. It felt like I was inhaling a slice of Heaven.

"This," she paused for the drama, "is my garden. It's so beautiful in June, wouldn't you agree?"

"Absolutely. I've never seen anything like it."

"No? You must not read *Town & Country*."

"What's that?"

"It's a . . . oh never mind. After all, you *are* from the ghetto."

Her words sent a shot to my heart that I would've otherwise responded to—and it wouldn't have been nice either—but Tia touched her hand to my cheek. It was a compassionate touch, as was her smile. I felt a bizarre tug at my senses, like a puppeteer was towering over me. Her touch melted me. "Now here's what we're gonna do," she went on.

We? Shit, lady, doesn't your "we" mean "me"? I ain't seen you get down and spit-shine shoes or scrub the tub!

"Run over to the shed and find the long pole. It looks like a giant fly swatter, but it's actually for the pool."

I finished lacing up my sneakers and I did as she asked, trotting back to Tia like a soldier armed for battle.

"Now we're going to sweep the pool for the things that don't belong there . . . like that, see it?"

I squinted.

"There."

I leaned in. "You mean the dead bee?"

"*Exactly.* If you look closely you'll see a lot of those . . . and flies, and moths . . . *ecchh!* I can't stand swimming with insects. And, oh . . . see over there?"

Tia was close to me, her arm brushing against mine. I could smell that incredible fragrance again. It was something that penetrated my soul. I leaned further to see what she pointed to. That's when I felt her hand. She popped me on the ass, much like the basketball players do after a hell-of-a-shot scored. I jumped, jerking my neck abruptly, ending up in the pool. *In the pool!*

The lady was standing at poolside cracking up. I mean, *really cracking up!* And she was pointing to me like I was some sideshow freak. I didn't know what to think. As I made breast strokes to the edge of the patio, I tried real damned hard to maintain some kind of sanity, but I swear I wanted to slap the shit out of that bitch.

Laughing like Mrs. Santa Claus, Tia said, "You look so handsome when you're wet! *Mmmm . . .*" She said that like I was about to be a good meal. "Well, at least now I know you can take a joke." There was that goddamned motherly smile again, wagging her head and looking at me like she was so proud of me. How could I be mad? *Just a zany, burnt-out actress*, I told myself.

"You really got jokes, Tia." I said this and even found myself laughing at the whole mess. I pulled myself up and out of the pool, all soaked up in my jeans, sneakers-n-shit. *Squish, squish, squish.*

"I'm glad we can get along, young Spencer. Now do me a big, big favor." She lit up a cigarette and puffed.

"What's that?" I said with my hands on my hips, my expression saying that I'd *surely* done her a handful of favors already, especially being her boy toy and all. Still, I managed to keep a crooked smile.

"Clean my pool," she said, and spun off with authority and her ass switching in that short dress. This was the first time I looked at her differently. I actually noticed the shape—nice ass, strong legs and calves, with a choreographed walk that men would die for.

The sun was still out, keeping my wet ass warm, so I just went along with the program. If this was as bad as it got, then *whatever.* That $800 couldn't look any better than it did right now. Maybe I'd buy some new tires with the extra money. I went back and forth over this in-ground pool, skimming the surface for anything that didn't belong. Just for the hell of it I counted all that I caught: four flies, six bees, and a cigarette butt. I probably went back and forth a hundred times, figuring I was being paid close to eight dollars a trip, if you didn't count the shoe job and Jacuzzi cleaning. How did I guess Tia would be behind me when I was done?

"Great job. You're really impressing me, Spencer." She was real close again. Even ran her hand along my short hair. "Not mad about the li'l dip, are you?"

I made a face and said, "Nah. It's all in fun, right?"

"Hmmm . . . yeah. All in fun. You all dry?"

"Just about. An hour and a half in the sun, ya know."

"Mmmm." Tia put her hand to her mouth, her elbow in her other hand, thinking. She cast her eyes at my feet and her gaze crawled up my body slow as an inchworm's movement. I felt as though I was undergoing some kind of inspection.

"Turn around," she instructed. I obeyed. My back was to her now and I swore she was about to push me over the edge again. She said nothing. And then I felt her warmth. Her body couldn't have been more than an inch from mine. Her breasts grazed my back. In my ear Tia said, "See the lawn on the other side of the pool?"

"Yes, ma'am. I mean, Tia." There I was again, Spence, the stuttering fool.

"Well . . . there's a lawnmower in the shed. I want you to go over the lawn nice-n-thorough. I want you to cut my grass until the sun goes down."

Her arm reached around in front of me. In her hand was money. "This is your eight hundred I promised. Take it." I did, tickled both by her lips next to my ear and by finally holding the money I slaved for. Now her other arm came around, barely embracing me, her breasts now pressed against my back. With both hands in front of me she counted out more money, looking over my shoulder. "One hundred . . . two hundred . . . three hundred—here's another five hundred," Tia said, and she took the folded money and smoothed it up and down the front of my body, from my chest to my groin, as if the money was a paintbrush. "Now why don't you be a good boy and put on a show for the lady."

She said this and thrusted me forward. *Thrusted me!* I went into the pool, money and all. When I finally looked up she was gone again. I waded around, treasure hunting for hundred-dollar bills floating on the surface and after counting all $1,300 I got out. I felt funny holding on to thirteen soaking-wet hundred-dollar bills, but money is money. I stuffed them in my pocket. There would be drier days, I figured. I found the lawnmower in the shed, *a manual one*, and I began pushing it back and forth along the grass, praying for sundown while asking myself what kind of crazy bitch did I just hook up with?

It didn't look like the grass needed cutting. No impressions were showing where I'd passed over. But I soldiered on nonetheless. Tia was in the distance, sitting on a lawn seat, one leg bent, smoking her lung poison, probably looking at me through those dark glasses.

I paced myself, because, as much as I was proud to be active, I was running out of steam. My thoughts were consumed to make the best of this mundane job, thinking that if only Troy could see me now. I wondered if he would be proud of me or if he'd call me a sell-out. But then, I'd wave my $1,300 in his face and make him sorry he wasn't the one who bagged this woman's groceries. I also thought about Roxy, wondering if we'd ever get together again, or if she'd spot me with one of the girls while she was on another of those lonely weekend visits to see her pops. Finally I was determined to tell Tia that I wasn't down to do this type of stuff every day. My body couldn't take it. But the other side of me, the side with all the common sense, was saying I must be out of my cotton-picking mind to jeopardize good money. Already, for just one day's work, the woman paid me more money than I'd make in a month at Waldbaum's. Unless lightning was about to strike, wasn't no way I was gonna open my mouth. *Just roll with it, Spencer. Roll with it.* I swear I was about to drop to my knees from the fatigue my body was experiencing. But it was sundown, finally. My day was through.

"Hungry?"

"I could eat a cow," I said, meaning every word. Tia sniggled under her breath and had me follow her into the house. I could still feel the squishing in my sneakers, vowing to buy the flyest pair of Nike sneakers money could buy.

I was confused as to why we were headed upstairs again and not to the kitchen.

"I want you to get cleaned up for dinner. I have something special in store for us."

Us. We. Now, I came to the woman's house for a damned job interview and we're suddenly partners—she the *absent* partner. Absent-*minded*, that is. Tia directed me to a guest room, also with its own bath. Warm water already filled the tub.

"I prepared your bath."

"I'm not use to baths. I usually take showers at home."

"At home? With *mommy*?" The way she said that hit hard, like she was criticizing me, as so many did to an eighteen-year-old still living under his mother's roof. "You've worked hard all day. You need the bath crystals to penetrate your pores . . . get all the grime out of you. Go on. It won't hurt."

Tia stood at the doorway of the bathroom, her hand on the door jamb. Unease came over me. I slowly took my shirt off, turning away, half-expecting her to be gone when I turned back. But she was still there with those inspecting eyes.

"Really, Tia, I can handle this."

She had that pout on her lips and her nostrils flared. Her eyes were partially lidded in a leering way.

My words had her shake the spell. She said, "And I assure you, Spencer . . . I've seen all types in my years. Brought up three kids. I'm old enough to be your mother. You embarrassed?"

I uttered a slight chuckle and said, "Well . . . y-yes, I guess I am, ma'am."

"Well, don't be. Remember . . . you're still on my time. I'm paying you to do as I say, not to question me or out-talk me."

Her arms were folded now and she levied that scornful gaze. I couldn't tell if she was kidding or not. If she was performing again. Then she left, and I was entirely relieved.

I had a war with my jeans, pulling the soggy denim off of my lanky limbs. I found myself half-falling to the bathroom floor to finally get them off. I stood up again to strip off underwear, looking forward to the so-called bath crystals penetrating my pores. The sudden draft made me swing around.

"You okay?" Tia was there at the threshold. Again.

"Mrs. St—!"

"I heard a thump. I wondered if you . . ." Her words faded as she became aware of my full nudity. It didn't even make sense for me to cover my privates, she'd seen it all. "You have ab-so-lutely nothing to be ashamed of, Spencer. You need to relax, really." And she was gone again. I went to lock the door behind her.

"And you need to stop drinking Clorox, lady," I said to nobody in particular. I finally soaked into the bath, its soothing effect chasing all of my cares away until I fell into a brief nap.

[THREE]

MRS. STERN, OR TIA, as she wanted me to call her, wanted to be adventurous.

"I want to accomplish something bigger than me," she told me.

"I'm all ears," I told her. She was sitting there in one of two high chairs, the pool cue standing between her legs, waiting for me to miss my shot. We were in the basement at the time—the playroom, she called it—well into my sixth month as her nurturing confidant, personal assistant, gofer, and, well, house boy. "Six ball, corner pocket."

"I was hoping you had a plan or a goal. I'm almost out of dreams. Being a successful actress was one of them, been there, done that, isn't that how the saying goes?"

"Yup. Four ball, cross side," I blurted. Tia had stripes. I had solids.

"See? Seems like you've *still* got a whole lot of dreams," she said, implying that I'd miss my shot.

"Very funny," I replied, and I *did* miss the shot. "Your turn."

"You're about to see a lady go for hers."

"Oh yeah?"

"Twelve . . . straight up."

"Mmmhmm," I said once she made the shot.

"Ten in the side."

I was silent when she made the next shot. *Hustler.*

"Fifteen ball, dirty off the eight, in the corner."

"Hold up! Hold up! You can't use the *eight ball.*"

"Who says?"

"Aw, come on. *Everybody* knows *that* rule."

"Oh. You mean like house rules?" Tia stood up, to break in her rhythm.

"Y-yeah . . . right," I said.

"Well, ah . . . whose house is this?" Tia had the tip of the pool cue up under my chin and that seductive gaze dug into my own eyes.

I swallowed, still overwhelmed by her ability to bring the drama. "Yours."

"Exactly. Now zip it, before you catch a beat down." Tia poked lightly at my groin. She made the shot, too. "Now . . . I'll make this last shot a little difficult, just to keep the game competitive."

"Mmm-hmm," I said, the Doubting Thomas.

"Eight ball . . . two cushions."

The eight ball fell as directed. I wagged my head in disappointment and exhaled audibly.

"Now. As I was saying . . . isn't there anything that you dream about? Some large goal you'd like to accomplish? Put it this way, Spencer . . . if money wasn't an issue, what would you buy? What would you venture into?"

Tia sat back in the high chair. I took her stick and the

one I held and put them back on the rack as I listened. My mind wandered.

"Well, the first thing I'd do is buy a nice car."

"Okay."

"And . . . I'd probably get a nice place, maybe a penthouse in downtown Stamford. Something where I could see all of downtown, the Sound, and even my neighborhood where Mom's at."

"Alright."

"And, well . . . there is one thing I've always wanted to do."

"What?"

"Run a modeling troupe."

"A *troupe?* What's that?"

"I mean a bunch of beautiful women. Women of color."

"And . . . what, may I ask, will you do with these, ahh, beautiful women?"

"Aha! Wouldn't *you* like to know?" As I said that the house phone rang. Without mention, I went to pick it up. "Mrs. Stern's line." This was the standard procedure for incoming calls ever since she announced she wanted a divorce from Mr. Stern.

"It's your lawyer," I said with my hand over the mouthpiece. "You want to speak with him?" I said in just over a whisper. I also gave a slight nod, suggesting that she should go ahead and talk with him. It was like that with us now, where I knew all about her marriage, her want for a divorce, and also how her husband was more than a little ticked off about her sudden change of heart.

"Yes, Roland," Tia said with the sigh, expecting more disturbing news. David Stern had been dragging the divorce proceedings, hoping to play it all out in a messy court battle, which would serve to tarnish the actress's name forever. In the meantime, she was left to live in the home on the Sound—as lavish as a divorcée could ever have it—with a weekly allowance of $15,000.

"Roland, we've gone over this, haven't we? He has much more than he's claiming. I know this. Before he was a judge he ran a practice here, you know this. Everybody knows this. His name is still on their business cards for god-sakes . . . of course, Roland. He has *more* than a stake. It's *still* his business. It's been ongoing ever since he was appointed. How can you be a lawyer in Stamford and not know this stuff? Has he gotten to you, too? Huh? Tell me, Roland? Does he own you, too?"

There was a moment of silence during which I had second thoughts about having encouraged her. She should've never taken the call. I wanted to kick myself.

"Listen . . . let's keep this real simple. You tell that bastard, his lawyer, *whoever*, that I want twenty million, plus the house and my car. You tell him that I'm not bending one inch. No compromises. He pays me the settlement, or he'll see a mess he never counted on, trust me. I've still got a few power moves left in me. Now you get me that settlement, Roland, or you, too, can kiss your ass good-bye." She hung up and took a great big breath.

"It's gonna be fine, Tia. Don't let that stuff—"

"They're stressing me out, Spencer. It's your fault, *too*."

"My—?" My head nearly snapped back off of my neck.

"My bath," Tia pointed in the direction of the steps. It was a direct order.

"But—"

"Draw—my—*bath*," she said with more determination. I'd grown to learn how that tone of voice was a dangerous one. One that threatened my job security on at least one other occasion.

"Yes, ma'am," I answered in a mumble, that heaven-sent salary hanging over my head as usual.

This was the way it was. My newfound reality. I felt like a surrogate son sometimes. At others, I was an ear and a voice that she could confide in. Still, at other times, I was treated like an indentured servant. It was a twisted relationship, but only months away from my nineteenth birthday, and having saved an average of $3,000 a month, I was building a nice little nest egg for myself. So what if I was impressionable, manipulated, and if I was kissing her ass left and right. What did I care? Like she said once or twice, I was from the ghetto with ghetto dreams and ghetto potential. Thing is, if my friends could see me now I'd be a little ashamed, but I figured another year as Tia's personal assistant and I'd not only have "cake" myself—close to $30,000 of it—but maybe she'd finally invest in my dream. So what if I was too ghetto; soon I would be ghetto *fabulous*!

"ROLAND, PLEASE. This is Spencer Lewis calling, Mrs. Stern's assistant. Yes, I'll hold." While the Mrs. was taking her bubble bath I took it upon myself to call her lawyer back. It wasn't outside of the scope of my usual duties, having frequently called her accountant, her hairdresser, the housekeeper, and even her children over the course of our partnership.

"Hi. Yes, this is Spencer. Listen, you know and I know that my boss is a bit stressed out, probably not thinking straight . . . I don't know, doesn't that type of stuff stop after a woman's forty-five? Yeah, I thought so, too. Maybe it's that other thing they go through—some kind of syndrome. Plus the kids are all grown now and, between you and me, she ain't been seeing no other men since her and her husband broke it off . . . Nope . . ."

He asked me what that had to do with anything.

"Well, it could all be weighing on her decisions right now. I mean, twenty mil is a lot of money . . ."

Roland said I was right.

"For any woman, forget that she was . . . I mean, that she *is* an actress. Hollywood or no Hollywood, someone could live five life times off of that much dough."

He asked me to get to the point.

"I think I can help you change her mind."

I think I offended Roland.

"No, Roland, I'm not trying to be her lawyer, but you know she confides in me. Trust me on this."

Roland asked what I had in mind.

"I heard a quote of fifteen million, what was it? Last week's discussion?"

He said yes, that it was offered in monthly payments of $25,000. I took a minute to do the math.

"Damn. That's, what, three hundred thousand a year, which means . . . man, *Roland*. She'd have to live to be ninety-five to get the whole fifteen million. Not only that . . . What happens when her ex kicks the bucket? Will she still get paid?" Now I understood Tia's dilemma. I suddenly wished I had stayed out of the negotiations.

Roland said something about an interest-bearing account. Stern would only have to put up a percentage of the money into bonds and what-not. His wife would be paid the interest from the investment. It was said to be guaranteed regardless of how long David Stern lived.

"So, in actuality, he's not really giving her the money as much as he's investing it. He gets to keep the overall principle, while the interest goes to pay off the nuisance settlement."

Roland asked me where I got my smarts from.

"I was an A-student. I just couldn't afford to go to college like you." I felt like I jabbed at him. He made a sound, implying that he understood. But I doubt that. "Tell you what . . . if I can get her to agree to fifteen you think a balloon payment could be arranged? A sort of good faith to kick off everything?"

He said he was sure they could work something out. I told him to "go to work on your end and I'll go to work on mine. If we come up with an oral agreement how soon can the settlement be achieved?"

Roland said he felt they'd be ready within a week's time. I told him we had a deal, as if the agreement had already been made. I felt like a big-time negotiator, like I was on Wall Street somewhere. But the reality is that the Mrs. and I had grown close. We had discussed her finances, her past life, and her future. Spencer, the therapist.

I KILLED some time by straightening up the guest room where I slept from time to time. These days I was feeling as though I had two homes, two mothers, and two ways of life.

Back home it was our distorted color TV with only the antenna to provide us with four or five channels—Public Broadcasting was the clearest of them. Back home it was leftovers from Kentucky Fried Chicken; Troy was managing the store now, so he always brought home the chicken, corn, potatoes, and biscuits that weren't sold. There was a point when I was having chicken for breakfast, lunch, and dinner. And, of course, back home I had to cope with the stench that hung in the air from Mom's home-beauty salon. African braids were the trend now, so there was a lot of that going on. Sometimes the smell got so wicked, I wondered if the women who were her customers even wore any underwear. *Something* was letting those carnal fumes run free.

At the Stern home life was different. Desirable. A world away from stray dogs barking, babies crying (should one of Mom's clients decide to spend the night out), and synthetic horse hair everywhere I sat down. The Stern home had the 54-inch television with a 500-channel satellite. There was the pool, the Jacuzzi, the playroom, a warm fireplace here and there. The livin' was lovely. Tia liked to dine on seafood and salads that I would've never tasted if not for her. She took me on quite a few shopping sprees, and she even made the people at the pier allow her to use David's yacht. They were unsure of whether or not to do it, not able to get Mr. Stern on the phone. But her willpower and how she said, "Dare you question my authority?" made them comply with her wishes. Tia and I spent the whole weekend on the yacht—it was Labor Day weekend, too, when boating is in heavy demand during end-of-the-summer flings. I found out later that the yacht crew and an employee of the pier were fired. I laughed so hard about that. The life of a personal assistant, what a time I was having. Tia would act crazy sometimes, directing me to scrub her kitchen floor or to hand-wash her panties and brassieres. But I put up with those humiliating tasks and the perks that I got once in a while. My wardrobe was on blast now. Tia even had a credit card issued to me, in her name and mine, so that I could pay for the things she needed and which I often shopped for. Many times I left my Volvo parked in her four-car garage and took a hired limo out on the various errands. Other times I drove her Jaguar. Even sported it back in the 'hood, feelin' like the ultimate pimp.

That day was crazy, too. One moment I felt like the big fish, like I had it all goin' on. The next I was a slug again. I came back to tell Tia about the experience and she flipped. At first she sucked me in, made me think I did good.

"So you got a kick out of that, huh? Did they all stare at you?" She had her arms folded with a smile.

"I felt like a celebrity or something, Tia! It was bananas. I even showed off to Jody, an old girlfriend."

"Bananas, huh? Jody . . . the old flame." Tia hummed and said, "Sounds like you had a good ole' time."

"Yeah," I sighed, success oozing from my smiling lips.

She nodded, a grimace across her grill. "Well . . . now that the fun is over there's work to be done. When you finish with putting those groceries away come to the patio. I have a job for you."

"Something wrong?" I asked.

"Oh . . . now what would make you think that, playboy?" I shrugged. Tia was already leaving the room. "And don't drag your feet."

The house had an indoor and outdoor patio. And since it was mid-October, I knew the Mrs. wanted me in the room that sat off of the dining area. It was a glass-enclosed patio, all types of greenery growing like an atrium greenhouse effect.

When I got there Tia was relaxed in a wicker lounge chair. She was wearing one of those T-shirts that exposed her trim midsection and a terrycloth towel-skirt. It was the summer wear that a young sexy, voluptuous woman would have on at a beach. I had to admit, even she looked young, sexy, and voluptuous.

"You wanted me?"

Tia said nothing for a moment. She looked over at me. "I wanted you . . ." There was another pause that seemed like forever. "I sure did. Go get the lotion," she said and laid back on the chair. "Some champagne, too," she called out just before I left the area. *Champagne. Lotion. A glass. Ice and a bucket.*

This was the kind of self-talk that I'd grown accustomed to as I went off on gofer tasks. It was a routine that enabled me to remember things without writing them down. I returned and automatically poured the Mrs. a glass of champagne.

"Did I say I'd be *drinking* champagne, Spencer? Are we assuming again?"

"I, uh . . ."

"I—uh—*nothing*," she said. "You really think you call the shots around here, don't you?"

My eyes widened. I couldn't imagine why she said that. Or maybe this was another of her tangents. Her games.

"Doing things I haven't asked, like . . ." she reached out

and took the glass from me. She tossed it to the ancient stone floor where it shattered in its own tiny puddle, ". . . like pouring champagne. Like parading my car all around your ghetto neighborhood. Like negotiating *my financial affairs!*" Her eyebrows furrowed. I swallowed and told myself, *Oh shit.*

"Boy . . ." Tia gritted her teeth and slightly wagged her head, "what you really need is a good old-fashioned ass whuppin'."

"But I—"

"What'd I tell you about talking back to me? Give me that bottle," she commanded. I obeyed, passing her the champagne. I figured she was gonna throw it at me. "On your knees," she said.

"*Whoa.*"

"Whoa?"

"No," I protested. Then I explained, "It wasn't a reply . . . more like a-a-a response. A reflex. Not an answer. I . . ." I just did as I was told, ran out of excuses. I also closed my eyes knowing for sure she was about to bash the bottle over my head, or worse. For three grand a month I was every bit of the punk she wanted me to be.

The next thing I knew champagne was dribbling, streaming, pouring over my hair, my face, and my body. She emptied the bottle over my head. Tia was positioned sidesaddle on the lounge chair now, hunkering over me as if she were on a toilet seat. I was still kneeling before her, wet with champagne, with that sorry-ass look on my face.

"For your information, I'm going to accept the deal," said Tia, her eyes changing their meaning from fearsome to proud. "But the next time you do something like that behind my back . . ." Tia had her face inches from mine now. Then she closed in and kissed me open-mouthed on my lips. "I'm gonna break your neck. Got it?"

I was in bad shape right now. My heart was jumping in my chest and I squeezed my rectum as if my insides were about to rush out of me.

"*Answer* me," she ordered.

"Y-y-yes ma'am . . . I m-m-mean Mrs. Stern . . . I-uh-Tia."

If I could've flopped over and lost consciousness I would have, except so much was going on in my head and my body right now, none of which amounted to the coma I wished for. Was I supposed to feel guilty or accomplished?

"Good. Good. I believe we have an understanding. Now clean up that champagne, the broken glass, and I want you to lotion my feet and legs." She swiveled back into a lounging position, her bare leg and thigh exposed from under the towel-skirt. "What are you waiting for?" She flashed me another look. Tia, the drill instructor. I shook out of the dumbfounded spell that overcame me and hurried to clean up the mess. I didn't even get to towel off the champagne she poured over my head; it just dried on me like a sticky film.

I massaged her feet, wearing the most concerned face I could manage, in light of the intimacy. She knew my touch pretty well by now, since I massaged her back and shoulders once or twice a week and I applied ointment once when she caught a heat rash from lying in the sun too long. Except there was something different now.

As I rubbed the lotion in between her toes, and on the tendons, giving added attention to the top of the foot, ankle, and heel, I happened to look up enough to see that she had nothing on under the towel. Bigger than that, her legs were slightly parted. Concerned that she might've seen me looking, I remained busy. I squeezed out more lotion and worked my thumbs and palms into her Achilles tendon and calf. I went as far as the knee before I began on the other leg. Not once did I look at Tia's face, but something told me her eyes were searching for mine.

"You have to do my knees, Spencer; you know I played tennis yesterday." Tia stretched her left leg out for me to work on and I was glad the view to her genitals closed up. I duplicated my effort on her right leg.

"How's that, Tia?" I said this, trying to maintain some semblance of professional behavior. But in actuality, my loins were stirring.

"Ohhh . . ." She let out the combination of a sigh and a moan. "It's such a relief, Spencer. I hope . . . I haven't . . . ahhh, that's good, *real* good. I haven't been too hard on you, have I?"

"Not at all, boss. I understand. Really."

"That's good. I was . . . *ooh* . . . right there . . . yeah. Work my thighs. Please. Yeah. Rub harder. Massage it really good, Spencer." Tia drifted off into her own world, laying back, slowly spreading her legs, muttering instructions. Eventually her legs were spread apart, her feet touching the floor on both sides of the chair. This was getting out of control. Now she had her arms up, reaching back behind her head, her hands raking through her length of black hair. At one point she pulled at her hair, grabbing it down over her face until some of it fed her *teeth*. I swore I felt her shudder during one of the more outrageous cries. Part of me wanted to get up and out of there, the other part of me was happy to make her feel good.

"Oh please—*please* don't stop! Don't stop, Spencer. *More. Higher!*" She managed to utter these pleas during bouts of heavy breathing and panting.

My hands reached her upper thighs, kneading her with gentle pressure and firm attention from my fingertips. I was inches from her body's furnace. I wondered how far this would go, but as I did Tia let out this hell-raising scream. It froze me in my tracks. She shook and her body squirmed. She was experiencing spasms, like an epileptic fit. I removed my hands and backed up, feeling entirely out of place. I turned to grab the lotion and raised up to give the lady some privacy. One last look before I got out of there. Some discharge from between her thighs. Oh *God*.

While her eyes were closed, her teeth clenched in some strangely amusing grimace, I got out of there. I cleaned up as fast as I could, showered, and I took the Volvo for a long drive.

[F O U R]

ROLAND ARRANGED FOR a $250,000 good-faith
payment at the signing of the settlement. The boss took me
along for support and we were driven into downtown
Stamford by chauffeured limo. And it was David Stern's
chauffeured limo.

A bunch of suits were there at the settlement, most of
them white men, distinguished, working for David his
Royal Highness. I noticed the name of the practice, "Stern,
Worchovsky and Fleisher," as I remained no more than a
backseat observer. Even after Tia signed a pile of paperwork
there was a lengthy wait for the check to be cut. Something
about it being certified at the bank across the street. In the
meantime I went to take a piss.

In the last stall, as I drained myself, I traveled back to the
day, months earlier, when my boss asked me about my
dreams . . . *if money wasn't an object, what would you buy?
What would you venture into?* Those words kept dancing
around in my head. But while it felt great to revisit that
moment, I wasn't willing to be spun like a turtle on its shell.

People always changed their minds, depending on the weather, a whim, whatever. Something was always putting a damper on my dreams, like Jody did at my senior prom . . . like that girl Roxy did when I wanted to get with her for a long-term relationship. I wasn't willing to have Tia lift me up to bring me down.

As I swam through those thoughts others came into the restroom. The stall where I was had its own walls, a door, and isolation from the rest of the bathroom, but the top was open to the air above where I could hear their voices.

"Phew, I'm glad that shit's over."

"You're tellin' me, Frank. That bitch was a pain in the ass. She could've sunk our ship, but good."

"You think she knew?"

"Well, shit, she hinted that she knew. Just imagine the scandal . . . the headlines. Senior Court Judge Stern still in private practice—offers clients immunity for a fee. Story at eleven."

"Yeah. I can see it now. Every client that we got off at trial would come under scrutiny. The Bonzo Mob. The junk bond traders. And what about that nonprofit fund that abused contributions said to aid the families in the World Trade Center tragedy?"

"Like I said, she could've sunk our ship, but good."

I heard a flush. Then another. There was the sound of sinks running water, and then the door opening and closing.

I came down from where I had climbed onto the toilet stool and finally zipped up my pants. I made sure to take a look out in the hallway before I left the bathroom, and when all was clear I slipped back out, down the hall to the conference room where the negotiations had been ongoing.

"Where were you? I got the check. Let's go," said Tia with the glimmer in her eye.

I cut a look at the few suits in the room; even if it was impossible to match voices with faces, I couldn't help being curious. My gaze rested on David Stern. Now I could read him. Deceit. Cunning. The master manipulator. It was great to have such inside information. Judge Stern, the scoundrel.

"I DON'T know about you, but I'm hankering to shop my rich ass off. Shall we?" Tia managed one of those evil smiles as she showed me her check.

I smiled back at my boss and returned the check after a nice long study: $250,000.

She kissed the check and folded it. In the bra it went. Always putting the finances in her bra, I noticed.

"Aren't you gonna cash it?" I asked.

"For what? Do we really need money?"

"It would be nice to have the cash in hand. Just to know it's real." I lifted a skeptical eyebrow.

"For the umpteenth time, Spencer, I think you're right. Driver? Please make a U-turn. I want to stop at First National Bank of Connecticut."

At the teller's window, the bank manger looked at us like we were crazy. He said, "We just don't keep that kind of money on hand, ma'am."

"Well, how much *do* you keep on hand?" Tia asked.

"We might arrange fifty thousand or so."

"Let's have it," my boss replied.

The manager had her endorse the back of the check, he arranged a wire transfer of $200,000 to Tia's personal bank account, and eventually had a teller count out $50,000 in stacks of thousand-dollar bundles. We left First National floating on air.

"This is for all of your help." Tia grabbed a handful of the money and let it spill in my lap.

"No, boss. That's your money. Really." I took up the cash.

"Please. Money means *nothing* to me, Spencer. What really makes me happy is the security it offers. Plus, I'm through with that man once and for all."

She pushed my hands away and sat back. Her eyelids fluttered as though she was in heaven. She inhaled air that promised her a fresh start in life. I could see that glow about her that all but erased the age of her camera-ready looks.

"Now . . . let's go shopping!" She tossed up a bunch of money and a lot of the bills took to the atmosphere of the limo like fallen leaves.

I DON'T think the Stamford Mall ever experienced a wave of commerce like Tia put it down. We started on the ground floor where there was a furniture store, a sporting goods store, and a place filled with antiques.

The salesman inside of Sheffield Furniture & Interior started to make his pitch, "Oh, our furniture is built to last, with unique construction like Quadra linear posts and solid cherry or Quartersawn Oak . . ."

"Young man . . . please. Save the spiel. I wouldn't have come in here if I wasn't interested. You don't need to sell me. Now get out your pad and pen. I want that, that, that, and that. Throw in the mirror with the gold trim and I want it delivered to my home by next week. Spencer, handle the particulars. And you, have a nice day," she told the salesman. Then she went next door to the antique shop.

Now, it was my turn to direct. "Okay, buddy. Here's the address. Give me a call when you're ready to deliver. Meanwhile, let's swipe this credit card and show me where to sign. Gotta get goin'." It was Christmas in November.

"My, my," he said, breathlessly, and he led me to the cash register.

By the time I got next door, my boss had already decided.

She said, "Stunning work of art, don't you think?"

"Wow. That's you, boss!" I was serious as a heart attack, staring up at a painting of a woman who was seated looking over her shoulder at us, with some kind of dragon-painted silk robe falling off of her bare shoulders and draped all around her, the chair, and the floor. The woman's face was partially shadowed, and she was done up like a southern belle—or maybe it was a Spanish rose. (I wouldn't know the difference.) The painting was somehow set within a massive chunk of dark, rusted bronze and appeared to need a half dozen people to carry.

"You think so? Or are you just flattering me again?"

"Really, boss. You lucked out."

"Good, then. Make the sale. I'm going into the sports shop." The boss lady spun off, her skirt behind her, calves just calling out to me. Come to find out she got his-and-hers ski suits, a carload of bathroom, dining, and kitchen accessories, plus a half dozen sneakers, watches, and hats. I was already the owner of an incredible wardrobe, so I deferred on a lot of things. But the Mrs. found things I wanted.

"You really need to be introduced to some intelligent

music, something other than that hip-hop you play all the time."

"What's wrong with hip-hop?"

She made a face and went digging into the CD bins of Musicland. I stood by her side with the shopping basket we borrowed from the store across the way. I guess Musicland only expected people to buy one or two CDs. They would never be ready for a rich black woman who had a hard-on for what she saw as *important* music.

"Okay. Let's begin with the As and Bs . . . Oleta Adams, After Seven, Gerald Albright, Herb Alpert, Atlantic Starr . . ." The boss was pulling up CDs like they were apples and oranges. "I know these are before your time, but trust me . . . we're gonna have a party. Anita Baker, Regina Belle, George Benson . . ." The basket was filling up pretty fast and I glanced over my shoulder, shrugging at a few of the Musicland employees, who were looking over at us like we were stealing the whole store. By the time we reached some dude named Miles Davis, I went to go and empty the basket on the front counter. When things were totaled up there were six hundred CDs in all. Too much shit to take home with us, so it all had to be delivered.

By day's end we had the limo half filled with goodies and decided to stop at a restaurant that overlooked the coastline.

"How about a toast?"

"You deserve it, boss. It's been a struggle, hasn't it?"

"But you've helped me to make things that much easier, Spencer. So here's to our partnership and all of its future encounters." She winked at me. I had to think about her words for a time, the creamy tune of it all just causing my breathing to lock up, and there was a tremor in my chest.

"Yes, of course," I said as I raised my glass of champagne and tapped it against hers. "To a *bright* future," I continued, wanting to specify our objectives. I had experienced my boss going off on her tangents now and again, and I also grew accustomed to bringing clarity to things. A confidant's work is never done.

While we waited for a seafood platter for two, Tia struck that note again, about my dreams and goals. She said, "So . . . now that David is out of the way, I was thinking that you could be more useful to me as a live-in. Maybe one of the bedrooms down the hall."

"But I thought you didn't want live-ins? I thought you wanted your privacy."

Tia looked out of the window toward the dark waters of the Long Island Sound. She seemed to be in a moment of deep thought, or searching for words.

"There's a life out there for me, Spencer. Something greater than I've ever imagined. I know it. The acting was good. Ever since I was a little girl—the talent shows, the school plays, eventually Broadway, then the television shows and finally the sitcom. That damned show ran for ten seasons, and when it was over it was as though part of me died. I was pigeonholed as a mom. There'd be no way I could compete with the Halle Berrys or the Nia Longs or the Jada Pinketts of the industry, only because of my wanting to be consistent and loyal to one show . . . to one effort, one man's idea. I did the same with David."

"I guess you have to commit yourself to something in life. And it probably comes with its negatives and positives. I read once that *every success has its downside."*

"And whoever said that is most certainly right, except I'm sure it doesn't say *anywhere* that the downside of success is to shrivel up and die. God, Spencer, I'm not *that* old . . . am I?"

Tia seemed to say all of that just to get to the age issue. I could tell. We hadn't discussed age at all from the day we met at Waldbaum's. But now, almost a year later, after so many important changes in her life, this felt like the moment of truth. And it felt like I was a big part of that moment. She required an answer that more or less found me stuck between a rock and a hard place. I said *no*, that she *wasn't* that old (and she *wasn't*). But I realized I might be asking for more than I *could* handle—and at my age, the last thing I wanted was the introduction to a lifelong commitment with a woman who had already experienced many of life's peaks and valleys. She already had certain mental luggage that had accumulated for over forty-five years. Me? I had my whole life ahead of me. And being more than the employee would be something like stepping in on a major motion picture, a movie that started an hour earlier. However, on the other hand, if I agreed with Tia (and it felt like that was where she was headed) and I said that she *was* too old for this "new life" she spoke of, I'd be the worst for my opinion. If I suggested that she lay back, relax, and maybe vacation some and enjoy all the lush life that David Stern's money could afford . . . if I said to her that she was no longer competitive on any level, and that she should shut up and be happy with the devil, she'd get rid of me quick, fast, and in a hurry. And that would end the dream, as well as my *knock 'em dead* salary. I was in a no-win situation.

"Spencer? How about an honest answer?" She reached across the table and affectionately placed her hand over mine.

"Honest?"

She nodded with one eyebrow slightly higher than the other.

"The truth is, you've seen a lot of life. No doubt, Tia. But . . . I'm sure there's so much more to see . . . to achieve. No. You're not too old. You look great. I'm sure you'll do the big things you want."

"What about love? Do you think I'll find love again? Do you think I can make it in this new age of dating? It's been quite a while since I've been on the market, you know," she said matter-of-factly. I found it humorous, her idea of seeing love as a marketing plan, and I told her the same. But still, we were in those waters again, that discussion of animal attraction with all of its "what if's" and "maybe's." I wondered where this would lead.

I kept it broad, saying, "I'm sure you'll find love again, Tia. Someone . . . the right person is out there for you. Trust me. Just don't look *too* hard. I've never been in love before, but from what I've heard, it's not something that you look for. It's something that finds you." There was that eerie silence after having said that, but I realized how much the conversation shifted here and there. I hesitated to say, "But . . . what does your love life, dating, or your age have to do with the privacy issue, or me becoming a live-in?"

Tia seemed to gather some courage to say, "I want you to be a bigger part of my life, Spencer."

"Bigger? I already discuss your finances with the account-ant, set appointments with your hairdresser, I juggle the hired help around the house, and . . . Tia, I handwash your doggon *underwear*. How much bigger can this get?"

She stared into my eyes. Her hands were clasped there in front of her, the thumbs making circles around one another. It *felt* like indecision.

"I . . . well, let's just say it would be more convenient, wouldn't you agree?" Her attention dug into me.

"Uh . . . well, I guess," I said, somewhat unsure myself.

"Come on, Spencer," her intentions gaining more momentum. "My house, compared to where you live *now*? With *Mommy*? With the roaches and the horse hair you told me about? This is a *no-brainer*."

"I don't want to impose on your—" I was cut off.

"Nonsense. I want you to move in this weekend."

"Okay. Is that an order, boss?" I asked with my surprised sound.

"A *direct* order."

[FIVE]

I ASKED TROY to help move my things, but I had very little to move. The real deal was that I wanted him to come and see. I wanted to show off, have him see how I was livin'. I wanted to let him recognize for himself that chicken and gravy wasn't everything.

"Ta-da!" I trumpeted when I opened my bedroom door. "It used to be the guest room, but now it's Spencer's room," I said to Troy, proudly.

He stepped through the doorway with that crazy look on his face. "Damn, Spence! You got a *balcony* in your bedroom? I ain't never seen nothing like this."

"Actually, this isn't the bedroom, it's the living area. Upstairs is the bedroom."

"And you got a terrace, too? Overlooking the *garden?*" Troy said, breathlessly. "Wait till I tell Mom about *this.*" Troy went from one feature to the next. He pushed the sliding doors and stepped out on the patio, and then he came back inside and stood in front of the fireplace, looking at it with total disbelief. After that he gravitated to my work-study area where I had a computer, a scanner, and a color printer. To the other side of the room was my entertainment center, complete with a large-screen television, multitiered stereo system, and a catalog of CDs displayed on a wall rack. Troy took the remote control and activated the various devices as if he were a kid in a candy store. I laughed, but not like I was surprised or that I forgot where I came from. It was more of a joyful laugh, where I was feeling the amazement *with* him. Because no matter what, blood came first. What's mine was his.

"And what was your job again?"

"I'm a nurturing confidant," I supplied.

"A who? Man, Spence, I'm gonna be honest with you . . ."

"Go 'head. Keep it real," I said.

"Yo! When you told me about this nurturing confidant stuff I thought you were off your rocker. I thought it was some type of B.S. scam you concocted just to get paid—a hustle. But *maaan, look at you!* This beats packin' groceries any damn day."

I showed Troy my bedroom, which he claimed was bigger than my room and his put together. I also had a big-screen TV in the bedroom, part of another fully loaded entertainment center.

"What's *that* TV for?" Troy asked, pointing up at the monitor set inside a wall close to the bed.

"That's an intercom system that my boss set up."

"With video?"

"Yeah. See the camera? There's one in her bedroom, too, and in the kitchen and the front of the house."

"So . . . she can see us right now?"

"I guess—if she wanted to. But she's sleeping now, Troy."

"Yeah, but she be watchin' you at night-n-stuff? Gettin' undressed and all that?"

I sucked my teeth and said, "It's not like that, Troy. Stop jumpin' to conclusions. It's purely for security purposes. I have to check up on her from time to time, make sure she's okay. It's my job."

"*Mmm-hmm.* And guess what . . . it's gonna take a lot more than words to convince me that your, ah, boss isn't watchin' your black ass get undressed. Lemme meet this woman! Wait'll I tell—"

"Cut it out, Troy. Look here," I said stepping closer to the digital camera mounted in the corner of the room. "See the little dot there? It's dark now—know why? Because it's not in use," I had to explain.

"You sure it works? No funny business here?" he asked for assurance.

"It works, and no. No funny business, bro."

"Just checkin', dog. I don't wanna hear about my brother on the six o'clock news, involved in some older woman's sex-charged, hair-brained exploitation scheme, where she's tapin' your butt-nekked ass for the world to see on the Internet."

I chuckled together with Troy, but as I did, I cut a side glance at the camera, somehow considering my brother's hints as warnings.

"So . . ." Troy had that little deceitful glint in his eye. "Can you cut it on so I can get a look?"

"Troy!"

"Only playin'—only playin'," he laughed.

WHEN THE Mrs. woke up, Mr. Kim had a Japanese cuisine prepared for the three of us. Mr. Kim came in once a week to do the Asian dishes. There was also a French cook and an Italian cook, all of whom I rotated by the week so we'd never get bored with the meals. A lot of times Tia and I sat alone over dinner, imagining what it would be like to have a big dinner party for, maybe, thirty people, with all *three* cooks at work. But for now, we were happy to have Troy over.

Tia and I shared a smile as Troy dug into the rice and fire-roasted chicken legs. I wanted to say, *See? I told you he'd like chicken.* But I think Tia read my mind.

"So, your brother tells me you help manage a KFC franchise."

"Mmm-hmm. Almost a year and a half now," Troy said, uninterested that Miles Davis's saxophone was playing softly underneath our conversation. "I'm really an assistant manager now—probation they call it—but in six more months I'll have the champion's belt. And the paycheck."

"Sounds like you've got life pretty much in check. And what're you, nineteen?"

"Twenty."

"So handsome and so accomplished at such a young age. I should've been so lucky to meet a man of your stature when I was younger." I caught Tia's saucy gaze at my brother and my eyes immediately cut to Troy to see his response. In a way I was sending him a message: *Don't you dare feed into that shit.*

"Thank you, ma'am. Its just hard work and knowing what you want in life," Troy responded thoughtfully.

"Hmm . . . a lot of people don't even have half that much going for them," Tia said, stretching the subject.

"Well, I got it, and I *know* Spence has it . . . maybe we'll show others by our example that you can't get something for nothing. I try to show the staff that at the job, but . . . sometimes I feel like a schoolteacher. A parent even."

"I feel for you," I interjected my two cents, tryin' to be cute.

That night I drove Troy home, and the first words out of his mouth cut straight to the chase.

"Spence. You expect me to believe that you ain't hittin' that?"

Even though I had my eyes on the road, I could sense Troy's eyes cutting into me.

"Come on, Troy. Give me a little credit. The woman is at least twenty-five years older than me!"

"Dude, that don't mean jack. Some women, *especially* her type, age like fine wine."

"Where'd you hear that, in a movie?"

"It's a fact, dog. An experienced woman? Whew! She's gonna rock your world because she's been there, done that. She's been around enough to know what you like and how to treat a dude. She's gonna cut through all the nonsense 'cause she don't have the patience for it. Plus, there ain't no ties? MAN. She's got you, bro. If she ain't turned you out by now, then it's comin! It's definitely comin'!"

"You trippin', Troy."

"Watch my words. You're in her house now. Part of her property. And she's payin' you lovely, too . . . got you all swanked-out with all kinds of big-boy toys. And what's next? A new car?"

We had just pulled up to Dakota Street. And I swear I couldn't wait for him to get out.

"Good night, Troy," I said short and sweet.

"*Mmm-hmm* . . . I ain't gonna hate on you, Spence. As long as you're happy. Word up. But just know what you're gettin' into." Troy got out of the car and I headed back home. *Home.* Wow. That was the weirdest thought. Home wasn't on Dakota Street anymore. It was way across town on the water, far away from the misery of the ghetto, with its many sounds and smells. Home was laid out, pampering me like a sweepstakes winner. Home was with my boss, Tia.

The landscape inside the oval drive was lit up like a brilliant Christmas night, with accent lighting along the walkways, directed up at the trees and at various parts of the house. From the driver's seat I could see that all the lights were out in the house but for my bedroom. For a moment I swore I recognized a shadow in my window. But then it was gone.

When I got upstairs the fireplace was blazing in the room outside of my bedroom. There were also candles lit. Tia was sitting on the camel-skin couch she just purchased as part of her redecorating—*de-Stern-izing* the home, she called it. Tia was also wearing a full-length fox fur that was full of various earth-tone colors like sand, bone, and bits of tree-bark brown.

"Wow. Surprise, surprise, huh?" I said this only because I

had a hole in my face and a voice. Otherwise, I was just lightening up a seemingly heavy mood.

Tia moaned and grinned, with her lips closed in that crooked smirk. Then she said, "We haven't finished celebrating. Now that you're officially a resident I thought we'd pop a cork. Whaddaya say?"

I made a half-ass attempt to yawn, which didn't go over too well, and then I said, "Okay, but I wanna get some sleep. It was a long day for me." Troy's warning weighed in on my response. Tia smiled again and indicated the bucket of ice and champagne on the low table in front of the couch. She did this with the mere extension of her arm and hand. In the meantime I ignored her smug position on the couch, sort of laid-back, her legs folded, smoking a Virginia Slim.

"Just one thing before we do . . ." I approached Tia and reached to confiscate the cigarette. We already talked about her smoking. I was supposed to help her quit. Now, she was passing me the cigarette and at the same time blowing a sarcastic stream of the smoke up into my face. I ignored her and popped the cork of the champagne, poured, then handed her a glass.

"Here's to my new living arrangement," I said, putting it out there first.

"Oh no-no-no . . . we must be more meaningful than that. How about . . . here's to new beginnings."

I shrugged and said, "Okay, to new beginnings in my new living arrangement." I tried real hard to keep this above the table.

"Sit down, Spence. I like that. Spence. Your brother's nickname, is it?"

"Basically. He's been the only one to call me that."

"Well, I like it. So now it'll be Troy and I who call you 'Spence.'" Tia gulped down her champagne in an uncustomary fashion, more like a dude in a local bar. She indicated that I refill her glass and I obliged.

"Spence, I've been meaning to have this talk with you . . ." She sat up in a way so that we'd be face to face for a heart-to-heart talk. The fox fell off of her shoulders some and I could see her bare collarbone. I couldn't help wondering what she had on underneath and at once I found it difficult to concentrate on what she was saying.

"A . . . a talk?"

"Yes. Remember our conversation about dreams? I know we discussed it at least twice, maybe three times."

"Sure," I said, coming to attention in my position next to her. I could smell Aura on her, the perfume I came to know and which I even went to purchase for her. "About my model project."

"Exactly. Well, I'm ready to take the dive, Spence. I love the idea, and in fact I'd like to lend a hand, too. I can even endorse the project and give the young women pointers on modeling, maybe even acting."

"Wow! That's great, Tia. I can't tell you how excited I am about the project. Made up a bunch of plans and everything."

"But there's more, Spencer . . . I mean, *Spence*," she added with those sultry lips of hers, like she knew something even more intimate about me than before. "Remember what else you wanted?"

"You mean—"

"The truck. I've already got it on order. The Eddie Bauer edition, right?"

"Wow! Oh my *God*. Aw man . . . I don't know how to thank you, boss. You don't know . . ." I had to back-step. "Wait a minute, Tia. Is there, ah, anything special I have to do for these things? I mean, there's no strings I need to know about, are there?"

She made a face, and then said, "No more than what you've *been* doing, Spence, taking good care of me. Now pour me another." I did as she asked. "We're gonna make everything official on New Year's Eve . . . consummate the new venture with our own little celebration. How's that sound?"

"Uh . . . fine. I—I don't know what to say."

"Don't say a word. Just come give me a big hug."

She pulled me into a warm embrace. When we came out of it I realized that her fox fur had come further apart. *She didn't have a blouse on.* Her breasts were exposed inside the folds of the coat.

"Something wrong?"

"No," I said and looked away, pretending not to notice.

"Look here, Spencer . . . you've seen my body on many occasions. There's nothing to be ashamed or embarrassed about." She leveled her eyes at me. "Is there?"

"N-no, not at all."

"You're not *feeling* anything, are you?" She cocked back her head as though that would be unthinkable. Then she made the grand gesture; the grandest of all. She stood up and had her fur fall to the floor. Her pelvis was a foot or so away from my face. I froze.

"Take a *good* look Spence, and don't forget it. This is me. All of me. Like it or leave it, this is your boss, with all of her jewels right here, for your eyes only." She said this with her

hands on her hips. "Now I'm gonna let you retire for the
night," she said as she stepped around my legs. I watched her
lanky frame as she was about to pass the fireplace. That's
when she turned. She caught me checking her out.

Oh shit.

"By the way, I want you to clean my Jacuzzi tomorrow."
Tia's statuesque frame was backlit by the fireplace.

"No problem, boss. Was there something wrong with the
job I did this morning?" I had poured another glass of
champagne, saving face from (so to speak) being caught
with my eyes on the prize. Tia approached me again. She
took my chin in her hand.

"I'm very happy with the job you did this morning,
except I'm gonna take a dip tonight . . . you know, have
some time for myself. Relieve some, ahh, tension. A woman
has needs, you know."

Dumbfounded, my lips partially sucking in air, I said
nothing. She bent down and kissed my forehead. "So make
sure to give it a good cleaning, you hear?" I nodded with my
wide eyes. She simply said good night and turned to leave
me alone. I felt like a stud without a plan. I swallowed the
rest of the champagne, wanting very much to be subdued by
whatever alcohol content I could get down my throat. In the
meantime I tried to focus on December 31 and what that
day would mean for my big dream. It was as close as I'd ever
come to a "sure thing" since I knew that she (in fact) had the
money to invest, and also that I'd developed a working
relationship already. There was no way this wouldn't work
out.

THE HOLIDAYS came around quicker than expected. It was a little strange to know that so much gift giving was going on everywhere else in the world, everywhere but my boss's house. We had done so much shopping during the proceding months that both she and I had most of what we wanted. Still, on Christmas Eve we went out to eat, just as we did for Thanksgiving. And I readied a gift, something I knew she wouldn't expect.

"Guess what?" I asked.

"Okay. Is this about a Christmas gift, Spence, because you know . . ."

"I know how you feel about Christmas, boss, but I'm still with the spirit of giving. And you've given me so much that I had to give back. It's only right."

"Okay, I give in," she said rather quickly. "What's the surprise?"

I signaled the maitre'd, who was waiting with his staff of five. They wheeled out a large gift-wrapped present. It had a huge red bow over its shiny green wrapping paper. A staff member handed me a bouquet of flowers.

"Wow. Now this looks big, heavy, and expensive," Tia said with an expression I'd never seen before. She looked like a child with her mouth agape like that. The restaurant staff had the package on a big easel, and they turned it so it was facing us.

"Now . . . I'll be very upset if it turns out you don't like this," I told Tia.

"Is that so?" she said with the small audience of diners hearing every word. Then Tia curled her forefinger at me. I approached her and she whispered, "And if you should be upset, how shall you seek redemption? Will you punish me?"

If there was any time I would've turned red in the face it would've been now, with these folks as close as they were to me and the Mrs. I gave Tia the flowers.

"She's always kidding," I said for all to hear. Then, to Tia, I said, "So . . . if I may do the honors . . . this gift isn't about Santa Claus, jingle bells, and all that jazz. This is mainly," I cleared my throat, "a gift for me to show my appreciation to the best boss in the whole world." I reached to shed the gift of its wrapping.

"Oh my . . . oh my . . ." Tia put her hand over her mouth with a look that held both shock and amazement. She appeared to be trembling. I went to her side and put my hand on her shoulder. Then I crouched down next to where she was seated. "You might've forgotten this. Remember the day at Stamford Mall? I had the antique shop deliver this to an artist I found out about on the Internet. She does refurbishing and touchups of paintings . . . so I asked her if she could make some changes . . . I gave her your photo, and here it is."

"Oh, Spencer," Tia sighed and tears fell onto my head as she pulled me into her side hugging as much of me as she could. "This is so special. Nobody ever—" and the boss's words faded into thin air as she buried her face in the crook of my neck. I signaled the staff to take away the painted slab of bronze and we finished dessert.

I drove Tia home and, as planned, I went to Mom's house with the gifts I bought for Troy and my mother. I also had a big canvas sack of gifts that I told Mom to give to her clients at random. Plus there were stuffed animals for the children she babysat for.

"I see you all had a ball decorating the tree," I told Mom

when I noticed the Christmas tree. I could still remember buying it weeks earlier from one of those truck drivers who camped out at the exit of the thruway. Now it was no longer just another evergreen, it was colorful with lights and tinsel and ornaments. There was the bright star up on top that helped to give the tree some life. And I noticed that the house had more life, too. More life than I remembered from when I was there every day, all day.

"This is for you, Mom. Just a little something to help out." I gave my mother an envelope.

"Oh, good Lord. My son started sellin' them drugs. *Jesus!*"

"Mom, that's good hard-earned money there. Every dollar of it."

"Whatcha you doin on that job, sellin' y'self? I never seen you with this much money all at once, Spencer."

Not wanting to get into details, I said, "No, Mom, I'm not selling myself. I'm selling my services. And there's a lot more where that came from. You just put that to good use, okay?"

"I swear on Jesus' name, boy, if you sellin' them drugs or something—"

"Merry Christmas, Mom." I kissed her and went through the front door. Troy was coming in at the same time. "Merry Christmas, bro."

"You, too, lucky stiff. I got you somethin', but it won't come to your house . . . your job that is, until sometime next week."

"Thanks, Troy. Your gift is inside." I gave Troy a hug and said, "Talk to Mom, would ya? She's trippin'." Troy made a face as I went out to the car. Seven days until New Year's Eve. That was the only thing on my mind now.

[SIX]

I OVERSLEPT ON Christmas morning. Laying there awake, looking at the ceiling as though my own picture show was going on up there, I replayed the highlights of the past year. Things had progressed so fast thanks to my new job. It was pointless to even concern myself with money, how much I had, or what I'd eventually do with it, because—as the Mrs. had suggested—money was no object. And all I could do was dream about it. There was a freedom that I was growing accustomed to, a universe away from scrimping, scratching, and saving as we did for most of my childhood. It was hard to shed that poverty consciousness where I never quite knew where my next dollar or dime was coming from. But Tia ushered me into realizing wealth, for what it was worth, was a state of mind. It was amazing how just across town a whole 'nother way of life was ongoing, with a roller coaster of ups and downs like the rent parties, payday, ghetto love, and our loved ones returning home from prisons every now and again. There were also so many downs such as gunfights, murders, and stray bullets taking the lives of innocent children. There were the statistics of broken families, (whether voluntarily or with the help of law enforcement), hungry babies, and drug abuse that leaned heavy on our overall consciousness. And then, of course, there was AIDS, the deadly virus that claimed its victims both unexpectedly and by the perpetual acts of others.

I imagined that I might one day be wealthy, too, with money enough to fix the ills back on Dakota Street, even if it was a slight adjustment. But I knew that idea, and those issues, were so many miles and years away. Right now, I had to be content with making things happen for me. And, of course, in order to do that I had to help make things happen for the boss lady.

"Breakfast is *served!*"

I laughed so hard to see Tia almost prancing into my bedroom with a tray of food in hand. She was also wearing a maid's outfit, one that I suppose had been hanging in the closet where the hired help kept their belongings.

"You've got to be kidding, boss. I'm supposed to be the one serving *you!*"

"That's right, and don't you forget it. Get use to this type of good deed and you can best go find yourself another job." Tia sat on the edge of the bed.

"You actually made omelets? What's in these, tomatoes?"

"And peppers. And onions. And broccoli. Oh . . . and cheese," she explained. I cracked up laughing again.

"So what's with the whole maid's outfit?"

"You don't like it?" Tia said this and then got up from where she sat. She did a quick turn, a half-baked attempt at modeling.

"No . . . ehh . . . I guess if that's what you wanna wear . . ."

"Maybe I should take it off."

And the woman was dead serious, too, already pulling the little hat off, shaking her hair free, and then loosening a button on the white uniform.

"Tia! You look fine. Don't you dare go there. It's Christmas!"

"Exactly. And I had such a wonderful time yesterday, and last night, that I thought I'd surprise you today." She sat down again, her leg folded underneath her. "Be sure to eat it all, Spence. It's gonna be a big day."

"What? You mean, for me? I got a Jacuzzi to clean. Plus, you wanted a massage."

Tia smiled a devil's smile and said, "Oh, believe me, you'll get to both of those tasks . . . eventually. But I have something else in mind. We're going to Foxwoods."

"The casino? Today?"

"Absolutely. Any objections?"

"No way!" I said, excitedly eating the eggs and toast. "Last time we went there was . . ."

"Just after you started working for me."

"Right," I agreed.

"And this is Christmas, our second—and your first as my, uh, house guest. So I want it to be special. I want you to feel free to have fun for the next few days . . ."

"Few days?"

"Exactly. We're gonna stay in Foxwoods until New Year's Eve. And on *that* night we'll consummate our partnership." I thought about that and the forkful of potatoes stopped on the way into my mouth. "No . . . don't worry yourself.

We'll have separate rooms." When she said that I pretended
it meant nothing and went ahead with the potatoes. And
besides, the food was so delicious I vowed (in secret) that
the next massage I gave my boss would be one of my best.

EVER SINCE the settlement we had a contract with a
limousine company that boasted a fleet of forty cars from
Mercedes to Volvos to Rolls-Royce models, all stretch
vehicles that dazzled the eyes. It was a thrill for me to
request which model I wanted sent for whatever occasion.
For the Foxwoods trip I requested the stretch Lincoln
Continental. It was white, with (of course) a fully stocked
bar.

At the resort, we did have the separate rooms Tia
mentioned, except there was an adjoining door with locks
on both sides. I wasn't even a little skeptical about us being
somewhat "connected at the waist" since, after all, it was
part of my job to be close to Tia, and to protect her when
necessary. Who knew? There might be some disgruntled
casino worker who could crash through the hotel room
door and hold my boss hostage. Of course, if that did
happen, I would be limited in my ability to respond. I didn't
own a gun. I didn't know any martial arts, and I couldn't
recall more than three fights I had as a child—the benefit of
being big brother Troy's tag-along. In the worst-case
scenario I would grab one of the knives that came by way
of room service—or maybe some boiling water? The truth
is I wasn't prepared for such an emergency. All I'd do is
follow my heart and do the best I could.

Of all the gaming attractions at the casino, be it

baccarat, craps, poker, or the slot machines, I found the blackjack tables the most exciting. It was a simple game. The rules were easy to follow, and the odds seemed to be stacked in my favor. Seemed.

We started at the $25 tables—that was the minimum bet, where only $25 dollar chips were at stake. After a half hour of winning and losing we stepped up the level and began betting bigger chips. Tia was right by my side, like we were romantically involved, with her sequined top letting on to her healthy cleavage and all. She was the one in my ear, urging me to go higher, to bet bigger!

"Get some more chips," Tia said in a volume enough for the card dealer to overhear.

"You sure? We're down, like, four thousand," I replied.

Tia leaned in and whispered, "Are you questioning me?" I immediately put my hand up so that the pit boss would come over. He was all in my business anyhow. I handed over my credit card, the Platinum Visa that was attached to my boss's account.

"Three please," I told him. It looked as if he knew already to bring $3,000 and he turned to make the transaction. But Tia made a face, as if I asked for the wrong amount. I looked at Tia for some acknowledgment.

"It's fine," she said, again in a whisper. I didn't bother to ask. I just stopped the pit boss and changed the request. And he added another $2,000.

The first $1,000 disappeared in three simultaneous hands. I stayed at seventeen for the second hand. On the third hand I caught a king and a queen. But the dealer quickly wiped the smile from my face by giving the house blackjack—*shit!*

"Let's go to another table, boss. This one's the pits."

We got up to leave, but Tia pulled my shirttail. "Tip the man," she said. I looked at the dealer and forced a smile. I pulled a ten-dollar bill from my folded cash. Tia saw this, grabbed my hand, and pulled it back. She wagged her hand at me and explained, "That's not how it's done, Spence." She smiled at the dealer and slid one of the $100 chips his way.

"Thank you, ma'am," he said. I swore he'd stuck his tongue out at me when he said that. Meanwhile, Tia took my arm in hers and we eased over to the thousand-dollar tables, and $10,000 was the maximum bet that could be placed.

"See, Spence, the key here is to relax. You've got to play to win, bet to win, and relax. If you play scared, you'll lose miserably. And you have more to answer to by losing money than you do by taking risks, so you might as well go for it." *Oh shit.* She was holding me responsible for losing. But at the same time she was giving me more and more rope to hang myself. *Whoa.* Talk about being caught in a spider's web!

"Get some more chips," Tia told me. And I asked for another $5,000. Now, that dammed pit boss was following us like a vulture, with that dammed wooden smile of his. His phony smile reminded me of a politician who bragged about *No New Taxes!*

It turned out that the $10,000 table brought good luck. The first hand got us two aces. We split them and caught blackjack, which paid two-to-one. The other hand drew a nineteen. Both hands on the split were winners against the dealer who only copped a jack and a seven. The house rule was that he had to stick seventeen. In that one deal we made $3,500.

"Bet it all," Tia said.

My eyes widened and I looked to see if she had too much to drink. She didn't even make eye contact with me. I think she was flirting with the pit boss, but still pulled back with her lips at my ear again. *"Do you work for me?"*

"Yes, boss, but we just won. We should . . ." She shook her head, curling her finger at me again. I turned my head to hear her whisper again. I swear her voice was sexy, her tone teasing my eardrum and her fragrance pulling at my senses all the while.

"If you do work for me, then do as I say and bet it all."

I took a deep breath and pushed the $3,500 in chips out over the betting mark.

"All bets in," the dealer said, maybe wanting to be sure that's what I wanted to do. Then he said, "No more bets," and he started turning over cards from the deck. We caught another blackjack. At two to one we won—$5,000.

"I really gotta pee bad, boss. Excuse me," I said and made my escape. In the bathroom I felt like a boxer between rounds.

When I returned, Tia was gone from the table, and I was both relieved and worried. The dealer, an Asian woman, indicated that my boss went that-a-way, and I did so. I found her at the window cashing in chips. Finally.

"You did good today, Spence. We won in the end, but considering what we spent, it was only a couple thousand— not bad for five hours."

"I guess. Where to now?"

"I was thinking a bite to eat and front seats at the casino's Motown Review."

"Now that's a plan." Tia faced me, handed me the cash

that the teller passed through the little metal tray beneath the bulletproof glass, and fixed my collar. She said, "Tomorrow we'll bet big. We'll play to win."

"I can't wait," I lied.

The next day found us so busy that we had no time to gamble. We spent two hours horseback riding, and then Indian escorts took us out in a canoe and we even joined in a ceremony at the Mashantucket Indian Reservation.

Thank God for the bonfire because I didn't want to spend *one more* hour outside in the cold December weather. Tia loved it all like she was a warm-blooded polar bear or something. The whole time our Indian escorts smiled those same one-size-fits-all smiles that you always see resort employees wearing.

On December 27, we were back at the blackjack tables. Tia didn't intend on staying at the $500 tables, but that's where we started off, just to get warm. We won four out of six hands and moved on to the $5,000-dollar tables with just over $2,000 in winnings. To begin with, it felt like it would be a good day.

"Place your bets," announced the dealer.

"Bet it all," Tia said. We had $5,000 in chips—the $3,000 that we came to the game with, and the $2,000 we won at the $500 tables. I pushed $5,000 in chips out to the betting mark.

"No more bets," the dealer said, and he began peeling cards. We caught a pair of queens and split 'em. The dealer laid out two more cards for us—a jack of spades and a four of clubs. I asked for a hit on the fourteen—we got a seven of hearts. My mouth never opened so wide. Then the dealer took a hit on his king of diamonds and six of clubs.

LADY FIRST   79

"Yes!" I exclaimed, once the dealer pulled a face card for himself; busted. He immediately piled on chips that amounted to $10,000. Wow! If I smoked, I'd be high as the heavens right then!

"Okay—time to eat," I said.

"Oh no you don't. We're hot now, Spence. We can't quit."

"One more hand?"

"We'll see what happens," Tia replied, with all her attention on the blackjack table.

"How much?" I asked, but I somehow knew what the answer would be.

"Everything."

Shit.

I got up from the table and walked toward the exit. I didn't want to have any part in her losing $10,000.

I heard her start to say something. "Where are you—" But I didn't stop. As I got close to the exit a big dude stepped in from of me.

"Going somewhere?" he asked with his deep voice and his hand on my shoulder.

"Get offa me!" I exclaimed.

"Ma'am? Has this man done something to you?"

"No, no, it's alright. Thanks just the same. You can let him go," Tia said, breathing as though she'd just completed an extended volley on the tennis court.

"Yeah! You heard her. You can let me go."

"Excuse me, sir. It's just that you were in such a—"

"Save it for yo' momma, Andre the Giant." Then I turned to Tia and said, "Can you believe this? Racial profiling in a casino. What will they think of next?"

"Oh, don't be silly, Spencer. He probably thought you took something from me. I would've done the same thing."

"Yeah, but why couldn't I just be a black man who was upset, or a black man who had to catch a bus . . . or who had to get to the toilet? *Damn.*"

"Well, now that I got your attention, let me speak with you over here." Tia directed me over to a wall where an ATM was nearby. It was the nearest privacy we could find considering the circumstances and where we were.

Before she got a chance to speak, I said, "Boss, I can't sit there and bet that much money."

"Why not? You *won* that much money."

"That's different."

"How so?" she asked with her hands on her hips.

I couldn't explain. Instead I tried to walk away. Tia pushed me back against the wall. It was more of a shock than an assault, and it could've qualified as the first such rift since she pushed me into her pool, twice, so long ago.

"Listen here, boy . . ." The way she said that, with the salty edge, and with her eyes turning to fiery slits, I was finally feeling assaulted. "This is the last time I'm gonna tell you . . ." Tia poked her finger into my chest, stabbing me with an emphasis behind every word. "Don't question me!" Her pointer could've been the tip of a broomstick as hard as it dented my chest. Then she grabbed a hand full of my shirt and jerked me forward. Our lips met in a rough kiss, Tia doing all the work. It lasted for a hasty two seconds. "Now get your black ass over to the table, and you place the bet I told you to place. Now!"

I moved like a robot. Or like a sleepwalker, almost stumbling like a drunk in someone else's *Twilight Zone* episode. I noticed the Jolly Green Giant finding humor in the altercation between me and the boss. I wanted to disappear.

All it took was one hand. We caught a queen. Then we caught an eight of hearts. My heartbeat was not only a riot in my chest but it was loud too, drowning out all the other sounds in the casino. At least, to me it was. I thought I heard every slight movement of the dealer's hand as the card slid out from atop the others and as he turned it up for the gamblers to see.

The pit boss stood by to witness the heavy bet, having already approved the wager that was too high for this table. Tia was there by my side rooting me on. At the same time, there were at least ten people standing around the table with high anxiety.

The dealer had sixteen and had to take a hit. I thought I'd die when he pulled up a five of spades. The whole $10,000 was lost.

I looked at Tia after a second or so of a self-imposed blackout. It was like one of those slow-motion gazes, and I truly didn't want to see her response. Tia just stared at me with the strangest expression. It could've been anger or upset or she could've just frozen, but I didn't stay to find out. I just slipped off of the stool and stormed toward the exit. Again.

The big Andre-the-Giant security guard was there again and I came to a stop expecting some kind of confrontation. When he did nothing, I cut past him and marched back to my room.

Some time passed before I decided to go and see Tia, but the door that connected the rooms was still locked on her side. Plus she wouldn't answer my calls. I figured she was mad at me and that it might take a day to cool off. And sure she'd cool off, because after all, what was $10,000 to a millionairess? Yet, I still couldn't help wondering if she'd changed her mind about the partnership.

FOR AN entire day Tia ignored my attempts. I know she was in her room because the hotel staff told me there was activity. She'd been ordering room service, and no, she hadn't checked out of the hotel.

On December 30, at about midnight, the phone rang in my room.

"Tia?"

"The door is unlocked," was her only response.

"Tia, I'm sorry, I . . ." It took a second before I realized she had hung up and that the phone went dead.

When I got through the door the room was immediately dark, illuminated only by candles, at least ten of them, placed in various spots around the room. Two or three of them were next to Tia on the floor. I also smelled the absorbent aroma of incense in the room as the scented smoke wafted through the atmosphere. And there she was, sitting there on a pile of pillows on the floor in front of the bed. I was in so much of a rush to see Tia that I never changed out of my robe, a thick brown one that she brought for me. Meanwhile, she was in a bra and panties.

I started to speak, but Tia put her finger to her lips.

"Shhh. Come," she said softly. She gestured for me to come down to where she was, so I lowered myself to one knee. "There's work to do," she said, and she laid a towel on the floor between us. Then she stretched out her legs and rolled over onto her stomach. "Massage," was all she said. There was a bottle of baby oil to her side. There was also a small basin of water and a razor. I didn't ask why, I just got to work figuring Tia was stressed from the loss. Maybe it wasn't the amount of money as much as it was the mere idea of losing. I unclasped her bra, as I did on many occasions, and I began to rub the oil into her skin.

There was only the faint hum of the central air vent in the absolute silence of the room. I worked the shoulders, the back of the neck, the spine, the lower back, and her upper arms. I made sure to do my best work, something I had promised myself and, maybe, one that would take all of her cares away.

"Hold on," Tia said in her raspy voice. Then she turned her body, flipping over on her back. This was a first—how she exposed herself like this, with her breasts lying like half-filled balloons and her arms up over her head and eyes closed.

"Well?"

"Boss?"

"My massage. Thank you. And don't miss a spot."

There was no way to be professional about this; no way for me to ignore how far this had come. I just did as she asked. As delicately as I could I massaged the front of her neck and shoulders. I worked my hands down the sides to her ribs and—

"Spencer." Tia's eyes opened suddenly. "My breasts, Spencer. Massage my breasts." Then she closed her eyes. And so did I while my hands roamed, and traveled her body. Tia moaned soft moans and uttered sighs of pleasure. I was eventually enjoying her body; enjoying the feel of it, and the smell of it. For the first time since we met, I wanted her the way I wanted Jody, and in the same way I made love to Roxy. It was finally now that I was saying to myself:

Tia . . . I want you.

I gave no indications about my innermost feelings, but I wondered if she could tell by my touch. I was taking extra time with her breasts, her ribs, and her abdomen. I found myself wanting to kiss her nipples, her navel, her—

When it seemed there was nothing left to do, and Tia expressed her satisfaction, she rose up and sat against the pillows again. Then she stretched her legs out and laid back, arching herself to remove the panties. I swallowed hard.

After tossing the panties, Tia reached for the candles and positioned them closer to her lower region.

"I want you to shave me," she said so casually, taking the razor and handing it to me. "Use oil and water. And be gentle. Pay attention to detail."

Tia lay there and spread her legs. Her eyes leered into my own, sucking me further into her spell. I was so drugged up by all that was happening, and all that was happening to me, that I simply complied. I just went along with it.

The lack of light made things easier to swallow, with how taboo this all felt. And "paying attention to details" meant I had to get close. Closer and more intimate than I had ever been to any woman's private area in my life. I took oil in my hand and coated her pubic area. Her hair wasn't all that long as far as I was concerned, but it wasn't short either. Something like the buzz cuts I've seen on the heads of a lot of Mexican men. I put water where I'd placed oil and gently rubbed it into her hairs. I could hear all kind of messages shouted, whispered, called out, all of it through Tia's eyes. She was saying so much without saying a word.

I pulled the blade in small strokes, picking the hairs from it and dunking it into the warm water after each stroke. When I finished the top, Tia turned to the side, fixed the pillows underneath, and hooked her leg with her arm to permit me a full on view of the unfinished areas of her genitals. My boss, the contortionist. My eyes could've popped out of my face at that moment. *Wow!* I thought to myself that I'd seen a whole lot in so short a period of time. This woman was showing me *everything*, even more than before when she'd disrobed. She was virtually introducing me to all of it, leaving no stone unturned, and looking me dead in the eyes the entire time. With all that I knew and all that I'd come to know about my boss, she still never ceased to amaze me. And, naturally, this was all making me hard as a rock. This woman was as old as my mother, and yet none of that mattered. She was a force that was calling me; calling up this desire that beckoned in my loins. *I wanted to be inside of this woman!*

I eventually finished shaving Tia, to the end that she was bald and smooth as a peach. She had me massage the shaven area with a warm washcloth when I was done. Of course, she did her own examination, smoothing her fingers slowly along her genitals.

"Put the stuff away. Clean up," she said. And I immediately became busy, nervous as hell about where all of this was going. Every moment felt like another level of revelations and anxieties.

When I came back in the bedroom there was a single

candle left, its glow flickering onto Tia who was on the bed, still without clothes, with her head propped against a pillow.

"Take off your robe and come over here," she instructed. I did, crawling up over her in my boxers alone.

"You want me, don't you?" she asked. But it didn't sound like a question. And before I could answer, Tia put three fingers over my lips. "You don't have to say it. I know what you want. I also know what you need. And don't you worry; it's all here for you. Don't be so nervous. Do as I say, and things'll work out just fine," she said. At this point I'm wondering if there's a label on my forehead: *Spencer the adjustable wrench.*

So, I did what came natural. I hovered down to kiss her and she let my tongue in. But, just as quickly, she pushed me back.

"Slow down, Mister," she said. "Patience. There's a way to do this." Tia put her hand against my face and smoothed it back over my scalp. She pulled my head down to her breast and I was encouraged to take her nipples in my mouth one at a time and together, as best I could. Something inside of me was pushing me to try and eat this woman alive; to devour her. "That's it," she said, petting my head as I sucked her breasts. "Nice and slow. Nice and slow. When I'm done with you, you're going to be a professional lover. Maybe the best whoever did it. *Ahhhh!* Easy with the teeth . . . that's it." Before I knew it, she was pushing my head down between her legs. From that moment on, I lost my mind.

"Okay, hold on," said Tia. "I want to make this an even more memorable moment. Do you mind?"

I was already shivering with urgency, but managed to answer her question by simply shaking my head.

"Good. There's another pan there. Right, that one."

I reached for the pan that had been there on the dresser all along. There was a towel draped over it, as if to keep it hidden or dust free.

"Careful, now. Don't spill it."

"What is it?" I asked.

"Something you'll enjoy, I assure you. Place it there on the floor. Good. And take the paper towel off the top."

When I did, I realized it was a pot of melted butter. And no sooner did Tia—

"What're you doin'?" I asked.

"Oh, from time to time I like to dip my toes like little shrimp in cocktail sauce."

I'm not sure if Tia was seeing the strange look on my face. *To each his own.* She sure did dip the front portion of her foot in the butter and I could see (and practically imagine) how slimy that must feel.

"Do they do this in the nail salon?" I asked.

Tia laughed. "Nothing like this, I assure you. This, young man, is about to turn into the tastiest treat you ever had.

Now I really wanted her to see my face and how I was onto her devilish plot.

Oh no, she is not gonna—

"I noticed you enjoyed tasting my skin, so I thought I'd make it all the more scrumptious for you. Enjoy."

Aww, shit! This woman went and had the nerve to butter her toes and lift them to my—this is the part that nobody but nobody gets to see. I wouldn't even mention it in a million-dollar Truth or Dare. But, man . . . I went for it.

The woman already had me hard as a rock. I already wanted her something awful. And, I wasn't sure if she was teasing me or not, having me with my hands all over her body and my eyes full of everything she previously had hidden. But, at this point all that didn't matter. I was just damned hungry. And I'm not ashamed to say that I licked those toes clean, butter dripping from my lips and everything. She laughed hard when I nibbled and she shrieked when I gave added attention to the spaces in between her toes. Truth is, I never tasted toes before. But if that was the plan, I sure wouldn't mind if they were buttered.

[S E V E N]

IF GOING TO work for Tia and moving in with her (all within eighteen months) was considered moving too fast, then I must've been flooring the accelerator. In the months following our New Year's Eve celebration, I had a cream-colored Ford Expedition, fully loaded, gold rims, with rawhide leather custom seats. And thanks to Tia, I had a new fetish for leather. My truck, my shoes, and even my clothes. In fact, Tia bought me an entire leather outfit, including a cowboy hat and boots. She also had a matching outfit. Not that we had many places where we'd wear such extremes, except for when we went horseback riding. I guess she had been looking for something else just to spend money on.

There was one occasion, I'm ashamed to say, when Tia actually lived out one of her fantasies, coming into my bedroom dressed in the hat, the bandanna, a vest, leather chaps, boots, and (of course) nothing else. And you know what happened next. That's right: Spencer, the stallion.

We also traveled some because we knew that there

would be work ahead: our Premium Fudge project was going to be launched in summertime. So, back to back, we took the ferry to Martha's Vineyard, we flew down to Miami's South Beach, we went cross-country on the Amtrak Express, and from Los Angeles we flew to Venice, Italy, where Tia and I took our first gondola ride—one of those long and narrow flat-bottomed boats with pointed nose and tail. I stood on the rear on the boat, directing us down the canal with a long oar while Tia relaxed up front, wrapped in a blanket, a scarf, wearing sunglasses like the retired actress she was.

These were the calm, relaxing times we spent together: the outings on the water, the picnics in the park, and the isolation of other worlds. I never wanted these times to end, they were so peaceful and full of things to do. This was a paradise that we created for ourselves; memories that we could take anywhere we wanted for the rest of our lives.

At times, there were others who looked at us as the mismatched couple that we were, but I didn't mind and I didn't frown on it. Even if they cast those *shame on you* thoughts our way, I just ignored them. There's no way they could know or imagine what went on behind our closed doors. And they wouldn't be wrong. There was a lot going on behind closed doors. I'll be honest; sometimes I felt like a punk servicing so many of Tia's whims. Other times I felt empowered, knowing that I was the sole source of her ultimate pleasure. However, whether it was in our experimenting—such as when she had me fuck her with my foot—or if we did the ordinary missionary position, Tia was the type of woman who made a lot of noise. She shrieked, she grunted, she howled, and on at least two occasions, our climactic bump and grinds led to screams that hurt my ears in a good way. I liked Tia's animal cries best of all. That was always something that kept my spatula stiff with me trying like hell to get every bit of mayonnaise I could out of her jar. Sure, she may have been an actress to the rest of the world, but when she was in bed with me there was no acting. It was always dramatic, always like a rocket launch and then a much-anticipated blast-off. And I know that the actor's job is to lie and to pretend, but she wasn't lying when it came to sex with me. At least, not that I could tell. Her shudders, her muscle spasms, and the way she bucked under my thrusts couldn't be phony. Her discharges couldn't be fabricated.

Once we stayed at the Stamford Marriott in the penthouse suite, with a view over the entire city. I realized that there was a perfect view of her ex-husband's offices, but I didn't mind Tia's plan. I figured it would be a one-time encounter where she could get her shit off. So we prepared the room by pulling the bed across the floor to where it was snug against the sliding glass doors. It was late spring at the time and the night air was convenient and pleasing, which meant two sweaty bodies twisted in some outdoor sex wouldn't catch us a cold. Tia also had extra pillows brought to the room and we piled them at the center of the bed, one on top of the other, in a kind of pyramid.

All this extra shit got me so horny; had me all full of desire for this encounter. Not to mention that Tia and I hadn't made love for weeks. I still gave her the massages, and more than once I nearly begged to come to her room, or for her to come to mine. But for those two weeks I was left to do without sex, something that had become a big part of everyday life. And besides, more than just a working relationship, I was becoming addicted and obsessed with this woman. So, that night at the hotel promised to be worth the wait. To put it in Tia's words, she wanted me to slam her like I never slammed her before.

With the bed and pillows ready, and the nightfall upon us, Tia began the show. We were out on the patio with four dozen candles all lit and haphazardly arranged about the terrace, its tables, and even the ledge of the terrace. The two of us stood there in our brilliant setting and raised our glasses for a toast.

"Here's to two weeks of torture," I suggested.

"Was it that bad, Spencer?"

"No, it was worse! I feel backed up like a jailbird."

"We'll just have to do something about that," Tia said, and she took a sip of the bubbly. She turned to look out over the railing "Do you think he's watching?" She referred to David, her ex-husband.

"I hope so! You went through all of this trouble to put on a show! I'd hate to think you went through all this for nothing."

"No. It wouldn't be for nothing. I have you here, don't I? I just wanted to feel the satisfaction of rubbing it in his face, Spencer. But, even if he's not watching, just the idea of it is satisfying enough. And besides that, to be honest with you, I'm just plain horny. I don't even care about the exhibition fantasy anymore."

"We may as well run with it. We've come this far," I added as I looked out over the skyline. "And if he's not looking then, maybe, a million others are." I chuckled as I said this. I could even pinpoint Dakota Street from the terrace. So, maybe there was some satisfaction in store for me as well.

When I turned back to Tia, I noticed she wasn't smiling. She put down her glass, took mine, and swallowed what I had left. I could hear her gulp.

"Kneel down," she said.

"Tia, don't you think we're over the whole slave-master era? I mean, it was exciting and all at the beginning, but we're lovers now. We're partners. You know, like on the same level. You and me?"

Tia took her hands to her lips and craned her neck back in a slight curve. Her eyes turned to slits and her brows furrowed.

"Since when are you on my level?" she protested.

"Since I started bangin' that ass, until you hollered," I said. My response came across in a sexy way, not interested in feeding any argument. I stood almost nose-to-nose with her. "Since I started making you scream like a bitch," I added. And I didn't get to say another word before Tia came around with a smack that stung my cheek like a thousand pins poking me all at once.

"Don't you ever, I mean *ever* talk to me that way again. Is that clear? You will *never* be my equal, Mister Ghetto Fabulous. *Never!* And never ever will I be *your bitch*. You've got some nerve. I might have to pull the plug on your little model project. Repossess your truck. Ship your ass back to Waldbaum's!"

"You wouldn't!" I said boldly.

"Try me!" she countered with the attitude.

I was hot. There was no way I would put my hands on her aggressively, but I wanted to. I wanted to smack the shit out of her! But in the end, she was in charge. She had all the chips and all the cards. They were her house rules. And now, more than ever, I could see what Judge Stern went through and why they divorced.

I softened my face and said, "I'm sorry, Tia. I don't know what got into me. I just thought—"

"You thought *wrong*." Tia put her hand inside my shirt; it was the expensive linen one that she bought for my birthday. In an instant, she snatched it open, the buttons shooting out into the night. "Now do as I told you. *Kneel!*"

I couldn't look at her anymore. I was still angry and I didn't want her to read my eyes. Once I was on my knees, Tia ran her hands through my short hair, her fingernails raking at my scalp. She positioned my head so that I was looking up at her.

"Repeat after me. I'm your humble servant."

"I . . . I'm your humble servant."

"Here to do as I please!" she said.

"Here to . . . do as you please," I replied like a parrot.

"When, and how you ask me to . . . so help me God."

I repeated the words. *So help me God.*

Tia pulled my head into her, my face below her waist. She was laughing out loud like a witch in the night. In between laughs she took another swallow of champagne straight from the bottle.

"Such a silly fool you are. Ha-ha-ha-*haaa*!!! Now come inside and fuck my brains out!"

Tia spun off, and there at the edge of the bed that blocked the wide opening, she stripped out of her strapless body suit and those matching above-the-elbow gloves. She bent over to pull down the embroidered black stockings and stepped out of her pumps. Fully naked now with her back to me, she unfastened her hair so that it fell over her shoulders. Then she looked over her shoulder and said, "Come on!"

Crawling onto the bed, Tia laid perfectly on top of the pillows. I remember us watching this in a porno flick she rented, where the woman laid face down over some cushioned chair. The furniture was flipped over like an upside-down V and there were handles for both the male and female. There was excessive grunting and screaming in the flick, too.

So when Tia lay there on the pillows, her body arched so that her ass was high and her face was down, I knew what I was about to do! I immediately came out of my clothes and climbed on the bed after her. She was wet and if she wasn't, I don't think it would matter. I was planning to be less than gentle. I pushed up into her forcefully and abruptly. I had no intentions of satisfying her, I just barreled into that forty-something-year-old pussy until she screamed herself hoarse. There were moments when she looked back over her shoulder at me and snarled like a wild beast, sending messages to me through her eyes only how she hated me and detested where I came from and that I didn't belong in her world. I could read all of these things she was conveying. And it all mixed in with the skyline of Stamford. Suddenly, it didn't matter if the whole world was watching; it was just as well that they all witnessed me banging the daylights out of this has-been actress! Put *this* on *Entertainment Tonight*!

By the next morning I had already left the hotel. I was hell bent on leaving Tia; let her keep her fucking money, her house, the truck, all that shit. *Fuck her!* I just wanted the money that I worked for. It was squeezed under the mattress. Close to $60,000—the $1,000 per week salary that I'd saved over eighteen months of kissing this bitch's ass. I thought about taking a shit and dropping turds of it in her shoes . . . in her fuckin Jacuzzi! But I didn't want to wait around too long and maybe run into her. I didn't really want to see her again.

I heard the taxi's horn outside and thought it to be great timing. I stuffed the money in a leather knapsack and said, "What the hell," before I took the collection of Gucci watches Tia had custom-made for me. I'd give one or two to Troy and another to my old boss at Waldbaum's. I figured he'd get a big laugh out of it all and take me back on board. Maybe I'd even get a manager's job if I put in a solid effort. I knew this nurturing confidant shit was too good to be true.

Just as I got to the foyer I was stopped in my tracks. The bronze slab that I had repainted with her face was up on the wall. It was the first thing she'd see coming in the house. On impulse I climbed up on a hall table and whipped out my dick. I urinated all over the art, hoping that the fumes and smell of it would catch Tia's attention. I hoped the acid in my urine would eventually eat away at the paint and eventually make the painting as unrecognizable as her career had become.

I hopped down from the table with my piss dripping all over it, and zipped up. The front door opened.

"Spencer?"

I was startled at first, but I'd already convinced myself I didn't care anymore. I looked away from Tia and told myself, *Let's go. Just leave!*

"Spencer, where are you going? Why's the taxi outside? What happened over *there?*" By the looks on Tia's face, she caught on to the offensive odor in the midst.

"Good-bye!" I said and proceeded to pass her.

"*Ohhhh* no you don't," she said, putting her hand out to stop me, still sounding so much like a disciplinarian.

"Excuse me, *ex*-employer," I said, hoping that she'd get the point.

"Spencer, what are you saying? You're leaving me? How *can* you, when everything is about to take off for us?"

"You've gotta be kidding. After all that shit you did and said last night? Did you honestly believe I would be your, ahh, *humble servant?* Did you truly believe that I'd be here to please you? Huh? Are you smoking tissue paper?"

"Spencer, Spencer," she said with her hand soft on my cheek. I turned away, not wanting her to touch me. The taxi's horn blew again. "Spencer." Now Tia was snickering. "Look at me. Look—at—me, please?" It was the first I ever heard her say *please.* Through my nose I pulled in a long flow of air. The urine was sour to my senses.

"Spencer, last night wasn't all that it appeared to be. I am not your master. You're not, I repeat, *not* my slave. Do you hear me? Last night I was on stage with all the lights, the audience . . . the night was mine. You were part of my fantasy . . . my fantasy come true. That's all it was. *I was acting.*"

I stared at Tia in total astonishment. "An *act!* You're telling me it was all an act? The slap? The master-slave bit?"

"Yes, Spencer. It was all one big movie—like on the porno film we watched together. Except last night you had a real actress. You got *the real thing*. You came real good, by the way, which was the whole point."

"I don't believe you," I said, still finding it hard to swallow. My arms still folded.

"Then believe this, Spence . . . ," she said and pressed up to my body. There was a pause as Tia looked at me with her glassy eyes. "I never meant to hurt you or chase you away. It was just a fantasy . . . you are my equal. You're better than my equal. And if you'd like, I'll be *your* humble servant. I'll be *your* slave, *your* bitch . . . whatever you want, whatever you say. I'm *yours*, Spencer. Yours."

Tia lifted up on the balls of her feet and gave me a passionate kiss. I allowed it. Then I immersed myself in her assurances.

"You're crazy, you know that?" I could barely get the words out.

"*Mmm-hmm* . . . crazy . . . for you," she managed to reply.

"And one more thing . . . ," I said, pulling my lips from hers. "You are some kind of actress."

"No, Spencer. I'm some kind of *woman*." We went back to kissing, tongues tossing and flipping and dancing as if our lives depended on it. Meanwhile I heard a loud motor outside the taxi making a screeching noise off of the property. *What-ever.*

[E I G H T]

NOW I WAS king.

And never was Tia more obliging than she was after that day I peed on the artwork, that same day she explained how she was mine and we reconciled. She also gave me a gift on that day when she returned home.

"I want you to hire somebody to do the menial work," I said to Tia. "Things like cleaning shoes and Jacuzzis, and washing your underwear? That's dead. Somebody else can do that from now on."

"Not a problem."

"The pool, too," I said. "And any other little nuisance that I decide I don't wanna do, that's for the hired help."

"Whatever you say, baby."

"And just to make clear our commitment . . . to confirm our arrangement, I want you to deposit a hundred thousand in my personal bank account as a show of good faith. This way my plans for the model project will be guaranteed." I didn't really need the money, but I thought I'd toss that in just because I could. I was fucking this woman so good these days that she was making me feel superior. Her attitude was enjoyable and her attentions were all about me. So, I figured I'd go for it.

"A hundred—?" she started to say.

"Now if there's a problem with that—," I threatened.

"No. No problem. I was just wondering if I could afford that."

"You can. I should know. There was four hundred and fifty liquid last time I spoke with your accountant—last week, to be exact. Plus you've got settlement money comin' in hand over foot. Not to mention all the property and possessions you now own."

"But—"

"I'm tellin' you, Tia. You put your money where your mouth is, or else . . ."

"Spencer, it's not that I don't want to. It's that . . ." Tia was wearing a trench coat made of red leather. She subtly reached in a pocket as she listened to my terms. She took out what looked to be a bracelet. "I just spent a hundred thousand for this. It's made of uncut diamonds. I planned to give it to you on New Year's Eve—but I had to have it custom-made and everything."

I took the bracelet and at once I knew she was truthful. I didn't know too much about diamonds, but I did know that I could easily have the bracelet appraised. Tia wasn't fool enough to give me something fake at this stage in our relationship.

Damn, I told myself when I saw that the links of the bracelet were composed of block letters all the way around. The "S," I guessed, stood for Spencer. And the letters were glistening like drops of heaven.

"You *are* serious, aren't you?" I said in amazement.

"And willing to prove it," she said. And from that moment on I felt liberated, free to move ahead, to go with the idea. The Premium Fudge project was about to blast off.

"SPENCER! SPENCER! Are you home? Spencer?"

I could hear Tia's voice from the study, but I was on the phone. Instead of shouting I simply went on with the call. Surely she knew that I was hard at work; she'd find her way to our little home office. After all, this *was* supposed to be a business environment, not a day at the park. What was all the excitement about, anyway? I guess she heard what I was thinking because she made her way to the study.

"Spence, didn't you hear—*oh . . .*" Tia lowered her voice when she realized I was on the phone. "*Sorry,*" she whispered.

I waved hello and noticed that she wasn't alone, and it was back to the business at hand.

"Okay. Listen, I've gotta hang up now, but see if you can get us in the next issue, Jamie. You've got our commitment for six print ads for your next six issues of the magazine." Jamie asked me if that was a promise. "You got my word, Jamie. You scratch my back and I'll scratch yours. Bye-bye, cupcake." And she responded in kind, making me believe that I was a Hershey's Kiss. My focus turned to Tia and company.

I said, "Just placing the last of the advertisements. I still have to work out something with *Essence* magazine, but otherwise we're all ready to go. So who's our friend?" I asked, turning my eyes to the short-stuff with the long braids and Camay completion. She couldn't be more than five feet six inches, considering the stiletto-heeled boots. I immediately guessed that Tia had recruited our first candidate for the Premium Fudge project, and I said so, too.

"No," Tia responded. *"Yes and no*, that is. Remember we spoke about you having an assistant?" Tia made the gesture that a magician would, with the whole *ta-da* expression.

"Oh yeah. You mean the girl we wanted to scrub the toilets and shovel a ditch out back?" I lied, but I never expected Tia to join in.

"Exactly. But don't forget that oil spill in the basement," added Tia.

The visitor looked to be no more than twenty years of age with a mysterious, sleepy gaze over her picture-perfect nose, cheeks, and lips. Her features were sharp, surreal, like those Japanese animations. When I got up from my desk to approach I could see how the hint of mascara and the brush of lip gloss were helping to enhance what was so attractive.

"Excuse me?" she said, falling for our prank hook, line, and sinker. Her expression turned to an appalled one. I wondered if looking too close into her eyes might get me cut or stabbed!

"Jokes," I said, and I put my hand out to shake hers. Tia had her hand on the pretty one's shoulder as well, an assurance that we were only kidding. "I'm Spencer Lewis," I said. "Nice to meet you."

"Cassandra . . . Cassandra Evans," she said with the deep, smoky voice and the firm-but-feminine handshake. Her face softened to an appreciative expression, as well.

"She's the daughter of a lady at the tennis center. We got to talking, she's done some college, been in the business a little . . . Cassandra? Why don't *you* explain? Go on. Just like we discussed. I'll leave you two alone." Tia started to leave.

"Ahh . . . Tia?" I excused myself as Cassandra had a seat. When we were alone in the hallway, I asked Tia, "Can't *you* tell me who she is?"

Tia smoothed her fingertips along my cheek. She said, "I found her for you, love. It may not look like it but she wants to work for us *real* bad. Go on, break her in. Do what you do best." Tia smooched closer for a quick kiss. "I know she'll work to our benefit."

"How qualified is she?" I asked, trying to maintain focus.

"Very qualified, I'm sure. See for yourself."

I took a deep breath. "You're the boss," I said.

"No. I'm your lover. This is *your* dream. I'm just here to put up the money. To lend support."

Back at my computer. Two clicks and another printout emerged. Cassandra circled the words and gave the new printout to me. She offered to redo the ad we were placing and I was willing to hear her out.

"Now look at *this* one," she said.

I read the quote. It had been changed:

THERE'S A BRIGHT FUTURE AWAITING YOU.
WE WELCOME YOU TO COME AND LIVE YOUR DREAM.

At the bottom of the headline, there was small print that read,

ASPIRING MODELS AGES 18 TO 22 NEED APPLY.

"Now this is more appealing . . . not something that would scare me."

"You? I'm not trying to sell *you*. I want that superfine college dropout who always wanted to model. She's not ditzy, but she could use a bit of, let's say, manipulation."

"Well, Mr. Lewis . . . I *am* a college dropout. I may not be superfine, but yes, I always wanted to model. Except no one is checking for a pretty girl who's five-five. They want tall girls with the face of America. They want long luxurious hair, not braids like mine—too Afrocentric. Basically, they don't really want women—and you heard me say *women*, not *girls*—like me. So in all reality, you *are* trying to sell me. My opinion *does* matter because, based on what Tia said, you're looking for women *just like me*. And guess what? I don't require *manipulation*—bad word. But I could use some guidance." Cassandra had her hands on her hips, but also a smile.

"Okay, Cassandra. I respect your opinion. And your confidence. But let's start from the beginning, okay? All the pointing and the saucy attitude ain't gonna get you nowhere but on *trailer trash TV*, Maury or Jerry Springer, maybe. That's where that stuff belongs. But here? We're a team. We work together. So how about you and I sit down and talk like we know better." I could see that Cassandra had been through some things in her life. There was a certain mistrust deep behind those stunning eyes. But beyond that, there was a savvy woman; it even showed in the way that she dressed. And quiet as I kept it, I appreciated how she was aggressive and edgy. All of that in the first ten minutes I met her. I knew that she could be a firecracker, a source of energy that would help propel my dreams into reality.

"I went to Stamford U for two years. The reason that I dropped out was because it wasn't what I wanted. I felt like I was wasting time, ya know? Like life was pulling me in another direction."

"What's your big dream?"

"The big one? I want to have some contribution other than being just another pretty face, or just *existing*. The best-case scenario is I'd like to be a part of something big. And honestly, it would be a thrill to be a part of a blastoff like this. The birth of an empire."

I had heard enough, but I couldn't help wanting to hear more. Her words were scratching an itch I'd had for a long time. They affirmed my own attitude about life. And the more Cassandra spoke, the more I couldn't imagine her not being a part of the project.

I asked, "And, so . . . now you're not working?"

"No."

"You'll have to spend long hours," I said.

"That's cool."

"You're gonna have to deal with a lot of different personalities," I warned.

"You mean, like those who think they have all of the answers?"

"Maybe. Some arrogance. Attitudes."

"So? How'd I handle *you* just now?" she asked with a slice of sarcasm. "Not that you're arrogant or that you have an attitude," she added.

I smiled a crooked smile and looked away from her allure. "Moving right along . . . the pay won't start out great," I insisted.

"What-*ever*. You want me to give you some of my time

for free, just say the word. You wanna give me a probation period? I'm with it, *what*. I guess . . . what I'm trying to say is that I want to be involved with you. You want an once of blood? A lock of my hair? Just tell me what I gotta do."

I looked hard into Cassandra's eyes. I looked for lies, deceit, anything phony. Instead, I saw nothing but truth.

"You can start with taking off your jacket, your hat, and helping me with these ads, they gotta be finished before FedEx gets here to pick up at five. Seems like you know more about this stuff than I do," I admitted.

Cassandra and I worked up a comfortable relationship. In the beginning we tiptoed, never getting too personal, keeping everything on a business level. It was fantastic that she had a driver's license because I'd send her out to the local Kinko's Copy Center from time to time, to handle the bigger jobs that our home copier couldn't handle. Cassandra also took it upon herself to create relationships with the beauty salons and clothing boutiques, the places that women of color frequented on a weekly basis so we could get wind of our big model search.

JUNE 1 was scheduled as our first day of one-on-one interviews. The advertisement attracted 2,200 responses from women who lived as close as Stamford and Norwalk, and from as far away as San Diego, California. We received the majority of the responses by e-mail, physical mail, FedEx, and we even had a Premium Fudge Web site where folks could register. At least half of the responses were tossed aside based on photos alone. We even let a few slip through because the photography wasn't all that hot—it was my idea to give those candidates the benefit of the doubt. With the thousand or so responses we had left, Tia, Cassandra, and I sat and read the most interesting profiles out loud. It was a mess down in the basement game room that day, with photos and biographies, letters, and e-mail printouts strewn and piled all over the pool table, the floor, and the bar.

Mimi was living with us now. Tia had mentioned our need for household help; someone who could do those menial jobs that I once did; perish the thought. She found out about Mimi at the country club where she played doubles tennis once a week. A number was passed to her and the rest was history.

Mimi was an au pair who was in from Norway and looking for work. When I first met her, I thought her to be novel, showing up at the house with a sort of Bohemian sloppiness: cuffed paisley jeans, a halter top, and clogs on her feet. She spoke charming English. Charming, because it was always sprinkled with the accent of her Norwegian birthland. I'd never forget how she sat there perched on the edge of the sofa, abundant cleavage pushing out of her top, submissive like a geisha, while Tia and I decided hard on whether or not to hire her. I was relaxed that day, in a *neither-here-nor-there* mood, which probably led to the easy decision to take Mimi on board.

We expected a horror flick to unfold in the house since this was Mimi's first job in the states. The worst-case scenario would be our atmosphere smelling like three-day-old trailer trash. But things turned out well once Mimi settled in. We were ecstatic to know that she kept herself clean. Cassandra helped her to shop for clothing more comparable to our tastes. Bigger than that, Mimi took it upon herself to clean tubs—there were five of them—she changed bedding and she even cleaned curtains. What was *really* crazy was how Tia and I would sometimes do small tasks ourselves just because we felt sorry for Mimi.

"I was thinking that it might be a good idea to have Cassandra move in, too. We do have plenty of room," Tia said over two piles of dirty clothes. We had just about separated the whites and the colored clothing for two washloads. "I mean, since Mimi's here for good now, what the heck?"

"We're gonna need the four remaining rooms for the girls, Tia. Where will they stay?"

"I was thinking about clearing out the space over the garage. It's big enough for two, really. Actually, when you first came to work for me, I was gonna put you up there."

"Oh yeah, put me in some crusty storage space, huh?" I tickled Tia until she begged me to stop. I ended up on top of her and the piles of clothes on the laundry room floor. From tickling, we went into kissing. Then I began to pull at her tennis shorts. She begged me to stop.

"*Spencer!* Mimi might come in. Cassandra . . . the *cook.*"

"Nah, Mimi's upstairs changing the sheets; the ones that you got wet last night. The others are working, too."

I ignored her and wiggled lower, burrowing my head between her legs. She had panties on still as I nibbled and snorkeled in a frenzy, driving her wild with squeals and moans. This was getting serious.

"Spencer! Come on!" she pleaded. "Take me to the *bedroom.* Not *here.*"

"Shit! It didn't *start* in the bedroom."

Tia took hold of my head. It was hard to tell if she wanted me to go on or stop, like she was having her own inner battle.

"No—no—no—*nooo* . . . let's stop before this gets out of hand. *Really.* Let a lady keep what little integrity she has left. Please, Spencer."

"Integrity? *Tia!* You know you're the biggest freak on two feet. Who you kiddin'?!"

"Okay," she laughed. "I'll give you that. But the others in the house don't know that. Now let me up. Come on."

I grunted and stood, looking down at Tia and knowing that I could've easily turned her *no* into a *yes.*

"Well? Aren't you gonna help me up?"

I gave her a hand. Meanwhile, my erection went limp and the lava in my body simmered to its cooling point.

"What's wrong?" she asked.

"What's wrong? What's wrong is when *you* want it, I give it to you. So it should be the same for me. When I want it, there shouldn't be no sniveling or excuses. *Fuck* what everybody else thinks. They ain't your man. *I'm* your man. You don't think they know what's goin' on? You don't think Mimi's up there smellin' your dried-up juices on the sheets?"

"Spencer?"

"Spencer, *nothin'.*"

"You're taking this too far. Blowing it out of proportion. I just want to keep apples separate from the oranges. I want us to have our own space. Anybody can walk in here."

I folded my arms. A lotta good an explanation was doin' me with my dick all shriveled up in my pants. My attitude in the clouds somewhere.

"Okay," Tia said. "You want to be the spoiled brat, I'll give you what you want." Tia stepped past me and closed the laundry room door. She turned the latch to lock it. Then she confronted me again, taking off her button-down blouse as she did, then the bra, then the shirt. I stood there with my arms folded as she put her hand on my shoulder to keep her balance as she stripped her underwear off of her legs.

"How do you want me? Come on, I'm *serious*," Tia said, her hands on her hips. "Should I bend over? Or get on my back?"

"On your knees. I want you to blow me."

She looked down at my crotch angrily and then back to my eyes. Without a word Tia went down to her knees. She began to fiddle with my zipper.

"Ahh, Tia?" I said, not the least bit impressed. My words stopped her before she freed the cobra. I took her chin in my hand. "Next time I ask for it . . . don't do that shit, *alright*?"

Tia looked at me confused.

"Get dressed," I said. And I left the room knowing Tia was still there on her knees, bewildered, bewitched, all that. Butt-ass naked except for her Reeboks.

WE CALLED in a three-man crew of hard-working Mexicans to clean up the attic over the garage. Tia said that most of the stuff was old memories and that she didn't care what they did with it. I told the guys the same thing. It took half a day, but when it was all over there was an extra room the size of a studio apartment that could easily suit two or three people. The only additional work needed was for a bathroom to be installed. But until then, Cassandra would have to trek back and forth across the driveway to the house to relieve herself, wash, or eat. I was happy with the idea of Cassandra becoming a resident because she was getting a lot accomplished. Now, coming to work would be more convenient for her. She'd always be accessible.

"Sir, there was a few things that I thought would be important. You might wanna check 'em but 'fore we toss it," a worker suggested and handed me a box.

"Thanks. The girl inside, Cassandra, will cut a check for you."

"Ah . . . sir? You mind if we take half of that in cash?" I was already looking through the box, but agreed without looking up. The man left.

Photos. Some antique jewelry. An address book and some sewing accessories.

I began to pick at the photos. There were a few white folks, one whom I knew to be David Stern.

"Spencer?" It was Tia calling for me.

"Yeah . . . hold on," I started, and I went to stash the box up on a board that served as a high, out-of-the-way shelf. I figured on checking into those items later. See what I could learn about Tia's past, better than the four Emmy awards and all of the plaques on her library wall or on her mantel could tell me.

When I reached daylight, Tia said, "It's the people from the radio station. They want to discuss a co-sponsorship for the June 1 interviews."

I widened my eyes. Any sponsorship was always helpful, despite our having substantial funds for the venture. *Exposure, impressions, and promotion are things that make a plan come together nicely,* Cassandra explained.

The phone call and other business had me forget all about the box and photos.

THE BIG day came upon us like a speeding car just ten or so feet away from a wall of solid brick. The preceding weeks were spent on the phone and Internet whittling down our thousand-plus candidates to two hundred. Most of the two hundred girls vowed to travel by their own means; however, there were two dozen who needed financial assistance for the trip and/or the hotel stayover. We made the investment, knowing that we were in fact organizing our own little family of million-dollar babies. We presumed that our final selections would be women so passionate about the project, with such a desire to achieve success with Premium Fudge, that it would be worth the investment. We had no doubt that our group would bring in heavy financial rewards as soon as we were up and running. We envisioned a swimsuit video, Internet productions, a pinup calendar, and fashion shows. We had a tentative agreement to promote a new line of perfume with a new *Essence* venture, a campaign where our models would be employed to promote in strip malls over the course of the forthcoming winter. We had an oral agreement to do a six-month photo shoot for a new line of lingerie called "Obsession." And there was a lawyer's convention coming to Stamford where the organizers needed our girls to perform as hostesses for the event.

What was so amazing to me was that Cassandra was the one to gather all of these commitments, sight-unseen. We didn't have one model signed to contract, and yet we could count on future profit. *I loved that damned girl.*

She also had an arrangement with Nikeema, a professional model who had won on the popular TV show *Top Model* and had been featured on the magazine covers of *Vogue* and *Young Ms.* Nikeema was on board to act as a spokesperson who we could integrate into all of our mass-media marketing. It was a commitment that might otherwise cost tens of thousands of dollars. But Cassandra convinced the soon-to-be supermodel that it would be an inspiration to others behind her, that it was a way of giving back to all the aspiring models who wanted to be like Nikema. *Go Cassandra!*

Although the Stamford Marriott held special memories for Tia and me, the interviews were a business-only affair. I'd rented the ballroom, which was up on the second floor, and had a cavernous, sky-lit lounge area with couches and coffee tables just outside of its double-door entrance. Cassandra employed a team of college students for the event and they arrived at 7 A.M. that Saturday morning for the setup. Hotel staff already had reception tables, chairs, and a breakfast buffet prepared inside the ballroom itself, as well as a podium, a stage, and presentation devices for a planned slide show.

Tia and I arrived at 8 A.M. And she was entirely impressed at how things were so extremely organized, and how many of the applicants were eager enough to check into the Marriott on Friday evening; either that, or they arrived much earlier that morning. I could see at least fifty of these women myself perched on couches in the lobby, sipping coffee, flipping through magazines, and chatting amongst one another.

I was floored by the human element of this idea and how the seed that I thought up in my head had now earned its weight in flesh and blood. Like so much else that had befallen me since my high school graduation, this, too, was getting serious.

All I witnessed in all of those images before my eyes made me think of a waiting room, any waiting room, only this was so colorful with whites and yellows and blues and reds. Pink and black and lavender and every earth-tone color. Tote bags. Carry-alls. Hats. Flowers in their hair. And, *oh my god!* The hair and perfumes in the atmosphere! Just to inhale felt expensive, cheap, and spicy all at once. I could see toe rings, ankle bracelets, belly chains with pendants, and pierced navels. Some had expensive earrings, while others donned hoops, or a trail of two, three, and four on one ear or the other. There was nervous energy with so many pairs of eyes swinging, volleying here and there, and beckoning for the attentions of anyone important, anyone in power who could change their lives.

My biggest weakness was my eyes, and I didn't want to be too obvious. So, I kept a pair of dark shades on, even if they did take some of the luster from the spectacle. I wanted to shout *Women!* at the top of my lungs. Never had I seen so much skin in one place, under one roof. *Wow.* My head wasn't right when I thought of how many collarbones, necklines, and cleavages were on display . . . when I thought of all those limbs peeking out from the fabrics that barely covered them. This was the summertime—*what an incredible thing!*—when women wear very little. Today, they seemed to be wearing less than that. And when I tried to change my focus, instead of the rest of it, all I saw were thongs, thongs, and more thongs. Again, I wanted to shout out loud: *Pull your pants up!*

There were so many pretty faces, too; so many colors of beauty, with their accumulative aromas tickling my nose hairs, playing tricks with my mind. I digressed when I imagined how many breasts were there, how much ass . . . how much pussy. I had to tell myself that there was nothing wrong to think this way, to be a man who was both amazed and inspired. *Black women!* I loved them all, and individually. It was hard to keep my focus, but I did. *Damn.*

Interviews were scheduled to begin at 9 A.M. All of the candidates would be let into the ballroom at 8:30. They'd be registered. They'd be encouraged to wear name tags and they'd find a seat. The buffet was open to all. Meanwhile, Cassandra, Tia, and I were seated at three adjacent tables that were set up for one-on-one interviews. Tia stepped over to me for a word just before we began.

"You should relax, Spencer. Really."

"You're blowing me up, Tia. I'm fine."

"I can feel you, Spencer," she said and she put her hand over my heart. "Beating like a jackhammer in there."

"Okay. I'm caught red-handed. You got me there," I said, still looking here and there. "What should I do, counselor?" Tia bent down and spoke into my ear in business-as-usual fashion.

She said, "You're only a man, Spencer. It's okay to have desires, but you can't fuck them all. Remember your commitment. No lusting. Hands off."

"So I lied. A little lust never hurt anybody."

"And what about the business?"

Whispering back, I said, "I changed my mind. I wanna fuck everything breathing in here." My response came without a smile. Then I quickly grabbed Tia. "Just kiddin', woman. *Damn!* You really believed me, too!" I said this for her ears only.

"Maybe we all have a little actor in us."

"Yeah. Maybe. Let's get to work," I said.

[N I N E]

THERE WERE TEN of them.

Denise Matthews was born in San Diego, California, but when her parents divorced she landed in Port Chester, New York, where she worked at the local movie theatre as a ticket taker. When she came to us she was hungry, willing, and struggling to be any part of the modeling or entertainment industry. She said she once sang and danced and that she even had a big part in a school play back in San Diego. But the divorce diminished her motivation. At least she knew she could keep a check coming in. One day, she moved, eventually able to get out from under her mother's protective world. And now her future was in our hands. Denise had a glowing pine complexion and a round face, and she was big-busted, curvaceous, with hazel-green eyes. Her honey-roasted hair fell to her shoulders as she told us she still loved to dance, and in her Southern California–flavored girlish voice, she said:

"I put my heart into everything I do."

QIANNA LYNN was a no-brainer. We lucked out the moment she stepped in with her sensational, unique, and stunning beauty. It started in her Asian eyes, her Indian hair (dark with streaks of gold), and her Hawaiian complexion. Her total look, at eighteen years old, spoke of adventure and all things exotic. She was full of sex appeal. And her presence promised to add another level to the foundation of our organization. Qianna was from Kansas City, Missouri, an army brat, and one of the young women whom we paid travel expenses for. I'd bet everything I owned in the world that Qianna would help us make money.

DEJA SMITH. Wow. I remembered seeing her when I first walked through the lobby of the Marriott, thinking that she was cut from the custom-made, supermodel world. I'll always remember how she filled out that black, slinky, strappy dress and fantastically high heels. I couldn't ignore how sophisticated she appeared to be, or how her beauty came complete with her thick, sweeping tresses of shiny back hair and those pearly white teeth. I'd always remember the things that she said:

"I'm nineteen. I've wanted to model since I was little. I won Miss New Jersey in a pageant two years ago, but the contest turned out to be a hoax. I hope this isn't. I'm not saying it is, but I'm just saying . . . They never paid me the prize money—five thousand dollars—and I spent so much to prepare for that event. Even hired a vocal coach. I was hoping

to one day model for catalogs and magazines—even
calendars . . . I used to dream of living abroad and riding a
horse in the desert . . . I'm one hundred percent real; no
implants, no lip job, not even a tattoo . . . I'm naturally
shaped. I'm five feet seven inches and I weigh a hundred and
four pounds. Oh . . . and I love listening to Michael Jackson,
R. Kelly, and Maxwell."

I sat there listening to Deja, knowing that she was
deserving, and that her Milky Way brown skin and nubile
looks were just itching for exposure to the world. It even
crossed my mind that for her (and a million dollars) I'd
leave Tia in a heartbeat.

ELISE WILSON caught us off guard. I'd swear that she
was sun-kissed, as much as she glowed. She was a little
lighter-toned than Deja, like a Snickers bar from Nigeria.
She had that incredible doll face, with high cheekbones, a
slightly exaggerated pout, and black marble eyes with the
fluttering lashes. Elise was what I called *approachable*. Her
lips were a natural pink and her short, black hair was wildly
styled as if by electrocution. I asked her some of my own
IQ questions, like did she know who our last two presidents
were. She said *no*. I asked her how many pints make a quart.
She said *two*. I asked her what her favorite pastime was. She
said she *didn't have one*, but that *television was interesting
here in America*. I asked her if she had some goals in life,
and she didn't know what that was. Regarding goals, she
asked, "Are they expensive?" And we laughed. At least she
knew her age. She was eighteen. And how did she found out
about us? *Over the radio*, she said. I didn't care what Elise

knew or didn't know, I just knew that she was gorgeous and had potential, but for the teaching we'd have to do.

VALERIE GREY was what we considered a 'round the way girl. She was *ghetto glamorous*. Representative of every fly-girl or chicken-head I've ever come across. Valerie had the looks I had become familiar with thanks to hip-hop videos, Black Tail magazines and the chicks from Dakota Street. She was twenty years old, five feet seven, and weighed 110 pounds. Her brown skin had stone red in it, her eyes were large like almonds, and her lips were full. Her dark brown hair swept over her forehead and formed a ponytail to the back. I guessed that she had a hairpiece in, except it appeared to be natural. Valerie was one of the girls with hoop earrings and she was nervous like a busy signal. But beyond that, she was wholesome. She didn't have a supermodel's icy pout, but that was compensated for when it was time for the girls to show off their bodies. Valerie stood out like a sculpted marble statue. And at the same time, she could've been a gymnast! Tia was the first to interview Valerie, but eventually I had to give a final approval on all choices. Once Valerie came before me, a tear rolled down her cheek. I couldn't imagine what was wrong. I pulled her aside and away from the others.

"What's wrong?" I asked, easily weakened by her sniffles and tears.

When Valerie regained some of her composure, she said, "I just want a chance to prove myself, and I know that I'm not as beautiful as all the other girls . . . I know it."

"What makes you think you're not as beautiful? Look at

those pretty eyes of yours. I couldn't wait to meet you myself and have those excited eyes dancing in my face. But now you're *ruining* everything, making everything all sad." I made a face, a mock scowl. Valerie smartened up. I gave her a handkerchief and she patted her eyes.

She made a final sniffle before she asked, "You really think my eyes are pretty?"

"You've got a lot more goin' on than just your eyes, girl. Now shape up. Get yourself together. I don't work with crybabies."

The words did the job. Valerie shook the emotions and discovered a new energy between us.

I said, "Just because the average model is five feet seven and thin as a twig, doesn't mean that's what I want. I'm looking for girls just like you, got it?"

She couldn't help but to smile.

"So you think you're ready to come on board with us?"

She nodded excitedly.

"Then welcome to Premium Fudge, baby. You're in."

LIA STONE. Now *this* twenty-one-year-old was so fine, *I* wanted to cry. I was drunk from looking at Lia. I loved her shape, her warm eyes that seemed to float in some kind of slow-motion empathy. Lia had that lazy stare, a gaze that melted me; my insides had to be mush. She had a soft voice and a sensuality about her, the kind that deserved pampering, with her slinky walk and fluid gestures. I guessed that everything including men, money, and magic came to her with ease, and if it didn't, then something was wrong. Lia was a fudge-dipped beauty with soft, curled brown hair and a five-feet-four-inches build. She was short according to the tall man, but just right for absolutely everybody else. There was no question that Lia was one of the chosen ten, but I didn't mind sitting, and watching, and listening to her. I could've stayed there all day doing just that. Lia was from Norwalk, Connecticut. She was a cashier at the McDonald's rest stop on I-95 when a customer handed her our advertisement. *God bless that man.*

TRINA ALLEN didn't appear to be a girl who grew up on cow's milk, corn, and homemade peach cobbler, until she said, *"I reckon,"* and that she was *"fittin' to take the world by storm."* I couldn't help falling for the novelty of meeting my first *southern belle*, another of the travelers we financed. Trina was from Georgia and smelled sweet in my presence.

"What is that you're wearing?" I asked.

"For You," she said.

I smiled, but didn't let on that I was flattered.

"No . . . seriously, what is it?"

"It's—*For You*," she said, and brandished a sweet smile under her luscious lips. I couldn't get a straight answer from her, still busy absorbing her full breasts, soft brown, and blemish-free skin begging for a camera's flash (and my touch).

"Okay . . . see, I knew I'd getcha . . . *For You* is the name of the fragrance. But it's not a body perfume, it's in my hair."

I admired her hair, too, a rust-colored fuss-free bob that rounded down and up under her ears and chin. Trina had a way of projecting a dreamy world with her rich laughter, heavenly cheeks, and the healthy bazookas in that pushup bra. Nothing but possibilities.

EGYPT McKINLEY was her name, but she made it clear that she wanted to be called Egypt; that is, *if* we were going to accept her. And that daring element—I liked that about her. It was as if she was saying "Take it or leave it," without actually saying it in that way. Egypt also provoked a kind of lust with her exotic eyes and how they pulled at me. She had a tattoo of a thumbprint on her abdomen positioned at four o' clock in respect to her navel, but all of this was nothing . . . absolutely *nothing* close to telling me about the *real* Egypt.

Before I got deep into the question-and-answer segment of our interview, she asked if there was somewhere we could talk alone.

"Can you tell me why? I mean, what is it that you can do in private that you can't do out in the open? After all, this is *all about* exposure, where you project who you are by your image or in a snapshot. Modeling is all about exposure and showing the world who you are."

"Exactly. And I'm *so* ready for that, but I wanted to show you something special. Something memorable. I want it to be so that no matter what decision you make today, you'll never forget me. Please don't get the wrong idea . . ."

It was getting close to 6 P.M., the end of the interviews, and I was *so* ready to go home to the Jacuzzi. After thinking it over, I was ready to give Egypt what she asked for. What would a few minutes of my time hurt? I knew we had a private room available to us behind the ballroom, and I didn't mind getting my stretch on, either. So I led Egypt away from the ongoing interviews. The atmosphere in the ballroom was beginning to feel so drab and discouraging; I was ready for anything beyond the ordinary.

Egypt took a beach towel out of her carryall and laid it on the floor. She seemed a little nervous, but hurried around to prepare her little, I suppose, *show.*

Out came the candles, five of them I counted. She also lit some incense and waved the smoldering stick around the small room, its swirls of smoke suspended into a mini fog. Meanwhile she said, "My whole thing is I totally understand what men like. It's all about tits and ass, right?" Egypt continued speaking, moving around, setting up a chair a few feet away from the towel. The stage? "So, in the next few minutes I'm gonna show you something you can't deny . . . something to express my sexuality, my appeal and, well . . . I'll just let you see for yourself, Mr. Lewis."

Egypt went to turn off the lights and the room went dark, except for the area inside the candles. Now Egypt's box tape player began to play "Beautiful Ones" by Prince, and the music filled the atmosphere with a soft drumbeat, and then the eerie organ. I just sat waiting for Egypt to appear.

"Sorry. I gotta start it again. I wasn't ready yet." Egypt flew past me in an illusion of limbs and skin. Oh *shit!* I exclaimed this with a thunderous roar inside my head. My eyes bugged out, just knowing I was seeing things. Egypt was naked! All the way. And now she was crouching down to rewind the tape. Then she went to the center of the bath towel, knelt down, and folded herself forward into a fetal position with her hands on the floor out in front of her. This might've been a ballet position, only without clothes.

When the music started again, Egypt, still with her knees, lower legs, and feet on the floor underneath her, began to ease her upper body into the upright position and continued on until she was stretched back, with her body in a slight arch. Egypt shimmered within the candles' glow, apparently from oil that she'd put on specifically for this occasion. Her breasts and her skin were fully exposed. Her sinewy frame was taut there on the floor before me, her face was expressionless. She spread her arms out and to her sides as she rose again. Her belly was so flat, and her navel ring was silver just like the bud that pierced her tongue. Egypt's hair was a disarray of brown curls that fell over her face, adding to her mystique and showing how she was so determined to do as she pleased. And now she had me, my senses, and attention in check, bound to her display.

She put her hands on the floor in front of her and stretched her left leg back like a gymnast, lifting it high like the long tail on a retriever. Before I knew it Egypt had lifted up into a graceful handstand, her legs spread into a V, maintaining her balance, and then opening them wider until one foot touched down for a fully exposed walkover. Standing up now, Egypt made this windmill move with her arms and she sank into a split. Even in the shadows I could see how Egypt's pubic hair was kept in a miniature line that reached the edge of her sex. From the forward split, Egypt made her body fold and twist in contortions that I winced at, not realizing such was possible. At various intervals she stopped for a pose, keeping with the rhythm of the music. I saw everything. *Everything.*

The second verse of the song began:

Baby, baby, baby . . .
What's it gonna be tonight?

All the while, Egypt held on to this deep, sensual attitude that seemed to block out all else in the world; like what she was doing was perfectly alright.

Stunned and amazed, I tried to imagine this was mere art in motion, although I was definitely aroused, hiding all evidence with my arms folded over my lap.

Egypt was on her back now making butterfly formations with her arms and legs. Her head and eyes swooned with the song. Now her hands were caressing her thighs, her pubic area, midsection, and breasts until her fingers weaved up into her abundance of hair. From the looks of it, she *really* liked Prince's music because as the song moved into its final stages, Egypt's body convulsed and gyrated.

You make me so confused . . .

Then while Prince began to scream, Egypt humped the floor as if there were a man there receiving her in full, feeding her back in his entirety.

Do you want me Or do you want him?!
Cause I want you!

The song drifted toward its end and so did Egypt, apparently exhausted, spent there on the beach towel.

I was numb. Dumbfounded. Openmouthed. And I didn't dare move because my dick was hard as a rock.

"What's going on in here?"

Oh shit, Tia. I looked around, but not in time to stop her from turning on the lights. Her face was frozen in horror. I turned back to Egypt, still on the beach towel, motionless as a corpse.

As if Tia and I were the only conscious persons in the room, I gestured for her to come closer.

"I can't trust you for a—"

"Shhh," I exclaimed with my finger to my lips.

In a softer volume, still with the cloud of rage surrounding her, Tia asked, "Would you *please* explain to me why *we* are out there needing you and why *you* are in here with . . . with . . . this freak of nature, laying on the floor with no clothes on?" Tia had her hands on her hips, astonished and demanding an answer.

"It's her audition, Tia. Keep it down."

"Keep it down? Have you gone—"

I got up, my erection finally wilted, and I escorted Tia toward the door. I found myself repeating words Egypt had spoken.

"It's not what you think, Tia. Apparently . . ." I said this, but at the same time I looked over to where I left Egypt, ". . . the girl is very sexual and she had an act that she wanted to show me."

"You . . . why you? Why not everyone?"

"I guess she was nervous. So many strangers, too many people . . . hell, I don't know, boo. But you can ask her that yourself, after we sign her up."

I stepped away from Tia, leaving her (I'm sure) spellbound as I reentered the ballroom.

SUGAR MITCHELL was another homegirl who came up from the Bronx, like Valerie. Her angelic smile sold me the instant we met. She had long whip legs, a coffee-brown complexion, and full lips over the happy smile. She explained the truth, that coming to be discovered was something like trying to escape from her neighborhood, its violence and whims. How did she know that we had such similar intentions? Just like she escaped 149th Street, I escaped Dakota Street. Call it sympathy, but I said "Yes" to Sugar.

THERE SHE was. Carrie Bunn. Why-oh-why did she have to show her face. Five feet six inches tall. Dreamy, optimistic eyes. Long, chestnut-brown hair down to her neckline. Carrie was nineteen. As she spoke I saw a flower; an orchid that was beautiful from the moment she woke up to the moment she fell asleep. While her eyes were closed, she was simply every man's dream.

"I was on the pep squad and then the varsity cheerleading team before I left high school. They voted me prom queen, girl most likely to succeed, all that stuff . . . but unfortunately you can't pay for college with good looks . . ."

And if she could, I thought to myself, she would've been the homecoming queen.

"I can't be my own judge, though; it's others who say I look good, that I should model, act, or something. But when I look into the mirror I see plain ole' me. I look ugly in the morning . . . I have my time of the month, and contrary to what the boys at school used to rumor, I *do* use the bathroom . . ." I took that as a code for *My shit stinks too.*

I sat there listening to Carrie, not jotting down one notation, as I had been doing for other interviews. I was stuck on stupid, my elbow on the table, my hand covering my mouth and mumbling to myself like some psychopath.

"My friends know me as Charisma, a nickname my father used to call me. He's gone now . . . to, ya know, a better place. My mom used to say he went to the other side of the sun . . ."

I'm not even hearing this. It's the perfect full breasts, the perfect waistline and hips, the tan, the eyes, and the smile that are intoxicating, sucking at my eyes and overwhelming my soul. Even though we were ten minutes into the interview, I was still caught up in the first sight— Charisma, strutting toward me like some surreal fantasy woman. She was repositioning the spaghetti straps atop her low-cut, form-fitting, soft pink top, smoothing her hands alongside her curves to be sure that she had her thin, voluptuous form together, as if anything could suddenly be changed about it.

"I've never modeled before. I guess I never met the right people. I did have a job at the Gap once, and they used my photo for posters. But I never got any money for it. Besides, people kept stealing the posters from the stores, so I got very little exposure . . ."

I wanted to marry this woman. Tia who?

"I've horsebacked a few times, I love parks, and flowers, and birds. I'm a happy person who likes happy things; even an ugly dog likes to smile if you're looking for it. What turns me off? Just everything negative. Wars, pain, and misery. Accidents and blood and stuff. Whatever hurts people, ya know? I prefer the sun over the moon, and springtime over all other seasons. I'm a Libra and I can't sing a lick." She said this contrary to her birdsong voice.

The group was complete. My future wife, Charisma. Sugar and Valerie, my homegirls. Egypt, wild, crazy, and unafraid. Trina, our southern belle. Lia, the angel of the group. Elise, the Nigerian doll face. Deja, the Milky-Way supermodel in training. Qianna, the cinnamon wonder with exotic roots. Denise, with the pie-face, the mulatto roots, golden hair, and good heart.

Cassandra was the manager of the group, the no-nonsense leader, a troubleshooter, and a very able assistant. No one smoked, they were all healthy and available to fulfill the demands of the Premium Fudge manifesto. Moreover, they were all now resident guests of ours.

From this point on, there would never be a dull moment.

[T E N]

MOVING TEN WOMEN into the house was more of a settlement than anything else. There were rules, first and foremost, that were explained before the move, which in turn made the move itself simpler. There was no need for furniture, electronic devices such as beepers, cell phones, televisions, or VCRs. Our girls didn't need more than one suitcase, each with their most valued clothing and/or personal items such as jewelry, mementos, and hygiene and beauty accessories. So that first day was similar to a college admission room with assignments. We had four bedrooms and ten girls. Two of the rooms would have three residents, and the other two would each have two residents. Instead of playing God in every sense, we had the girls pull straws. The combination landed Denise with Valerie and Egypt. Qianna was grouped with Elise and Trina. Deja coupled with Lia. And Sugar roomed with Charisma.

Cassandra laid down the house rules, including the mealtimes, the hygiene expected, and other routines that would allow for a pleasant living experience. It took some convincing for Tia to go along with my overall plan, especially moving all of these young women into her house, but the talk regarding the protection and guarding her investment ultimately sold her. Now, Tia was a believer in how we had to more or less oversee our models, groom them to be the best that they could be, and we had to have access to them at all times. No scheduling mishaps, no issues with being late for appointments and none of that extra stuff, the luggage that women had, such as male suitors, family problems—*Daddy wouldn't let me go, blah-blah-blah*—and other excuses that might otherwise seem like priorities. That was the beauty behind my project, how these girls might not be the most beautiful in the world—they might be average girls with exceptional looks—but in the end, Premium Fudge was built with those who were willing and cooperative. There were those who believed in the overall objective, to be a family of beauty—beauty being the ethnicity in them to whatever degree; beauty being the colorful images that the world would have no other choice but to recognize, if even by the imposition of our will.

The creative work that Cassandra was doing would find avenues that were outside of the norm, and outside of what most models and other modeling agencies pursued. She sought out contracts that would earn Premium Fudge the presence and branding opportunities on a variety of platforms by our individual representations and as a group as well. Beauty also spoke to the independence and the uniqueness of our approach; independent, because we'd be able to say yes and fly off at a moment's notice for this project and that. And we were unique, because of the rich and diverse personalities in the group. As much as people are all the same, with the same flesh and blood, with the same basic wants and desires, there was only one Qianna, one Lia, and one Valerie. Deja and Elise could never, ever be duplicated. And Egypt was the equivalent of that pond somewhere in the middle of a vast desert; you needed her *really bad*, and, of course, she (the pond) is just waiting for you to take a drink. And then there was Charisma: not another place on the earth could a girl like her could be found. There was just one Charisma, and she was with us.

We were built to win, making something big out of what these girls might individually see as impossible. Together, as a family, we were a powerful force, maybe the most inconceivably powerful force the world would ever know.

Not twenty-four hours after their move-in, Tia, Mimi, and Cassandra took all of the girls on a mini shopping spree where they purchased undergarments and other items that would help them settle into their new home, their new family. I watched them all load up into two stretch limousines, all excited about the adventure of shopping with someone else's money. Tia, Cassandra, and Mimi led the motorcade in the Jaguar. I breathed relief to see them leave, even if for a few hours. It was a break from the perfume, the various bodies gliding back and forth through the house and all of the questions that I had to answer as the "dreamer" that put this all together. As they left the driveway, I decided that I would address every question possible over dinner.

"Mr. Lewis, sir, will you be having lunch?" asked Mr. Kim, standing behind me inside of the front doorway.

"I think I'm gonna grab one of those sandwiches left over from earlier. But thanks."

"Good. Maybe I go to market. Pick up fish for tonight. Big dinner, yes?"

I responded, however I had already intended on also chasing the cook from the house. I wanted time alone to look into some things. To be a little nosy.

The moment Mr. Kim left, I went to the second-floor bedrooms, starting with the room where Sugar and Charisma slept. The room smelled of flowers, and then I saw them, one of a number of fresh-cut bouquets that Tia had delivered. The two beds were separated, on opposite sides of the room, with two room dividers made of bamboo and which opened up like accordions standing in the center of the floor. I had to order ten of them the other day as a last-minute task so that the girls would have a little privacy within each room. Each bed also had silk sheets and fluffy pillows.

I sat on Charisma's bed and idled, taking in the atmosphere, the leopard-printed wallpaper, the bearskin throw rug laying on the floor that already had wall-to-wall low-shag ivory carpeting. There was a night table next to her bed with a photo of her and her dad. No photo of her mother. There was a dresser up against the wall with two columns of drawers where I imagined there would soon be clothing and other feminine goodies.

Clairvoyance, intuition, or just plain old curiosity had me smoothing my hands along the bed covering, as if it was Charisma's body that I had touched, and then eventually wedging my fingers between the mattress until—*Bingo*—I felt something hard. I looked around again as if ghosts might be watching, but then I went ahead and I slipped the item out into the open. It was a book: a diary, with no lock.

I took a deep breath, knowing that this was *dead wrong*, taboo even. But I went ahead anyhow and opened the book, which had daily entries dating back to the beginning of the year. I was most interested in the current entries, hoping maybe to see something about myself, if not, then at least something about Premium Fudge.

As a marker, Charisma had a copy of our advertisement:

ARE YOU AN ASPIRING MODEL?

I recalled our interview the day before and how she explained that a friend gave her the ad. Doing so had provoked tears from the friend, some realization that Charisma had to outgrow Boston and the limitations it held over her.

June 1, Saturday (1 P.M.)
Dear Diary,
For the first time in my life I'm doing something that I want for myself. People have tried to get me into the fashion shows, into beauty school, and in pageants, but finally I've found something that I can luv. These people seem really nice. I'm nervous as can be. I hope they pick me since I've spent almost every penny I had to come here. Oh well . . . talk to you tomorrow.

June 1, Saturday (8 P.M.)
Dear Diary,
I'm going out of my mind! I had my interview! It was the

longest wait, but I finally had my turn. I first spoke with an older woman. They said that she was once an actress on TV and all, Emmy awards and everything. Wow, my first celebrity. And just to think, all this time I wanted to meet a rapper, a bad boy. She said that her name was Tia and that she was happy to know me. So, I calmed down. There were quite a few questions, but after that she said that I had to have one more interview. Then I met Spencer and he took me through the whole question shit again. There was a period where he just sat staring, like he was reading me or something. Creepy. And he looked so young to be the man in charge. Oh well, he gave me chills. I wonder if he's gay. Well . . . I'm holding my breath, until later.

June 2, Sunday (9 A.M.)
Dear Diary,
I received a phone call from a woman named Cassandra. She said that she had to speak to me as soon as possible. She used the initials ASAP. Excuuuuse me. The meeting is at noon over lunch. I hope she's paying 'cause I'm about out of money. In fact, if I don't get any kind of confirmation by 6 pm, I got to check out of the Marriott. Back to waitressing I guess. Wish me luck.

June 2, Sunday (2:30 P.M.)
Dear Diary,
Sorry it took so long. Lunch ended a half hour ago, but I've been crying my eyes out ever since. THEY WANT ME! THEY WANT ME!! I'M IN! I CAN'T BELIEVE IT! I CAN'T FREAKIN' BELIEVE IT!!! SOMEBODY'S GOTTA CALM ME DOWN BEFORE I EXPLODE! I'VE GOT SO

MUCH ENERGY AND EXCITEMENT RIGHT NOW. I
CAN'T BELIEVE IT! I COULD RUN TEN MILES RIGHT
NOW . . . NO. I KNOW WHAT I'LL DO: A CHEER!
YOU WON'T BE ABLE TO SEE THIS BUT I'M ABOUT
TO DO THE BEST CHEER I EVER KNEW RIGHT HERE
IN THE HOTEL ROOM, UNTIL I GET SWEATY LIKE A
PIG. HOLLA IF YOU HEAR ME!

I chuckled there in the bedroom, my head and eyes
turning up to the ceiling, picturing that caramel bombshell
jumping and shouting and chanting cheers up in the
Marriott hotel. As excited as she seemed, she had to give
the people in the surrounding rooms a headache. And what
was that shit that she said about, *Was I gay?* Something
inside of me burned to prove her wrong. When we get
married, when we have our honeymoon, and when I give
her every bit of dick I got in that one night, she'll never
have another doubt!

This diary was getting good.

I read the latest entry:

June 3, Monday (8 A.M.)
Dear Diary,
I had to get up early to talk to you. Wow! I can't believe
that I'm here. I've actually moved into the house. It's like
an estate! I've never seen anything more gorgeous! I feel
like I've taken a trip out of this world and ended up in
paradise. Can you believe they have an in-ground pool
here and Jacuzzis that we can use anytime that we wish?
The bedroom that I'm in is shared by another model. (I
can't believe I'm calling myself a model now!) Her name is

Sugar, she's from the Bronx, a little ghetto, but I can handle it.

Cassandra went over mad rules for us, like no fighting, arguing amongst one another, be polite and respectful, all that kind of stuff. We were shown around the house, introduced to the cooks—Wow! THREE COOKS! There's laundry rooms, a big game room with the whole lounge area and entertainment theater, and a dining room that can seat ten or even twenty. You know I don't swear, but I SWEAR I'm in heaven before my time.

Soon we'll be taking our first professional photos. They say it's all goin down in San Diego. Wow! This is so big!

Until later,
This is your favorite Supermodel. Over and out.

The rest of the diary was descriptive of different anticipations, anxieties, and fears about coming to Connecticut, of making the commitment, and about leaving her mother behind. I also searched for any notes about a man in her life, hoping that there wasn't one. Picture me lucking out with my future wife. Charisma, the virgin.

No such luck, there was a guy named Marvin. Apparently, she had given up the coochie to him for the last time, several months earlier, and eventually missed her period as well as she went through the anguish of wondering if she was pregnant. It turned out that she wasn't. She rejoiced right there in the diary. And I thanked Marvin in my heart and mind for disappearing.

In the dresser, Charisma kept it simple. She had just what we'd suggested. Two pairs of jeans, two skirts, two blouses, and so on. The girls only needed to bring enough for an overnight really, because we had big surprises in store, and the shopping spree was just the beginning. Beyond the clothes, Charisma had a couple of watches, feminine accessories, and perfume. I took a whiff,

"*Uhmmm,*" I said for no one in particular to hear. It was the scent that I remembered from our interview, one which I'd never soon forget.

Since Charisma was now exposed, I became addicted, soon craving to pick through Egypt's things, dying to find out what made *her* tick. What made that girl get all naked, showing me every nook and curve of her body?

I went across the room before I trekked down the hall. I immediately pushed my hands under Sugar's mattress, figuring this was where we all hid our precious treasures. Nothing. I checked her pillow. There was a paperback book. *Why Men Cheat.* I took the title to be a revelation of some kind; maybe Sugar was scarred by an ex-boyfriend. I didn't bother with her side of the room after that; I just cut out of there.

Egypt was rooming with Valerie and Denise. The wallpaper in that room was decked out in a haze of floral prints, with buds of blue, pink, and canary yellow. They also had the silk sheets, the expensive pillows, and the room dividers, four of them that divided the large room into three like pieces of pie. Egypt's area was to the far left of the room; I could immediately smell her incense having thickened the air in the room. I wondered if either Valerie or Denise minded. In fact, I wondered a lot about a lot if things. Egypt had a Bible under her pillow, but it was old, like it had been used every day for the past half century. There were dozens of handwritten notes filling in as, maybe, bookmarks in various sections. I was really feeling like a private eye now, wondering what in God's name *she* was doing with a Bible. *Not Egypt. Not Miss Show-it-all.*

There was a photograph of Egypt in her high school graduation garb. There was an astrology chart. There was a magazine cutout of Prince, the entertainer. There was a handwritten note that stuck out:

Some religious references say that a person without a vision shall perish, maybe not literally, but definitely in the everyday life that he or she leads. Surely, it's important that all people have at least one idea where their lives are going if they wish to survive. What is your vision, Egypt? Where is your life going?

That one note was stuck in the section titled *Genesis*. It made me flip to *Exodus*, where there were two more notes.

Egypt, you have within you a force that is so powerful that once you unleash or tap into it, there is nothing that can keep you from doing, being, sharing, creating, and giving whatever you envision in life. Go for it!

While I'm reading Egypt's notes, I'm saying to myself, wow, either I've met a different girl at the hotel the other day, or Egypt had split personalities. There was just no way that a girl so young—she was eighteen—could be so intense. I found myself recalling her aerobically thin body, twisted up in a sexy knot with Prince's music guiding her, controlling her as she mashed the floor.

The last note I decided to read was to the rear in *Revelations.* It said: *Be true to you.* I wagged my head and placed the Bible back under the pillow. I pulled open the drawer in the night table. There were a few one-inch candles, chunks like golf balls, contained inside the small glass jars. Egypt also had a nice quantity of incense in the drawer. I left the room, not much more confused about the girl than I was already, and I stopped across the hallway to where Deja roomed with Lia. There was a teddy bear seated between the pillow and the wall on Lia's bed. The bear had on a red baseball cap with white screen printing that read SQUEEZE ME! LOVE ME! I thought about Lia, how I became sick and dreamy-eyed just to look at her.

She's so damned seductive, I reminded myself.

On Deja's nightstand, there was a photo that could've been her brother or her boyfriend. I hope that it wasn't the latter; not because I was obsessed and wanted to hog her all for me, but these girls needed to be focused on the *overall* goals, not personal goals. There'd be time for men once we were firmly rooted and positioned as a market leader in our own right. I could already see our company slogan: PREMIUM FUDGE, WHERE THE BEAUTIFUL ONES ARE.

Since I was on a roll, I decided to cut over to the studio atop the garage. While I was up there I'd knock out two birds with one stone.

CASSANDRA HAD the place cleaned up and decked out. The place looked a million light years away from what had been a crusty old room over the garage. I was further surprised that Tia had sprung so much for the furnishings.

From the looks of it, the walls, arches, and eaves had been left bare but were somehow washed, maybe steam-cleaned to their natural dark wood surfaces. The floor was carpeted in a thick off-white shag that stood out brilliantly against the dark, shadowed walls and cascading roof. In the corners were tall, gray ceramic vases with branches sprouting up and out of them. Some kind of artificial white cottony buds blossomed.

There was a skylight which lent the attic some of the sun's rays, enough for me to admire Cassandra's good taste. And an uncomplicated taste it was, with a queen-sized platform bed, a plentiful arrangement of pillows, with black-and-white bed coverings. A small table with two chairs sat across from the bed. A small black leather couch faced an intimate entertainment center. Plus there was a portable wardrobe closet to the side of the bed, and the tree-lamp.

Keeping with the newfound patterns, I sat on Cassandra's bed, smiling at how great the place looked and smelled. A copy of Dennis Kimbro's *Think and Grow Rich: A Black Choice* was stacked on a small night table along with Iyanla Vanzant's *Acts of Faith*, and Omar Tyree's *Flyy Girl*. There was a Mickey Mouse alarm clock, too. I felt beneath the pillow and mattresses. Nothing. I pulled open a drawer underneath the bed. *Whoa!* Magazines. Back issues of *Players, Blacktail,* and *Pictoral. Shit! She likes women,* I concluded. I flipped through a few of the ten or so magazines, not as interested as I probably should have been, only because (1) Tia was performing every freaky act that I could imagine, and (2) I had more foxy, sexy, beautiful women around me these days than I'd ever be able to have or hold for myself. So what good would gawking at pictures of naked women do me? Women that were *nowhere near as fine* as those I now had in my company from day to day.

I pulled open another drawer and found photos, Polaroids taken of girls at the June 1 interviews. I had been wondering what had happened with those. I fingered through the photos like they were baseball cards, knowing that some had not been chosen, and others were now living with us as resident models. Four or five of the pictures had hearts drawn on them, framing the image of the subject with red magic marker. I saw this and said, *Damn!* She really *does* like women.

Cassandra had good taste because there was also a photo of Charisma in her collection. That photo had a heart, too.

I was a little more concerned now. My interest wasn't merely peaked now. I wondered just how far she wanted to go to pursue this heart-marked model—my future wife. I was serious as shit about Charisma being my wife, too, not just thinkin' shit. Not just dreamin' or fantasizin'. I didn't know how or when, I just knew one day.

I also knew that there wasn't any real opportunity for Cassandra to follow her heart, so to speak. After all, we had only just met Charisma for the first time days ago. I remembered the notation in Charisma's diary: *"I received a phone call from a woman named Cassandra. She said that she had to speak to me as soon as possible . . . ASAP."*

The only other thing that I recalled about Charisma's notes was how she'd been jumping for joy, cheering, and shit, only an hour after meeting with Cassandra. I found myself wanting to go back to the diary, to read between the lines for deeper meanings, signals, and hints. Wasn't it too soon for this? And did Cassandra get butterflies in her stomach, same as me? Did women have some secret gestures or understandings that I missed? More important, was Charisma down with this? If so, I'd have to move faster than necessary if I expected to have a future with that woman. No telling how thick my competition was pouring it on.

My other objective while in the room above the garage was to get to the box. I had totally forgotten that stuff (the photos and whatnot relating to Ms. Tia's past) since we were conducting the auditions and interviews and orientations. But now I got chance to look up to the rafters, to the shelf where I'd left the box. A number of weeks had passed since that day when the men cleared out the old furniture—all of it junk as far as Tia was concerned.

I could only hope that now, after Cassandra had her way with the place, that the box might still be there. And it was. A little soggy, but at least it wasn't discovered, moved, or thrown away. I was relieved, because that damned box was calling me.

As I pulled it down, a squeaking sound caught my attention from outside in the driveway. A car. I put the box on the glass table and checked the door, through a small window as high as my chin. It was Mr. Kim returning from the market. *Whew.* The last thing that I needed was for Cassandra to find out that I had invaded her privacy. There was no way for me to put a time limit on their shopping spree—that was up to the whims of thirteen women—so all that I could do was keep my ears and eyes open. Mr. Kim wouldn't be a problem at all; he'd do his usual, minding what he did best, the business of cooking delicious meals. Dinner will be served! For *fourteen*!

Still, I'd surely keep this all on the sneak tip, my little private-eye escapade. I turned to face the entire studio again, as if I had already seen Cassandra naked, as I'd seen Egypt naked, and maybe some of the others whose privacy I had invaded. I hurried back to the box. There were a few beaten-up envelopes with papers and photos therein. I went straight for the photos. I remembered a couple of them, those who I had glimpsed at the first time around. There was a photo of her ex, David Stern, with his white hair at the sides and to the rear of his pale, globed forehead. *Was this Tia's taste before she met me*? Old, white men? Mostly bald with law degrees and a lot of money?

There was another picture of Stern in his judge's black robe, and another wherein he stood beside two other white men, all of them in double-breasted suits, all of them showing their teeth in a ribbon-cutting ceremony outside of that law firm in downtown Stamford where the settlement took place. I could see the posted sign that read: STERN, WORCHOVSKY AND FLEISHER. It was clear that the other two men in the photo were Stern's partners in the law firm, men I also recalled seeing the day of the divorce settlement. Were they also the men I overheard speaking boldly about the law firm's unethical practices? No matter, I continued flipping through photos. There was a photo of Stern with a white woman. It was a younger Stern, and the two were holding on like they were lovers. There was a much younger Stern now, with a black woman in a collegiate bomber jacket. A big varsity letter "S" was stitched over the heart of the jacket.

And now I remembered seeing Cassandra with the same type of jacket, because as she told me, she attended

Stamford. So then David Stern went to Stamford University, too. Hmmm. And he liked black *and* white women. Hmmm . . . a diverse dude, *aren't* you, David?

Finally, I found a photo of Tia and a black man, both of them hugging with a cheek-to-cheek love that I'd seen in one of the previous photos. Another photo showed Tia and this other man standing behind two young girls, both of them surely less than five years old, with a newborn baby cuddled in their arms. There were more photos of the children. They seemed happy. All of the photos seemed like happy times. I had an urge to ask Tia about her past. Not just about her TV sitcom, her ex-husband, or the settlement. I also wanted to know more about the how's and why's. Who was the other black man? Were those her children? Or his, from another marriage? There was so much that I was curious about. Who exactly was this woman who I was fucking, who I learned to love, who had all of this luggage from her past?

I stuffed the photos back into the envelope and pulled out a second envelope, the one with the paperwork.

There was a birth certificate: Cassie Stern. There was another birth certificate: Linda Stern. A third one read: Courtney Stern. I picked through the papers some more. A deed for the house. And . . .

Oh *shit. That's Cassandra!* It was a school photo of a younger Cassandra in her trademark braids, seated at a desk with a pencil in hand. She wasn't looking forward at the camera, but down at what she was writing. I wondered why or how Tia had such an old photo of Cassandra there amongst other forgettable reminders of the past. It fucked me up to look at that photo. Did Tia know Cassandra from years earlier? Was she closer than just a friend's daughter, the friend she said she knew from the country club? Now, without a doubt, it was a must that I have a talk with Tia. What the hell was going on around here?

I put the box back up where it couldn't be seen, for lack of a better place to stash it. Then I stepped over to Cassandra's stand-alone wardrobe over near the tree-lamp for a last-minute peek. There were so many snazzy outfits in there. Party dresses, gowns, printed pants that were paisley, floral, or tie-died; outfits that were either leather, denim, or spandex. I thought of Cassandra's body and how petite and shapely it was. For some reason, I sensed that there was a lot more under the surface; indeed, under *everybody's* surface. And now, for the first time, I considered that Cassandra could be as scandalous and as cunning as she chose. I guess there was more to her than met the eye.

Horns were blowing all of a sudden, and I could tell they were entering the driveway, coming closer to the house. It was easy to sense that either somebody was excited or in trouble. I cursed and hurried to make sure that everything was left just the way that I found it. Somehow, my violating Cassandra's space felt like a more wrongful act than even murdering a helpless kitten. I looked out of the window in the door before I opened it. I slipped out and locked it from the outside with the spare key, and I hustled down the flight of stairs to the driveway. I immediately guessed that the noise was our band of satisfied shoppers. And within minutes my theory was proven right as the house became filled with shopping bags, smiles, plenty of comments about the future, and naturally, that thick, estrogen-rich atmosphere. I shot inside the house through the patio doors in time enough to catch the girls hopping out of the limos, loaded down with shopping bags, dancing and prancing into the front entrance of the house.

Tia and Cassandra admired this from behind and shared a smile that I felt a part of, but somehow was left out of. In the entry hall, I stood with my hands clasped behind my back as Mimi led the delegation of joy over the threshold and into the house.

"Mr. Lewis!" Mimi announced. "WE ARE BACK!"

"Hi, Mr. Lewis," said the two just behind Mimi. And the chorus of girls behind them acknowledged me as well. Nobody had left me out, making me feel so important, so official, and so proud. I hid my blush.

"Thank you so much, Mr. Lewis," said Deja. "I feel like Cinderella!"

"That's because you *are* Cinderella," I confirmed.

"We can't wait to show off our bathing suits at our little party tonight," said Sugar.

"Party?"

"Yes," Trina said in her southern drawl. "The *pool* party, Mr. Lewis. Miss Tia said so."

"Is that so?" I said, suddenly absent-minded as Charisma followed behind Trina. "And how are you, Miss Charisma?"

"Me? Oh, I—thank you for taking such good care of us. I *still* can't believe all of this. I'm still floating around like a child on Christmas morning." There were those twinkling eyes again, pulling at my heart and soul.

"Well, enjoy it all, Charisma. We wouldn't invest in you if we didn't believe in you."

"Thank you." As this conversation went on, Cassandra stepped in. I thought I saw concern in her eyes, even if for a fleeting second, as she approached. Then there was the close-lipped smile that I assumed to be practiced and always ready to fire.

"So what's this about a pool party?" I asked as Tia appeared inside of the doorway and turned to close both doors behind her.

"Oh, just an idea Cassandra and I had. A little fun in the water. Some lounging, you know, before we take off in the morning."

She was speaking of the trip to San Diego. "We had the girls pick up lingerie and bathing suits. They're planning to put on a little entertainment for you later. It's supposed to be a surprise."

"We gotta talk, Tia."

"Can it wait 'til later, Spencer?" Then she whispered, "*Please?* It's been such a day so far, and it's not even over with. We're waiting for the delivery, remember? Then there's dinner, and . . ."

I realized that Cassandra was within hearing distance, so I agreed. Later. For now, I was relieved, having avoided being caught in my little at-home expedition.

[E L E V E N]

MR. KIM LAID out an incredible spread of baked salmon, roasted shrimp with apple-and-raisin sauce, fried rice with Asian-style green beans in butter. After so many great meals at Tia's house (our home) Mr. Kim still never ceased to amaze me. He prepared the kind of delicious foods that made me wanna moan my appreciation, even though cleaning my plate to the last morsel was, Mr. Kim said, enough of a compliment.

In the hours preceding dinner, there was a big delivery from New York, something Cassandra set up, a strategic alliance with some of the black community's most notable clothing designers. Boxes upon boxes arrived with pants, blouses, jackets, shoes, and sneakers in sizes that would accommodate each of the models. Meanwhile, as the man of the house, and since Mr. Kim was busy cooking dinner, I was the only strong hand available to help the driver unload the delivery. *Woe is me*, the burdens of the man who swims amongst a pool of women.

After everyone received their wardrobe, it was finally time to eat our first big dinner together.

"Shall we toast?" Tia suggested. Some had champagne, others, juice or water. We all raised our glasses just the same. Then Tia said, "Why don't you dedicate the toast, Spencer?"

"Very well then," I said, all gentlemanly and whatnot. "Here's to Premium Fudge. No waifs, no strays, just the freshest beauty, the most brilliant personalities, and the baddest bodies of this generation. We're gonna blow their minds, ladies." I raised my glass high. "Premium Fudge!"

Everyone raised their glasses and repeated in chorus, "*Premium Fudge!*"

"Cassandra? You wanted to say something?"

"Thank you. Yes. I just wanted to make this my official welcome and all. I know that we've spent the day together, all the rules and junk, plus all of the fun that we had shopping. But when it comes down to it, this is a business. I'm the business manager, and any questions, problems, or issues, other than what we might discuss here at the table this evening, should be addressed to me. Don't be afraid to come and talk to me about anything. And I do mean *anything.* I'm so happy to have so many beautiful new friends, and I cannot wait to get started with our projects ahead. I applaud you all for coming this far and making the cut."

Cassandra stood and clapped her hands ceremoniously and it quickly caught on as Tia and I joined in, then everyone else joined in, too.

"Thank you, Cassandra," I said. "I second Cassandra's words about the congratulations. They are surely in order.

You ladies come from all over the world. Your cultures are all ethnic, and colorful, and diverse, but the one thread that you all have in common is your dark beauty. The world needs these images in every way, in print, on television, and for live events. Gone are the days when folks must accept the faces that have been forced upon us through the mass media. As you can see by the many shades of brown in this room, the world represents a lot more than one color, or lack thereof. My dream is to add a little fudge to the diet of images that we see from day to day. So one more time, give yourselves a round of applause. You represent a new beginning, and my dream come true." After the applause, I decided to have each individual introduce herself, officially.

"I don't mind kickin' this off," I said, standing to set the theme. "My full name is Spencer Lewis. I was born and raised here in Stamford, Connecticut. Yeah, a local boy. Went to school here and eventually side-stepped college to pursue my dream. Now, along with my partner, Ms. Tia Stern, er, should I say, the *Emmy award–winning* Ms. Tia Stern, I am the founder and president of Premium Fudge Unlimited, otherwise known as Premium Fudge. Okay . . . well, give me some love, ladies." I made a face and then flashed a warm smile when the applause kicked in. "Thank you. How about you, Cassandra?"

"Okay," she said and stood. "I think you all pretty much know me by now, so I'll keep it simple. I'm Cassandra Evans. I'm five feet six inches, five seven with these fancy boots . . . I'm from North Stamford, studied fashion, worked on some music videos . . . a lot of stuff in New York City. Anyhow, I'm a Gemini, June tenth for anyone checkin'. And that should mean only that I'm good with communicating. I'm also a perfectionist. I'm willing to break the rules in order to get the job done. You should know that in the long run, I'm the master of my own destiny. It took some pain to get to this state of mind; however, I believe that we are all the masters of our own destinies. If we're observant and cooperative enough, I believe that we will all learn from one another and grow to love one another to an ultimate end."

Cassandra sat down. For a time the room was silent with awe, and then the applause trickled and grew to a loud ovation, as everyone whooped it up.

"Gee . . . I guess I'm next. I'm a nobody, just li'l ol' Mimi, here to make you all comfortable. If anyone needs anything, like sheets, towels, ahh, whatever, just holler. Oh, I'm nineteen, from Norway, and . . . I love all people, but especially *you all*."

Mimi turned red when the girls applauded her.

"I'm Denise Matthews. Born in San Diego. Moved to Port Chester, New York, a year or so ago. I like entertainment and all, music, too, but I always wanted to model. I'd like to think I have a good heart and I pretty much get along with people pretty good. I'm nineteen and really glad to be here. I hope . . . I hope we can all be sisters and rise to the top together, cuz I'm not into those cat fights they always do on MTV and *Top Model*. I just wanna excel."

"Okay. My name is Elise Wilson. I'm originally from Nigeria. I'm eighteen, I'm a fun-loving person, and I like to help people. I don't know how to swim, so let me put that out there right now," she said with a mock scowl. "And besides that, I hope to change the world in some small way.

And, umm . . . that's it. Oh! And I'm a MySpace junkie and I'm really happy to be here."

"Hi. Deja Smith. Nineteen. January fourth," she said in a singsong voice. "I'm from Jersey, glad to be here, all that good stuff. I love anything to do with modeling, fashion, and beauty. I look forward to the traveling, the cameras, and I like music. I'm five-seven; five-eight in heels, and now that I think about it, I'm simply *fabulous!*" The way Deja said that with the whole Hollywood pose brought about giggles. "I'm just kiddin' . . . but I'm not, know what I'm saying?" She put on the glossy smile. "But seriously, I feel like I finally found my dream come true. I hope it lasts a long, long time."

The applause erupted again and Lia, Qianna, Trina and Sugar spoke. They mentioned their ages of 21, 18, 19, and 20 respectively. They pretty much sang the same tune about being happy to be in the group, that they couldn't wait to get busy with their dreams and so on. I thought Valerie was gonna cry again; and she was, until I winked at her, offering her a little motivation. Then she just spilled her thoughts on the table, made everyone feel compassionate and human. She made us all recognize how down-to-earth she was. My homegirl.

It seemed like the best (Egypt and Charisma) was saved for last. First it was Egypt who said, "I'm Egypt McKinley. I'll be nineteen on June sixth, which not only means my birthday is a few days away; it also means that I'm a Gemini, too, like Cassandra. Being a Gemini, too—like my favorite artist Prince—means that I have my own unique way of expressing myself. I tend to have problems with people when they don't understand me . . . how I, er, ya know, I kinda like the dark side of life. The radical side, period. I'm very defensive, so don't try and hurt my feelings. I hope I don't sound foolish with all of this, but that's me, ya know, and I like to keep it real. I . . . I guess that's it. Love me for who I am, ya know? Peace."

I couldn't help but sneak a peek at Egypt's roommates, Denise and Valerie. Egypt sat down leaving everyone, even me, stunned. The response was suspended in the air until the applause hesitated and then spread amongst us.

"I guess that leaves li'l ol' me," said Charisma. "My name is Carrie Bunn. My friend's call me Charisma, that means all of you. I'm nineteen years old, from Boston. I'm a Taurus. I don't exactly know what that means, but I do know Coretta Scott King and I have the same birthday. I like anything to do with nature, like flowers, birds, and clear air. I love the water, like the ocean, or even a quiet lake. I was a cheerleader in school, but you can't pay for college doing cheers. So, here I am. Maybe I can get lucky and become well known, but if not, at least I hope to learn something and meet a few friends along the way."

The applause that followed pulled me out of the spell that Charisma, so far, always managed to put on me.

"And last but not least, my partner in crime, Ms. Stern, otherwise known as Tia, otherwise known as Ms. Tia . . . give a hand to the lady with the big bucks," I said, clapping my hands to get the group amped. And Tia, too.

She cast a funny look at me. "I don't know about you all, but I smell good seafood . . . so let me just raise my glass to you. You young women are so very lucky. You have so many options and possibilities ahead of you. I never felt I had so many options. Hopefully, I can teach you and learn something myself. Cheers. And, bon appétit."

After dinner the girls made the whole big deal about me coming out on the terrace so I could be the audience. Mimi and Tia escorted me upstairs to sit where I could look down at the patio, with the in-ground pool and garden serving as an ideal setting. It was getting dark now and the solar-powered outdoor lighting gradually came to life along the perimeter of the property, the lawn, and demarking the patio and pool. I felt like I had box seats and down there at ground level was the stage with all its many footlights.

"Wanna at least give me a *hint*, Tia?" I asked this now that Mimi had left us alone.

"It's just part one of the night's entertainment, lover."

"And how many *parts* should I be looking forward to, Madam Superior?"

Tia's lounge chair was near to mine, close enough for her to touch my hand, letting me know the show was starting. It was only then that we realized the railing would impair our aerial view, so we stood up. Cassandra scurried out and set up a portable tape player while Valerie and Sugar stepped out to the center of the patio in oversized leather pants, jackets, and manly hats. Cassandra depressed a button and loud voices shouted into the night air.

I'M THE KING OF ROCK, THERE IS NONE HIGHER!
SUCKERS EMCEES SHOULD CALL ME SIRE!

I quickly recognized the old-school rap with the voices of RUN-D.M.C., except Valerie and Sugar were simultaneously lip-synching the words while pretending to be the recording artists themselves. Arms folded, shoulders at an exaggerated height, and gritting like tough guys, Valerie and

Sugar performed the whole homeboy act as best they could, making me laugh and cry at the same time.

Elise was next. This was a shock. Her black hair was matted down with a twist so that it curled left and dangled down over her forehead. The rest of her disguise did it for me. Highwater black slacks, an oversized blazer over a low-neck T-shirt, black shoes, and a black-and-white gangsta brimmed hat. Oh, and she had just one sequined glove on her left hand. She stood with her head down and just before the music's beat bopped in, Elise struck a Bojangle's pose. Elise was Michael Jackson, lip-synching and doing her damndest *Billie Jean* performance. She was *killing me!*

Afterwards, Trina showed us a convincing effort of impersonating Madonna; except she didn't convince me that she was *like a virgin.* Deja actually did a hellifying Whitney Houston act; Denise, Qianna, and Egypt tried miserably to be the Supremes. I could tell that Egypt would rather do her own bit. Finally Charisma came out and did a cheer.

"Gimme a P, Gimme an R, an E." Charisma went on until her cheer spelled Premium Fudge. "What's that spell?" Charisma hollered. And the rest of them were all on stage now chanting "Premium Fudge," doin' some kind of cheerleading maneuvers that, I had no doubt, Charisma showed them. Tia and I applauded. When the individual acts ended, the girls created a hasty chorus line and, after Cassandra loaded a tape and joined them, there was a big finale with all of them singing "I'm Every Woman," that old Chaka Khan song. Meanwhile, they all just danced in their own spheres or together, in some cases, until the outfits came off to reveal eleven sexy girls in two-piece bathing suits. Elise was the only one to sit on the ledge of the pool with her legs over the side

Watching all of this, sipping more champagne that Mimi poured, I couldn't help thinking: *This is the life.* I couldn't help thinking of myself as some resurrection of a young Hugh Hefner. Yeah, yeah, I know. I've seen movies and heard about books with the same stuff; but this was really happening right here in my face. I was Spencer Lewis, the playboy. And, because I know how jealous people could be, it was just as well that it was my big secret.

"Nice to watch, isn't it?" Tia noted, looking down dreamily at the scene.

"Ain't that the truth? It's heaven to just hang out around all of this beauty."

"Am I included in *this beauty*?"

"Of course, Tia. Don't be trippin'!" I felt her hand on my ass. Then she was in my ear.

"Come inside. I'll be waiting. I need to see you."

"I need to see you, too," I said, thinking about my earlier findings.

"Give me a couple of minutes' headstart, just to freshen up," she said. And she was gone before I could question that. I hoped she wasn't talking about sex. That wasn't my mood. My mind was on making the most of these beautiful bodies in our midst. Making the flight tomorrow and making money.

"Tia? Hello?" I poked my head into her bedroom. A candlelit glow flickered against the gold-trimmed ceilings, the ivory walls, gold-rimmed mirrors, royal-style furnishings, and heavy tasseled drapes. This was truly the queen's lair, with dark red and green upholstery soaking up the golden gaudiness, almost. Just like Tia, to be pampering herself as the rich and royal queen. I imagined she deserved it.

"Over here, lover," said Tia's breathy voice. I looked over her toward the master bath where she was standing in the doorway, barely visible. I could, however, see that she had a silk teddy on, the one that barely reached her waist and came with a matching thong. I could also see Tia had pumps on, too. *Oh brother.* I was *not* in the mood for this. Seconds passed as Tia approached me, her full-on image making it that much more difficult to reject her advances. Not that I was erect or even the least bit excited, I just didn't want to hurt her feelings and then have to hear her mouth.

In the faint light I saw a different Tia. An older Tia. I wondered if seeing her in this way was in direct contrast to the bodies I watched only minutes earlier. Of course it was. Those girls outside were young and beautiful. For *god-sakes*, they were girls that I should be courting, dating, laying down with. Those girls, any one of them, promised my future, my children, and my destiny.

When I thought of Charisma, I could see a young woman who would have my children. When I thought of Tia, it was just about sex and money. But now, in my mind, I was saying that this shit had to stop. But as usual, my actions were off on their own. I found myself gravitated to the bed where Tia undressed me. I was wearing my velour Sean John sweatsuit, something that was easy to strip off. And so it was, with Tia unzipping, shedding, and pulling off all the clothes I had on.

"We can go ahead and do this, Tia, but I want you to tell me a few things."

"Things? Like what?" She asked this as she laid me out

on the bed, crawling over me and now kissing my bare feet as she responded.

"Things like your past. I wanna know more."

"Now, why would you . . . be interested in . . . such things," she asked, not concerned in the least with what or why I wanted whatever. She was too into the moment, I suppose. She worked her way up to my kneecaps.

"It doesn't matter what I want, does it? I mean when it really comes down to it, you just want my body, don't you? You'd rather me shut my mouth, too." Tia was rubbing at my thighs as I said this and I felt that first spasm. I was limp no more.

Tia stopped to look at me. "Now that you mention it? I *do* want your body . . ."

I said to myself, *And I just want your money, bitch.* But my good sense said, "You came to the right place, momma." And now, at least to me, it was clear how it all came down to the money.

I laid back against her pile of pillows with my hands behind my head—the king's position that one of our porn tapes showed and told. In the meantime, Tia was busy with my dick fully engorged in her mouth. I watched her unfeelingly, wondering to what ends she was reaching for. I certainly wasn't ready for an orgasm; maybe that wouldn't ever happen tonight. Not at this rate, since it was already going past twenty minutes of this. I learned much earlier in our sex play that if I didn't ejaculate within the first five minutes of a blowjob, then she wouldn't be drinking. It was that simple. Sometimes I was feeling her, and sometimes I wasn't. But all the time I felt like a goddamned fountain of youth being tapped of my sole resources. My energy.

I might've looked at my watch, if I had it on, to see how long this was taking. Instead, not necessarily bored and not necessarily about to shoot a load either, I took the remote control from its place behind me. Tia had one of those caddies draped over her headboard where a paperback book and her "little man" were occupants along with the remote. Now that we were fucking from time to time, "little man" wasn't used as often, unless Tia was in the mood for some double penetration.

I depressed a button on the remote for a panel of the adjacent wall to lower. There were five screens in the wall unit. The four smaller ones could either show various areas of the house or different cable channels. Any of those signals could be switched to the one larger sixty-inch screen just under the smaller ones. In that instant, I had the swimming pool area on the big screen.

"What's wrong?" Tia stopped sucking to speak.

"I thought you wanted me to shut up?" I said, for lack of a better answer. Just as Tia was about to dip her head back down, I guess she realized the TV was on. She turned to look behind her at the enlarged view of the swimming pool. I had the camera zoomed for a close-up of the activity. It was too late to switch everything off.

Tia turned back to me and said, "You're crazy." Then she put her mouth back over my erection, more aggressively sucking and jerking now that she knew about her competition. At the moment I expected Tia to be disgusted. But when I gave it a second thought, why should she be upset? After all, how many times had we had the pornos on while we did this stuff? Had to be dozens.

"Take it easy baby, *damn*," I said, but I was steady

looking at the pool scene all the while. "Life's too precious to rush," I said. Tia seemed to be frustrated or full of anxiety, one or the other. And when she stopped with the blowjob, she lifted up off her elbows and maneuvered herself to squat over me. Now this, I liked. This could get me excited: Tia exerting herself like she was, seated on top of me with her hands on my waist, taking me fully inside of her walls and hopping up and down on me like a mother chimp.

I'd been here before, just relaxing there while she did most of the work. There'd be that one face she'd make, or that one noise or desperate cry, and that would do it. I'd blast off right inside of her and she'd eventually collapse on top of me. But that wasn't the case now. Now, Tia was interrupting my show. I was trying to watch Charisma, Cassandra, even Valerie. I was trying to imagine it was one of *them* I was fucking. I was trying to put *their* faces on Tia's naked body. I was trying to replace her *once*-incredible tits with their *now*-incredible tits.

But Tia was in my view, fucking shit up.

"Turn around. Lemme watch your ass while I'm getting' fucked," I told her.

She was already huffing and puffing like this was a race. I loved those sounds. I knew she wasn't acting. Tia tried to do both, to maintain friction and to turn around. When the move was over, she wasn't holding my waist anymore. She had her hands on my knees, but still she was in my view. I slapped her ass. Again.

"Ooo-hooo-hooo," she responded, liking it. I wondered if she was watching the screen as she bounced up and down on me. Then I saw her eyes open. I wanted to tell Tia to bend over so I could see the *damned screen*. I was *trying to get inspired here!* I spanked her again. She cried out.

"Yeah, baby, that's it. Work that ass," I said, knowing how she liked me talking dirty. Finally I was getting those spasms more frequently, a build-up that made the orgasm certain.

"Touch my toes, baby. Go—head," I ordered. And I spanked her again until she obeyed.

"Take it easy, Spence; you know I can't take it all in this position."

I didn't wanna hear that shit. Actually, I didn't want to hear her mouth at all. What I wanted was Charisma's voice. And the time was right for me to have that. I unmuted the sound on the screen so that the sound of the pool filled the speakers in the room, blending in with Tia's moans. Tia looked up at the screen, then back at me.

"You're so crazy," she said.

"Yeah. And you like it. Now, shut up. Shut—the—fuck—up." I thrust myself inside of Tia with every word. Then, I lifted myself and Tia up, took a number of pillows around and put them in front of us. Roughhousing now, I took a bunch of her hair and mashed her down into the pillows, banging her doggy-style. As I did this, I was looking up, concentrating on Charisma's smile. I kept a rhythm, too. I looked at Charisma, then I slapped Tia's ass. I grunted and looked up at Charisma, then I eased off of Tia's head so that she could breathe easily. That's when I demanded an answer.

"Whose is this?!"

"Yours, yours, yours!"

"I said, whose—pussy—is—this?!!"

"It's *yooooouuurrs!*" Tia cried out in a hoarse voice half muffled by the pillows under her.

The very last events I remembered were grabbing handfuls of this woman's ass, looking dead into Charisma's eyes, and feeling a rush of semen jetting out of me before I fell off of Tia and off to sleep.

[T W E L V E]

I HAD NOTHING but more accolades for Cassandra. She set up the photo shoot to take place over the course of the weekend right on the beach in San Diego, with an industry heavy—a photographer named Lynda—who had done it all, including cover shots for *GQ* and *W*. In the meantime, we all stayed at the Ocean Club, where one of Tia's Hollywood connects had a time-share in one of the club's high-rise residences. I guessed that this "Hollywood connect" was one of the few people whom Tia still meant something to considering how the business sort of let you down if you weren't what's hot and happening.

The place was one big great community with its stretch of sunny San Diego beachfront, including a few pools, a fitness center, European spa, tennis courts, and a bar and grill. All I could say to the girls when we arrived was, "*Don't get lost.*"

The residence that we occupied was large enough to be a three-bedroom house if it had been at ground level, and there was an awesome view of the water and horizon in every direction. Considering how beautiful everything was, we allowed the girls to enjoy the beach and the array of activities from Wednesday 'til Thursday. On Friday, Lynda wanted to do the first session on the sand, just as the sun was dropping from the sky. The club assigned us a tour guide for a few days so that, indeed, the girls would not get lost. Meanwhile, I was stuck with Tia. A good enough time for us to discuss some things, some things to keep us occupied with our minds off of the isolation that we were afforded, and the sex that would be inevitable during our stay. It was about seven, after dinner, when I set it off. I asked Tia to start with her first marriage.

"I never told you about him?" she asked.

"Stop the bullshit." I could tell when she was acting by now. "You know that you didn't say anything."

Defeated, Tia said, "What do you need to know? We got married. We got a divorce. End of story."

"*Why* did you get a divorce, Tia? That's the nitty-gritty. Why?" I could hear myself repeating and I knew that champagne was helping Tia take time to reflect.

"It was just a struggle. The show was taping in Los Angeles three and four times a week. Ken was at home in New Rochelle with his damned music career."

"New Rochelle."

"That's where I was really brought up. New Rochelle High School, then the College of New Rochelle, then I did the cattle calls in Manhattan, trying to get in wherever I could."

"Where'd you meet Ken?"

"An industry party. It was at the Rainbow Room in Rockefeller Center. The Emmys were in New York that year, at Radio City Music Hall. The after-party was where I met Ken."

"And?" I took another gulp of bubbly.

"And what? We, I guess, fell in love."

"You dated?"

"We dated."

"When did he hit it? First night?"

"Excuse *me* . . . I wasn't a first-night girl," Tia said with an attitude. "Maybe the second," she then said with a scandalous smile.

"And just like that, you got married."

"I was getting old, Spencer. Thirty-two, to be exact. I'd spent too much of my young life striving for my dream, never quite reaching the mark. And then the show came, took me in, and from that day on I became a TV mom. That's how everyone recognized me. Pigeonholed me. I wasn't a young starlet anymore. I was, well . . . *mom*. So I took the leap."

"How long of a leap?"

"It lasted long enough for me to find out about him back home, cheating, *screwing* some young nubile singer looking for a record deal. The thing is, *he* didn't even *have* much of a career until I came along. I paid for the in-home recording studio, all of the equipment, and whatever money he needed to make a name for himself."

"And meanwhile, you were being a good girl on the West Coast."

"Yes. I was."

"You're lying. You were fucking one of those producers. I read, ya know."

Tia shook her head. "Don't believe the *Enquirer.* Half of that mess is hogwash."

"Yeah, but the *Enquirer* isn't *fucking* you. I am. I know whatcha like."

"Spencer, you shouldn't speak about me like I'm some whore. I'm only human, just like you. Can't a lady like sex as much as a man without being cheapened as though she is scum? As though her fantasies aren't important or because I have them? You don't? Let me tell you something, Spencer, the same things that I want, you want, and vice versa. So if I'm a nut or a slut for wanting, what does that make you?"

"Okay, okay, but you're getting away from my original subject. Why did you break up with whasshisname . . . Ken?"

"Because he was a lying, no-good, son of a bitch, and a neighbor gave me details."

"A nosy neighbor, huh?"

"Precisely."

"No children by your first husband?"

"No," she said and then turned her eyes away. I didn't think much of that, her turning her eyes away.

"And then you got with David Stern."

"Yes," Tia said with choppy answers. "He was my divorce lawyer."

"My, my, my! How convenient. And the scandal thickens. Big-shot lawyer puts the moves on his client."

"I guess. Whatever. I've already heard all of the hate and disgust about my mixed marriage."

"You have?"

"I have."

"Did you ever answer them?"

Tia said nothing while she made a face. *Of course I have.*

"Then tell me *why*. What made you choose to go white and not black. Or is that even a valid question today?"

"Hmmm . . . maybe it's *not* valid. But just for your curiosity, I got tired of black men, black men's pain, and all of the luggage that came with it. Black men are ballplayers, singers, dancers, and laborers. Black men are pimps, hustlers, and dope dealers . . ." Tia was on a roll, another tirade. I was about to interject, but she said, "Wait . . . *let me finish*. Black men are the reason why so many children grow up in families headed by single mothers and because of this, these children who have families do worse as adults than the children who have families with two parents. Don't look at the *few* that don't fall into this category, look at the *majority*. Black men aren't leading in fields like logic, astronomy, atomic physics, or oceanography. They're not paleontologists or nuclear physicists or microbiologists or even archaeologists. My goddamned people want to be the next Michael Jordan. They want to be rappers or barbers. So my people are earning less, Spencer. They're earning less and they're *living* less. I can't wait a lifetime for them to catch up. If I did, where would I be?"

"Are you done?"

Tia said nothing.

"Number one, I may not have your college know-how, but I know this, it's not *blackness* that makes anyone dull or lazy, and it isn't whiteness that makes anyone smart or hard-working, Miss Thang. If you even took the time to come down off of your motha-fuckin' high horse, you'd see that blacks, or *any* underprivileged person for that matter, need people like you—*people who made it*—to show them the way. But *no!* You and the bourgies that you run with

rarely reach back into the 'hood unless it's with publicity—
a bunch-of-you-all at the soup kitchen on Thanksgiving
with your publicists on a leash, because it's good press. It's
because the folks down in the ghetto don't have images to
look up to, images to believe in, who will maintain good
standing. Every time I *think* we've found somebody, they
fuck up one way or another. Few ever fulfill the whole
picture. And if they come close, they get shot the fuck up.

"So when one of us makes it, it always ends up where
we're givin' ourselves to the *other* man—yeah, that's right,
you. You gave the pussy to David Stern. You put a cap on all
of your jewels, all of your acting know-how, you made a
million excuses for yourself, and you let him bottle you up
over on the creamy side of Stamford. The side that I ain't
never seen in my *life* . . . you keep saying *your people, your
people.* Where have you been for the past decade while *your
people* have been scratching around looking for a life or a
promise? How many young black girls do you think are out
there learning to do their hair or to take off their clothes
when they could be learning to act? Shit, you can even
teach 'em to speak proper grammar, all the fancy words that
you know. But now, as far as I'm concerned, you can't teach
'em much more than how to marry a white man and then
take his money . . ."

Tia stormed out of the room, but I was still running my
mouth like she was still there. "And the only reason you
ain't found no astronauts is because we like to keep our feet
firmly planted on the ground. *Bitch.*" I said this, then
finished what was left of the bottle. Even if I wasn't drunk,
I was ready to be drunk. Whatever the job required.

I don't know what had come over me. Why didn't I keep

my mouth shut and just let the chips keep comin' my way? *Damn.* I done scared the woman off. And for real, something inside of me didn't give a fuck. Something inside of me was satisfied. My dream was working. All of this model shit was set up based on how I imagined in my sleep. *My sleep!* Imagine that! Besides, I was also feeling good about my financial position. I had close to $150,000 saved now, all money from Tia. I'd found the woman of my dreams, even if she didn't *know* that she was the woman of my dreams or that we would be married. That was beside the point. I had proven once that my dreams could come true, so what? How much different could it be to marry a beautiful girl? How hard could it be to convince Charisma that we were meant to be and that she was my destiny? Fuck Tia. Fuck her and her limos, and her pool in the backyard, and her electronic surveillance and her blowjobs. I did good for eighteen years without it, and I'd do good for *another* eighteen years.

"SPENCER??? SPENCER... what's wrong? What... why... are you okay?" I had to get the fog out of my eyes, but eventually I saw Cassandra. Maybe two of her.

"Ain't shit," I said, still groggy. "I'm just acting up. You seen Tia?"

"No. I was with the girls and came up to see if you guys wanted to join us down on the beach. We're havin' a ball."

"I dunno . . . I'm not feelin' too great. I don't really want them to see me like this."

"Lemme help you up," I heard her say, the words bouncing around in my head like a pinball in a tin can. "How'd you end up on the floor anyway?"

"I dunno . . . I . . . what-ever. Cassandra?"

"I'm here, what's up?"

"Help me to the bed."

Next thing I know I was flopping down on the bed, looking up at the ceiling. I heard the bedroom door close.

"Cassandra?"

"I'm here."

"I fucked up." I said, my head as heavy as a tub of rocks.

"What? How? You're the man. How could *you* fuck up?"

"My big mouth. I think I pissed off the boss-lady."

"Y'all had an argument?"

"Worse. I called her a bourgie bitch."

Cassandra laughed. "And? You get six points for telling the truth."

"Ha-ha-ha-ha-ha . . . you got jokes, girl. But I don't think this is a joke. This could be serious. It could mean the end of Premium Fudge."

"Stop the shit, Spencer. There's too much goin' on for it to be the end. Hell, I'm just gettin' started. Did you forget the "Obsession" line? The Passion for Fashion Show? The company in Chile that wants our models for their groundbreaking ceremony? How about the lawyers' convention in Connecticut? Or the TV commercials Baby Phat wants our models for?"

"Baby Phat?"

"Exactly. I just got a verbal agreement from them. They saw our first photos, I made copies of them and FedEx'd them the other day. They said yes this morning to five or six of our girls. They took my suggestions, I put hearts around the ones I thought were winners."

"You mean, you're not a lesbian?"

"Spencer?! Where'd you get that?"

"Oh . . . ," I said, my hand to my mouth.

"Is that what you thought about me? Is that why you never made a pass at me?"

"A pass? I—"

"Spencer." Cassandra came to sit down on the bed where I was slumped. "We need to have this talk. And this time, it's alone, right now."

I was her captive audience. "Shoot."

"Even the day that I met you, when you scolded me that day, remember? At the computer."

"Mmmm."

"Well, from that minute, I wanted you. Except you were always on this *business-only* trip. I couldn't get an inch with you."

"Wanted me?"

"Yes, wanted *you*. Is it so hard for a man to believe it when a woman declares what she wants?"

"I—" I started to speak, but Cassandra put her finger over my lips.

"*Shhh*. Don't say anything. I think I understand you. I understand you because you are a lot like me. We have dreams; we're willing to do what it takes to achieve them. So . . ." I felt Cassandra's knee on the bed near my side. *Whoa*. "What are we waitin' for? Why don't we . . . just . . . make our dreams come true together?" She was serious.

First she pecked at my cheek, then my forehead, and then my lips. I thought that I'd shrivel up and die right there underneath her. The girl was tight-bodied, petite, and daring, the way that I've always wanted. My mouth, if only unconsciously, opened for Cassandra's tongue to come in. I felt her flat against me, and in the heat of the moment, my dick was hard as wrought iron pressing against her. As fast as my world was spinning, the fastest yet, I couldn't have met a more incredible woman; a woman who would go to such extremes to, as she said, "*achieve*." That mere aggression in itself had me hook, line, and sinker. The race was on.

Cassandra didn't have much on. The two-piece bathing suit and a wrap-around skirt to be presentable in her romp upstairs from the beach. I had house shorts on and a T-shirt. We both pulled and peeled at one another's clothing until we were naked with our mouths on every trace of skin that we could find. It was as if a dam opened or broke, all of our pent-up emotions hidden, harnessed, or saved for this moment.

What have I been missing?!

I could have cursed myself for letting Cassandra's interest pass me by like a ship ignoring a castaway. Like a train missing its stop. And as if in realization of that neglect, I paid homage to this woman like I had no sense. I was on my knees lying with her beneath me and I put my hands under her ass, lifting her to an arch until her temple was in my face. I could've stood there breathing her in, eating her, basking in her essence for the rest of my life, and I would've been an accomplished man. I would've found my destiny on earth.

This wasn't like the times that I had been with Tia. It just wasn't the same; not the same give and take that Cassandra and I were living at that very instant. It was more than Cassandra's looks, it was about her energy. I wanted to understand, take in, absorb, and consume her energy.

Somehow, I sensed that doing so would enrich *my* life. That it would *complete me*.

Cassandra swung around with her hyper breathing and panting, not saying it, but showing me that she had a *craving* to reciprocate.

We twisted our bodies to the degree that I was under her, she on top of me, both of us giving attention that was out of this world. I could feel her fingernails delicately teasing me as both of her hands cuddled my testicles, the warm exhaust from her nostrils serving some dual satisfaction, while she sucked on me like I was a wet and delicious blowpop.

I considered myself a professional at going down on a woman, especially since Tia had given me so many instructions in our earlier times together, when I was but a slave boy buttering her toes and sucking them. So these talents went to expert use on Cassandra. It turned out that, just like Tia, Cassandra liked it when I took all of her into my mouth, flicking my tongue from time to time, as my lips remained still on her genitals. It was that idea, that feeling of a man's mouth being firmly attached to their sex—that's what women liked. It was no different for me, how I liked it when she took control of me. My dick was both erect and throbbing madly, but pleasured as it was swimming in between her lips and curled within the comfort of her tongue. Things got even more intense when Cassandra said, *"Put it in me."* It was both an order and a request, both of which I agreed to.

I flipped her over and took her in the missionary position, her legs spread out for me, and her hands, fingers, and nails clawing at my ass in her want for more. My breathing was erratic now, as much as my heart was skipping around in my chest. This was *wild*. I thought about Roxy, the one-time affair, and I could've screamed at how I was so hard on myself, thinking that I'd never have such a marvel in my hands again. But here I was. With Cassandra. *Cassandra!* Who'd have thought?

We switched positions again so that I was taking her from behind—all of her, like it was the beginning and the end of my existence. Like nothing else mattered.

Harder and faster, I pushed between her walls, grabbing her waist, and pulling her in as I did. Cassandra yelled out. She growled and she shrieked in a way that sounded like an assault, but was actually the best feeling ever. It was an act of passion, passion that we both wanted and that we both wanted fulfilled.

I thought I heard a gasp, that's why I turned toward the door. Tia was standing there with the door opened just enough for me to see her entire face. I hesitated in the act, more startled than anything else, but I quickly resumed as if in spite.

Fuck you, I thought, as I pushed into Cassandra even more aggressively. I didn't care that Tia was looking. I didn't care who Cassandra was to her—old friend, niece, *whatever.* Fucking Cassandra while Tia was looking was just like fucking both of them at once. With Cassandra, it was pure pleasure. With Tia it was for being condescending, for leaving the 'hood behind and for crushing the black man with her pessimistic bourgeoisie ass.

After I was spent, and after I had opened my eyes, Tia was gone. Meanwhile, I realized that I had just come inside of Cassandra when I should have withdrawn.

Oh shit.

THE PHOTO shoots went along beautifully. All the while, Cassandra and I gave one another knowing glances from a short distance, knowing that we had had something special together. Knowing that we'd fucked more than a few times now. Knowing that it didn't matter if Tia went home that night without telling anyone. We never spoke on these things, it was just that *knowing.* That *believing* and that *faith.*

On Sunday while Cassandra and I sat together in the time-share observing the contact sheets—the miniature snapshots of the photos taken—all of the models were down at the pool. It was midday, hours before we were to leave for San Diego International Airport, and once we arrived in New York there'd be that quick trip up I-95 to the estate.

"We came and did what we were here to do, how could she be mad at you for that?" asked Cassandra.

"I like this one. Elise and Lia together. This photo should be against the law. They're so perfect together."

"Did you hear me, Spencer?"

"Yeah, I did. I'm just through with being concerned about Tia, what she thinks, yadda-yadda-yadda. You know? I love that woman for all of her help, but hey." I didn't want to say too much. I felt that Tia and I had still something that we could maintain despite our problems. No sense in spilling all the beans, causing more confusion. I'd have to deal with the old lady when the time came.

"Man . . . Charisma is such a *natural.*"

I chuckled under my breath.

"What?" Cassandra asked, reading more into my response.

"Can you keep a secret?"

"Mmmm . . . depends. Will it hurt somebody?"

"Only me. Cassandra, I wanted to marry that girl."

"No shit."

"Had the whole thing planned. The house. Picket fence. Maybe a dog named Bub . . ."

Cassandra looked at me as if she was gonna slice my throat if I had said another word.

"Relax. She didn't even know. We never even looked at one another that way."

"But you wanted her. That's against the rules."

"I know, but you know what they say. Rules are meant—"

"Don't you fuckin' dare, playboy." Cassandra said this, put the contact sheets aside, and straddled me there on the couch. "I'm gonna give this to you straight-no-chaser. If I find out that I am pregnant by you . . . if we go and get married like you proposed, and if you *dare* make a move on that girl, guess what?"

I didn't answer, but I cleared my throat. Cassandra was *this* close to me with her pointer finger in my face.

"I'll cut your dick off," she said. And then she smiled and kissed me. The kiss might've been meant to soften the sting, but that woman's word, just then, scared the livin' shit out of me. She meant what she said. For sure.

"Cassandra! Mr. Spencer!" Charisma was nearly skipping in the door as Cassandra climbed off of me. She caught us kissing and had her hands over her mouth to show it. "I'm sorry, should I come back?"

"No, ahh, it's alright baby," Cassandra said. "Nothin' to be embarrassed about, just two adults *in love*. What's up?" Cassandra with the convenient affirmations.

"Nothin' really. Just that we're all headed back up now. Tired of all of the attention that we are getting' down there. Like, everybody wants to take photos with us. It's a little annoying while we're trying to relax, ya know? On Sunday, of all days."

"Sure. Whatever. We'll have a bite to eat, pack up, and before you know it we'll be back home."

I thought about what Cassandra said. Home. Hmmm . . . I wondered if home was *still* home.

[THIRTEEN]

"SO YOU NEVER told me, Spencer. Why Premium Fudge? How'd you come up with that?" Cassandra asked me this while we were on the plane, both of us in adjoining seats with all those beauties-in-the-making doubled up in the rows of seats behind us. Half of 'em were sleeping, while others were taking in the flight's movie, *Mission: Impossible III.*

"Premium . . . you know, like some *value* . . . something worthwhile, even if it costs less, it means something. So I thought of amateur models who might not otherwise have a shot at this industry . . ."

"Okay."

"And I was thinking of how little value people place on themselves . . . that whole poverty consciousness. I guess I felt like flipping the game, whereas premium means *exceptional* quality, or *high* value."

"And fudge?"

"I guess that sort of speaks for itself. Who doesn't immediately associate fudge with chocolate? Chocolate . . .

fudge, right? Fudge makes me think of something rich, thick, and filling. Something soft and creamy with flavor . . . *like you*," I said with a grin.

"Cut it out, flattery might get you everywhere."

"But seriously, I needed to come up with a unique name, one I never heard before . . . something that would set us apart from X-Y-Z modeling agency. We're a family. We're all striving to reach one goal . . . to build on the one brand—and that brand is Premium Fudge."

"You know why I asked you? I had an idea. I was thinking that we could create a magazine and call it *Premium Fudge*. It could be monthly, and free, and it could feature one of our girls on the cover each month, maybe even two, for the special issues. We could have that girl's story inside as an exclusive and incorporate some sexy picture the general public could swallow without having a hissy fit."

"Free?"

"Sure. Distribute the magazines at all the hot nightclubs, restaurants, beauty salons, and barber shops. They'll never be able to keep them in stock. We'll always be in demand."

"Hmm . . . I like it, but how would we—"

"You're gonna ask me about making money; I know. The advertisements. We'll create a platform that businesses won't be able to deny. They'll *have to* advertise. Why? Because everyone will be checkin' us out to see our beautiful Premium Fudge." Cassandra's big smile made her words even more of a pleasure to hear. "Not only that, we'll have major celebrity interviews, community features, and business-to-business listings. Resources that folks will need."

"How'd you come up with all these ideas?" I asked her.

"I dunno . . . it's just like, all of a sudden, I feel like I've been . . . inspired by a certain someone." That smile again.

At least Tia didn't pull the plug on the limousines, I told myself as the two stretches carried the group of us up I-95 toward Stamford. I don't know why I expected her to be vindictive and spiteful after seeing me in bed with Cassandra. Maybe that was something I had to learn, how to be adult about things. Okay, so we had an argument, now let's get back to the business of living, of cooperating, and of coexisting. It wasn't as if I'd *shot* the woman.

As the limos curved their way through the oval driveway toward the entrance of the house, I could see a man at the front door. Mr. Kim was speaking with him, or listening. As we got closer I noticed the man was young and black, he had on oversized dungarees, a denim jacket, and a red fitted baseball cap reversed on his head. For a moment, I wondered if that was someone to see me, maybe Troy or somebody from back in the 'hood. Then I realized that he and Kim weren't merely discussing something, this was some kind of *argument*. This was a shouting match, and Mr. Kim had a frying pan in hand!

The vehicles came to a standstill away from the apparent altercation, and I saw Deja hop out of the first car before I could even address the problem. I opened the door to let myself out, about to be all the man I could be, when the dude had already turned to see our little motorcade. And now he was approaching Deja. An argument immediately broke off, both Deja and this thuggish dude in each other's face, suddenly in their own shouting match. We could hear it all.

The dude: "How you gonna all up-and-leave home like you ain't got no sense? Shit, you ain't old enough to make sense."

Deja: "Squirm, you need to take your sorry ass away from here 'fore you catch a beatdown!"

Sorry Ass: "Call me what you want, I'm takin' your black ass home with—what the hell is all this shit you wearin'? Where you get these rags!"

Deja: "Rags?! Nigga, what I got on in *perfume* is more than what your whole wardrobe costs!"

Nigga: "Lemme find out you turnin' tricks now, all done up like you—*whahh?* Who you?"

"I'm a friend of hers and . . ."

"So are we," said Sugar. And Valerie stepped to Deja's side, with head motions and hands on her hips.

"Yeah," said Denise from behind.

"Who's this, Deja?"

"It's not even worth getting into. He's a *nobody*," she said, facing him as she did. "Now take your lame ass home and stay out of my business!" As Deja said this, all of her new friends stood behind her, waiting for this Squirm guy to agree or disagree.

I said, "Listen, I don't know who you are or what you want with Deja, but it sounds like she doesn't want anything to do with you."

"Who the fuck you s'pose to be?" Squirm asked. "Where you goin' with Deja?"

"I told you, Squirm, go home. Leave me *alone*."

Deja hurried through the front doors, past Mr. Kim, and a few girls were right behind her. Meanwhile, Valerie and

Sugar were close by me, as if this were the sort of thing they were accustomed to.

Squirm shouted after Deja, "Go ahead and run, girl, but you can't hide! Nobody's gonna do that shit to Squirm. *Nobody!*"

"Alright, that's enough. You need to take your motorcycle and get off my property."

"Your—? This is *your* property?" Squirm looked around briefly, saw that he was outnumbered and (I'd imagine) unprepared. He squabbled, and then spit on the pavement by my feet. "Take your property and shove it up your rich ass."

I had an urge to charge at him, but Valerie and Sugar, and now Cassandra in my ear, kept me from blowing my top.

"Nah—nah, you don't want it with me, dog. Trust me. You don't want it with me. I'll be back to settle this. YOU HEAR THAT, DEJA?! I'LL BE BACK!!!"

Squirm hopped on his Suzuki and kicked it into a roaring violent monster, its exhaust filling the air enough to make my eyes tear up. Then he pulled his helmet on and made rubber burns as he darted up the driveway. When he cleared the oval, the bike's front wheel came up off the ground in a partial stunt before racing down the rest of the driveway toward the front gate. At the same time, Cassandra and I shared a look of concern, both wanting to see Deja.

"WHASSUP, BRO? Been a minute, ain't it?" my brother said.

"Yeah, it's the business, Troy. This thing has gotten so large, we got our models now; ten of 'em, and we just got back from San Diego this afternoon."

"You don't say. Find your wife yet?"

"Man . . . have I got stories for *you*."

"I bet. That's why you called? Or did you want to say *hello*? To your *mother*?"

I could tell that Troy was raising his voice for Mom to hear. "Troy. I ain't forget ya'll. Cut the shit. How's she doin' anyway?"

"Alright . . . ain't nothing change here, dude. Same ol', same ol', ya know. Nothin' like you, with an army of half-naked women floating around the house."

"ANY*way* . . . can you shoot over?"

"To your place? Shit . . . on the very next flight," Troy joked. "I'll bring some rubbers."

"Good, we'll have dinner," I replied, ignoring his testosterone-rich reply.

"I could make a joke here, but I'll keep it to myself."

"Mmm-hmm. You do that. Later."

While I waited on Troy, I had a couple other issues on the fire: Deja's past, or whatever she left back home, was catching up with her. But before I addressed that, I had to tackle my problem with Tia. Without Tia, there would've been no *Deja*. So first things first.

Mr. Kim told me that Tia had been hibernating in her bedroom for the past few days. He said she was hardly eating and that she didn't wanna see anyone. Sounded like she was more depressed than angry, and that made me feel a little guilty about the way I was looking at things.

As I stood outside of Tia's bedroom door, I took a deep

breath, gearing up for the all-star performance I had in mind. This would take a lot because I am definitely no actor. I knocked before I called out her name, then I knocked again.

"This is important, Tia. Please open the door." Maybe I was the person she was looking forward to seeing because she didn't take too long to open the door. When she did, I thought I'd never seen such an unfriendly expression on her face. It almost had me to change my mind—to make a U-turn, but I hung in there. *You can do this, Spencer. Stay strong.*

I sucked my teeth and walked past her, into the bedroom, as if I was just as much the proprietor as she. That alone took a lot of guts.

"I don't know what you all sad about, Tia. If you would've only hung out for a few more seconds . . . instead of getting all in your feelings, we could've had a real good time in San Diego. And I put on such a damned good *performance*! Tia! The stuff I was saying? The whole bit about you being a bourgeois bitch? That was all an act, baby. I was just trying to get you all riled up. I was trying to get you angry and excited."

"Humph . . . and, pray tell, why would you want to do something like that?" Tia asked. I swear, looking at her, with her hair a mess, no makeup, and her eyeing me like that, made lying harder and harder to do. As rough as she looked, that take-no-shit attitude, I had to stay sharp.

RULE 1 IN THE PLAYER'S MANUAL: NEVER TRY TO PLAY A PLAYER.

"Tia? I was so hot for you. I was drinking . . . feeling *real* good and I really wanted you. I was leading up to the big grudge fuck like you did with me during the holidays. Remember the Marriott Hotel? I mean . . . that was the best sex I'd ever had in my life. I was just hoping to do it again. So . . . the words I spit out were only the gas to get me and you goin'. I was so damned horny, tryin' to start a fire. And then you *disappeared.* Of all the times to up and leave me."

"I don't believe you, Spencer. Your words were too filled with hatred and . . . and . . ."

"And truth?"

Tia said nothing. She just stood leaning on her dresser, looking down. I finally got a real good look at her, her room, without her returning my gaze. She fucked up, like she might've thought about killing herself.

"Tia, listen. Maybe the alcohol got the best of me. You know I'm not a drinker. Maybe I was pushed into saying things that immediately came to mind, just to keep with the act. And so what?! That's my opinion. Since when do opinions have any real bearing on your realities . . . your decisions in life?"

"But some of what you said . . . it was . . . it was so painful. Things that I've always thought about, but never discussed." A tear rolled down one of her cheeks, then the other. I went to hug her. She accepted me. And I was relieved. I rubbed her back and shoulders as I hugged her, wanting to show her compassion. Wanting to keep her feeling wanted. "It doesn't matter, Tia. That was only a moment in time. Nothing more, nothing less. I still love you, ma."

Just then, Tia pushed me away. Like she'd just thought about something. Her eyes narrowed to slits. "You were fucking her!" she said, now with arms folded. "I saw you and Cassandra, you bastard."

I put my hands in the air, extended like a traffic cop. I had been waiting for her to bring that up. "You caught me red-handed. I admit it, but Tia, I'm a man. What'd you expect me to be, a punk all my life? *You* put this pretty girl in my face, she's in my face just about all day long, then just when I'm as horny as can be, you walk out on me . . . she walks in. Damn. Waddaya want? Call me an animal. Say all men are dogs. The shit just *happened*."

Tia, still with her arms folded, seemed to soften her disgust some. She asked, "So you mean she filled in for me?" Again with the question that didn't sound like a question.

But this was more than a question; it was the moment of truth for me. How should I answer? Would she accept the truth? Should I lie? I felt the tug-of-war that a soap opera stud might go through. On one hand, I wanted to tell her I loved that girl . . . that she and I had more in common, more to talk about, and more years to spare in life than Tia. But that would be too cruel of a truth, and as Tia already showed me, the truth hurts.

"Yes. Just a fill-in," I said, just knowing somehow I'd be able to have my cake and eat it, too, but also knowing that if Cassandra was pregnant, that I'd have to break the news somehow and soon.

"Does that mean we're lovers again?'

"We never stopped being lovers."

"And Cassandra?"

"I might have a little talk with her." Tia backed out of our embrace.

"A little talk?"

"Well, *damn*, how would *you* feel if a man laid with you and just all of a sudden said, *Sorry, can't do that anymore?* Let me handle this, Tia. Let her down easy, ya know? Wouldn't you appreciate that?"

"You're a dog, Spencer. I really thought you'd be different." There she went, balancing on that high wire again, wavering back and forth between love and distrust.

"I *am* different. You'll see." And I took her back in my arms, not letting her see my face and how confused I was. It didn't take much to indulge in a quickie.

All the girls were sitting in the room where Deja and Lia slept, all of them venting about their different trials and tribulations with men, boyfriends, big brothers, and fathers. I overheard some of it when I later approached the room.

". . . The bottom line is, men ain't shit, if they ain't got a pot to piss in. Without money or a life, without something worthwhile going on in their lives, they'll look for the first and easiest piece of ass that passes their way. Something for them to empty their frustrations . . . someone to swallow their anxieties."

"Oooohh . . . girl!" responded Sugar, and I heard a high five.

Then Elise said, "We have those kinds of problems where I come from. Love is a sacred feeling. A gift from God, but the men take us for granted."

"You tellin' me they got drama in *Africa*?"

"By drama, you mean troubles. Yes, there are troubles, but not like here. Troubles in my land might be ten times what you have here, because for years, for centuries, forever, men have been able to have many wives. And because they have so many, because it's so accepted, women just go for it.

We might leave our men, but we always return. It's like we have no other choice because that's the way it is."

"That's why you left?"

"Maybe, that's one of the reasons, but mainly I wanted the opportunities here. I wanted to be more than what my country would allow me. There were so many limitations."

"Well, to be honest, I ain't havin' that from no man. No man is gonna disrespect me. Regardless."

"Charisma, you gotta be havin' man issues, as pretty as you are."

"Honestly? I've only been with one person. He was a somebody in high school, but he turned into a nobody afterwards. It was like I was going one way and he was going another. No big spectacular drama like you guys. Boring really."

"Well, Deja, whatever you decide about Squirm, I'm one hundred percent behind you. I got your back, girl."

"Me too, Deja, but just one last thing . . . where in the world did he get his name, Squirm? *Geez.*"

"Sounds like something slimy," someone said, and then there was laughter.

"A snake."

"A slug."

"Something wet and gross!"

"I don't know," Deja said. "That's just his name around the 'hood where I'm from. Squirm. It's always been Squirm."

"Why would you get with that type of guy anyway?"

"Shoot, girl . . . he's a *thug.* Need I say more?"

"She's right, I heard thugs are some of the best lovers. Plus they'll protect you with their life."

"But that's not Squirm. I guess you got good-looking thugs that are about something, and good-looking thugs that aren't. He's the kind that ain't worth squat."

I'd heard enough to want to walk in on the conversation. As I did, I said, "The big question I have is, how much trouble will this thug bring our way?"

"*Oh* . . . Mr. Lewis . . . I'm so sorry for that outside. I never though he'd actually come here."

"Alright, apology accepted. But my question remains the same: what is this dude capable of? We can't live the way we do, with open doors and relaxed security, if there's a madman on the loose. I'm concerned for *everybody's* safety as well as yours."

"Honestly, I don't know. I called it quits with him about two weeks ago . . ."

"Right. You called it quits, but his photo is still on your night table."

Everybody turned to Deja, wondering how she'd slip out of that truth. And I knew she'd have a hard time answering me, so I just kept talking. Saving her the anguish. "That's exactly why you all are living *here* and not at *home*, where that other life is. The fact is, if that was such an ideal life, you wouldn't have come forth in the first place. You'd be satisfied with whatever hand life has dealt you. Whatever the opportunities were back home, would have been good enough for you. But Deja, they obviously weren't. Either you were unhappy or not quite happy enough. I'm not saying that you were exactly forced to leave home, but what I am saying is that we hope you'll unlearn the old habits and install some new patterns for living. Not that you have to act like a superstar, but maybe, just maybe, you can live like one. I'm hoping that the life we're offering you is a more desirable one, and like you all have said in one way or another, a dream come true. Can I get an Amen?!"

They all repeated, "Amen!"

"SO TROY, the bottom line is, to handle this problem, I gotta play soft and call the cops, or I gotta keep it gully, in case this Squirm guy decides he wants to be a threat to our smooth operation."

"Spencer, you and I both know you ain't keepin' nothin' gully, so you can kill that idea right now. Keepin' it gully means you would've pushed up on the dude the instant he posed a threat. You'd have let him know right then and there that you were a man ready to handle whatever it is here and now, not later. Face your fears, dog."

"You sayin' I'm scared? I'm a bitch now?"

"Nah, man, I didn't go that far. I'm just sayin' you didn't back his ass up enough to make him shut his mouth . . . to make him get some business of his own."

"You needed to be there, Troy. I *did* step to that dude."

"Alright, alright. I'm not going to get into a back-and-forth thing here. The thing is, what're you gonna do now?"

"Troy?! You askin' *me* that when you were the one I called for help?! Come on." My face said, HELP ME, PLEASE.

"You got my help, however you wanna go. We can keep nicey-nicey, like your uppity neighbors would surely appreciate, or we can do this like Dakota Street, call some of the boys up from around the way. Whatever. Thing is, if I'm not mistaken, you've changed a lot since Dakota Street, kid. You done stepped up in the world. Why would you ever want to take two steps backwards just to stay afloat? Nah. You want an easy solution to this. I know you, Spencer."

"I changed that much? It's that obvious?"

Troy nodded. He said, "You know who you remind me of? A rapper."

"Huh?"

"Yeah! A rapper. You used to live in the 'hood. You used to live the streets and breathe ghetto air. All of a sudden, you done gone platinum, traveled a little, met a few people, made some money . . . basically, you hit the big time. But just like the rapper, you still hungry for the street. That way of life is still in your blood. Sure, you're in love with your lush life, the shiny truck sittin' on twenties and the women, but you still have those tendencies . . . you crave the soul food or you itch for that fly girl who don't mind keepin' it real and tellin' you about yourself. She doesn't mind breakin' shit down in ABC fashion. Problem with all that is, you can't live both lives, Spencer. If you moved up, you gotta keep your head to the sky, 'cause that's what your dream was. That's what you wanted. So what if you call the police? That ain't gonna matter back on Dakota Street. They ain't gonna give a fuck about *you*. They busy with their own problems."

"I hear you, Troy. And you're right, I *do* want the easy solution. We got something big goin' here. We've only just begun, and I don't want nothin' to screw it up, feel me?"

"I feel you. Tell me more about this Squirm."

"The girl says he's a drug dealer with a crew."

"She know how many?"

"She only said he was too stupid to be in charge of any more than five cats."

"Okay, so we could be talkin' low-level or mid-level, but definitely not high-level."

"Definitely not. Otherwise, I don't think he would've come up here alone on a motorcycle."

"You're right. He came across state lines, all the way from New Jersey. Hell, even I'm smart enough to know you need your peoples with you if you got beef with someone on your turf."

"We don't have beef, not yet. And I don't have a turf."

"I'm afraid you're wrong, bro. From this second, you gotta look at this like you *do* have beef. Never underestimate your enemy. And make the first move whenever possible. And this house? It *is* your turf."

Listening to Troy made me harden. It made me change my attitude. He was right. I had the equivalent of the family jewels and I couldn't underestimate the need for security measures. That was for sure.

"What else? You think this guy is the type to use guns?"

I shrugged, unsure.

"Alright, we'll assume he does."

"Whoa, Troy. What's that mean?"

"It means, let me handle this. You just answer the questions as I dish 'em. How big is the dude? Does he look like a brawler or just a talker? How'd he dress? And what exactly were his statements? Come on, Spence . . . spill it."

I went over these things with Troy, along with a dozen other issues. By the time we finished working things out. Troy was hired on as part-time employee and security consultant. He called the corporate headquarters for KFC and explained that he had a family emergency to address and that it might take at least thirty days to attend to. They allowed him leave when he said there was no need to pay him for his time away from the store. Besides, Troy was the store manager these days. He had an assistant who could run things just as efficiently as he did. No problem.

I knew Troy wouldn't mind lounging around the house with all of our pretty residents. We arranged it so that his presence was felt most of the week; meanwhile, he was paid well, an influence I still had with Tia and the expenditures concerning the house. Convincing her about the need for security was a no-brainer. She told me whatever I needed would be okay.

Troy was excited, I could tell, when it was time for him to meet the girls. *Ladies, this is Troy, my brother. He's single, he's good-looking, and he's here to protect your bodies.* I didn't introduce him that way, but I may as well have considering how they were all looking at him. Like he was a juicy chunk of salmon that Mr. Kim had prepared. *Oh brother.*

[F O U R T E E N]

FOR THE NEXT few days, things were business as usual at the house. There were exercise sessions that we maintained, we had discussions about diets and eating habits, and Cassandra drilled everyone about keeping a certain image whenever they had to go out in public. Cassandra also invited a nutritionist, a fashion designer, and a beautician, all of whom came to the house and lectured the girls as a group, addressing questions and dishing expert advice in their respective professions.

It was great to have Troy around to shoot some ball and to have man-to-man talks. Then he had to go and remember. "So let's have it. You promised me that if I helped you, you'd give me the down-low. So? Are you hittin' it?"

"Man, you just can't leave that alone, huh. Ever since last Christmas you been asking that."

"Cuz I wanna know. Can't your brother be curious?"

"And nosy?"

"Whatever. So I'm nosy. Now how 'bout it?"

I faked left and then right before I did a spin-out and drove the basketball for a lay-up. Now, I felt better. You can fake the man out of the 'hood, but—

I got close to Troy and said, "That's game," still breathing heavy.

"Okay, you win. Now . . . how 'bout it," Troy said, also trying to catch his breath.

I looked to see if we had ear hustlers. When I saw we didn't, I said, "Alright. The truth?"

"The truth."

"I hit it, I shaved it, I kissed it, I slapped it, I flipped it, and I rubbed it down." I left the court, his mouth opened and his face frozen like a statue. Meanwhile I headed in for a shower.

EACH MODEL now had a headshot, a full body shot, and the pose of their choice from the photos we had mass-produced for distribution to potential clients—companies that would need our personalities for marketing campaigns, promotions, catalogs, and live events. Cassandra's philosophy was to reach out to any company, be it large or small, that could use a spirited smile and alluring eyes to sell products. She even took my suggestion to the next level, actually pulling dull advertisements and reformatting them on our desktop computer, incorporating one of our models in the ad. With ten different smiles and just as many sets of sparkling eyes, we were able to recycle our personalities for eyewear ads, automobile ads, soft drink ads, clothing ads, and hair care ads. Anytime Cassandra or I had time to spare we spent it experimenting and creating potential promotional tools for businesses. We also added a cover letter and a profile chart that showed small snapshots of all our girls. Basically, we wanted to make it hard for businesses to turn us down. And we stayed at it for a month. The concept caught on nicely. Inquiries began to trickle in. And once the Premium Fudge brand name was entered into phone books, business-to-business directories, and advertisements placed in *The Wall Street Journal*, even more credibility was presumed of Premium Fudge Unlimited.

We listed our catchy name with the local Chamber of Commerce, with the Better Business Bureau, and numerous Internet Web sites. Bigger than that, we also had our own Web site now, and the idea came up to have the model-personalities conduct chats with the Web site visitors. The only gray area that needed to be discussed was to what extent the girls would dialog with strangers. Ours wasn't a sex site or a porn site. It was a place where we exposed the personalities in our group. It was a home on the intangible worldwide electronic platform, much like our physical home in Stamford, Connecticut. For now, until we weeded out the dos and don'ts of our relationship with the public, the chat room concept was on the shelf as a future pursuit.

While we gave the big push in our for-profit efforts, we also contributed to community events like health fairs, parades, and food drives for the homeless. It was these activities that served to knock out two birds with the same stone, how we got so involved with charitable concerns, and at the same time, helped to earn further exposure for our brand name.

"MR. LEWIS, sir . . . there is a messenger at front door. He say he must speak to you only for signature," said Mr. Kim.

"I'll go with you, Spence. You never know," said Troy. Troy was the first one at the threshold, and I was right behind him.

"Mr. Spencer Lewis, I presume?" said the messenger.

"No, but who wants to know?"

"I have a subpoena for him, sir. I'm a process server."

"Lemme have that," I said, unafraid to answer to anything official. I took the envelope, signed for it, and thanked the man—I don't know why—before I stepped back into the house.

"This is a civil suit, Troy."

"Lemme see that," he said. After a moment, Troy proclaimed, "Shit, Spence. They're claiming that you're involved in child pornography. Exploitation."

"What?! That must be a prank. A *joke.*"

I don't know, bro. This looks pretty serious. Plus they got your lady, Tia Stern, as a defendant right under your name."

I saw the small list: *The Smith Family vs. Spencer Lewis, Ms. Tia Stern, Premium Fudge Unlimited, et al.*

"Who's the Smith family, Spence?"

I read more of the paperwork.

WHEREAS, Spencer Lewis, Tia Stern, and the proprietors of Premium Fudge Unlimited, hereafter referred to as defendants are engaged in child pornography and the exploitation of under aged females.

WHEREAS, the defendants have held captive, one known as Deja Smith for their exploitation scheme, and that Deja is in fact sixteen years of age . . . a minor in every respect.

That was all that I needed to see.

"Oh shit. That—she's sixteen, Troy! I can't believe it! She told us that she was *nineteen!*"

"Did you check her ID?"

"Ahh . . . I don't think so. I didn't think that we had to. Everyone knew coming in that we were looking for models from age eighteen to twenty-two. We assumed that—"

"She lied," Troy said matter-of-factly.

"She lied? I could kill that—"

"Relax, bro. Relax. Where's she at? In the room?"

I didn't answer Troy, I was already off and running for the room where Deja and Lia slept. "Where's Deja?" I asked Lia from the doorway, trying my best not to yell at the top of my lungs, something I needed to do really badly.

"I think she's in the Jacuzzi, downstairs in the playroom. What's—?"

I was a ghost again, darting down the hallway, down the winding staircase, and then down into the basement. Troy was right behind me the entire way, urging me to keep my cool.

"Busted!" I shouted.

Trina, Deja, and Qianna were sharing the Jacuzzi; all of them without part one of their two-piece bikinis.

The three of them screamed in unison. Not a horror-filled scream, but a shocked scream. A startled scream.

I moved straight for the towels at the side of the Jacuzzi. I grabbed one and raised it up.

"Out, Deja," I more or less ordered.

She hardly showed surprise. More like, *I guess this is it. I guess my charade is over.* I'd already caught a glimpse of Deja's headlights, incorporating the image with all else I knew about her, including what I'd just learned about her age. I cursed myself, wondering how I let her trick me. I turned to look at my brother, wondering if he could read my mind, me saying that Deja could pass for twenty-one with this body we're looking at. Meanwhile, Trina and Quianna were motionless in the jet-streamed water, wondering what this abrupt removal was about, half-covering their bare chests.

I GOT Cassandra and we sat with Deja in the study on the far end of the house—an intimate room that was full of books and offered a window view of the garden out back.

Before anyone said anything, Deja was already sitting, her shoulders depressed, her head down, her mouth pouted like a kid denied her lollipop, and her eyes watering.

"Deja," Cassandra said. "Is it true? Are you sixteen? You can tell us the truth. We're your friends."

Deja nodded. She muttered, "But I'll be seventeen on January fourth."

"That does us no good now, Deja," I said, more than not the bad cop in the conversation. "Your family is suing us. I could be in big trouble just for you being in my house."

"I'm sorry, Mr. Lewis, Cassandra, but I *hate* my family. They keep me in the house, my brother is a pervert, and . . ." Deja's words stopped. The tears started. "I just wanted a way out. I wanted to model. I know I can do it. I know I can."

I looked and noticed Cassandra's eyes watering as well, as though she could understand Deja's struggle.

I wagged my head and let out air. "This is crazy. Really crazy. All our work."

"Take it easy, Spencer," Cassandra said. "Troy, sit with her for a minute. Spencer . . ."

I went with Cassandra into the hall outside of the study.

"There's gotta be a way to work this out, Spencer. I mean, she lied to you, to all of us. So there was no way to know the truth."

"Yeah, but I don't think a jury, or a judge, or anybody else for that matter, will believe it. You know how the courts do us."

"How about if we speak with Deja's family. I mean, go out there, show them the work we've been doing with Deja, how it was all on the up and up."

"What choice do we have?"

"Maybe they'll drop this whole thing. Of course, Deja will have to tell them the truth."

"Well, what're we waiting for?"

I DIDN'T bother to mention this all to Tia. We just jumped in a limousine. Deja, Cassandra, and I took I-95 headed for New Jersey. "Where's Lodi anyway?" I asked. Deja spoke up. "Not far from where the New Jersey Turnpike begins."

In my mind I said, *"Wherever that is."*

When we exited the thruway, Deja gave directions, more

talkative now, and asked if modeling was over for her, if she'd be *thrown out*.

"Nobody can *throw you out* of modeling Deja. You just have to wait 'til you're eighteen."

"I don't see why. I was doing just fine. I beat out all those other girls at the interviews."

"That may be so, Deja, but anytime you're dealing with adult matters, or anything business, and you happen to be underage, parental consent is necessary. The world—the United States anyway—says that you're too young to make important decisions if you're under eighteen," I tried to explain.

"It doesn't feel wrong. It feels right. It feels like I was meant to model."

And to lie, I thought.

Then Cassandra said, "Maybe if your parents agree—"

"Forget it. They're so ignorant."

"But they're your parents still. You owe them that much. When you're eighteen . . . in another year or so, you can always come back to us. We'll be glad to take you on. Besides, we'll have many more opportunities for you," Cassandra added. Then I said, "Who's home now, Deja? Mom? Dad? Or both?"

"Probably my mother and brother—that jerk." In Lodi, on some street with small, one-family row houses, we pulled up in front of Deja's home. A yellow color that looked more like the stain on a person's teeth, than the color of fruit.

Deja had a carry-all over her shoulder and some clothes on, for a change, while Cassandra and I wore corporate attire—something you'd see on a CEO and his assistant, not a young playboy and a fine young nymph that he's sticking and dipping in.

The woman who opened the door seemed to be in her late thirties. She didn't look surprised to see Deja.

"Oh. So you decided to come home, huh?" The woman's hair was fingerwaved about her head and she was built like a woman who gave birth, and in the interim, earned the wider hips, the tummy, and the dead-end attitude. Her breasts sagged inside of her blouse—no bra—and she had 100 watts of teeth, inside of her tremendous set of lips, except they weren't smiling now, just another part of her big mouth. It was hard to imagine this woman pushing out something as incredible as Deja.

"Mom, these are friends of mine. They wanna speak to you."

"About what?" the woman asked as she reached for Deja's arm and pulled her in the house. Then she slammed the screen door closed and locked it. Before she could shut the solid inside door, I spoke up.

"Won't you at least give us a minute of your time?"

"For what? You're those people in Connecticut, aren't you?"

"Mrs. Smith. All we need is a minute. Then we'll be out of your hair," Cassandra said. And I thought to myself, *Forever.*

"So speak," Mrs. Smith said.

I let Cassandra do the woman-to-woman bit. And eventually we were let into the house.

My sense of smell was immediately reminded of long ago, where I was toted alongside Mom withstanding the conflicting aromas of this and that neighbor's residence. Only now, in Lodi.

"Mrs. Smith, we probably care about Deja as much as you. We're concerned for her welfare and we want what's best to see her succeed in life . . ." I was speaking, but I could feel a heavy barrier—maybe hours of hate-filled discussions that preceded our visit. Lawyers, promising to take us to the bank. An ex-boyfriend, vowing to rip my head off. Maybe some discussion with a cop, about Deja being kidnapped. Who knew what this woman had been through? "But you have to believe me. Our intentions are to do good by our people. I had a dream to bring more beautiful, colorful faces to the mainstream markets, more so than we've been seeing, and hopefully I'd make a living at the same time. But never ever had I intended on taking advantage of your daughter. What kind of man would I be? I'm from humble beginnings just like you are. I'd never turn around and exploit my people. It's just not in my blood. I ask you to look past the fancy lawyers and the hate that you've probably had for me . . . see a young man, like your son, who's trying to make something of himself. I may not be perfect, but in time, I hope to be. I hope to make my own family as well as my community proud of my hard work."

Just then, a young man strolled through the front door. He looked to be in his twenties.

"Ma, there's a limo—oh."

"William, we have company. This is William, my son. William, say hi to Mr. Lewis. He's in charge of the modeling—"

"The people in Connecticut? But—"

"You need to sit down and learn something from this here gentleman. He might be young, but he's got it on the ball. Seems like this was all one big ball of confusion."

I breathed easier, my eyes smiling at Cassandra. I couldn't wait to let Troy in on the good news, sure that he was out in the limo worried sick about me.

"Yes, it has been. I'm Spencer." I put my hand out to shake, but then smartened up and made a fist—the 'hood handshake was a pound, not that corporate shit I'd learned over these months. "You in school?" I asked.

"Nah. I'm done there. I don't do shit but—"

"Watch your mouth when we have company."

"Sorry, Ma. I sweep at B.J.'s," he said. And when I made a face, he said, "That's a barbershop down the way."

"Oh."

"But he wants to be on BET," Mrs. Smith offered. "Tell 'em, William. How you gonna be on the TV if you shy at a time like this?"

I glanced over at Deja, who was saying *oh brother* and rolling her eyes.

"Yeah. I, uh, work for this local cable show called *Big Time*. Ain't shit really—"

"William!"

"Sorry, Ma," he said. He sucked his teeth and went on saying, "We showcase amateur talent."

"Cool," I said, suddenly wishing I said, *That's wassup*, instead. "You like that?"

"They got me usin' the cameras 'n sh—and, uhh, well maybe I'll direct someday."

"That's *wassup*. Stick with it, William. Every success begins with a dream, but you gotta start taking a lot of small steps to reach the big time."

"My son, the director," Mrs. Smith said proudly.

"Mrs. Smith, we can't stay too long, there's a busy day

tomorrow. We're going to Manhattan . . . a fashion designer wants to dress up our models . . ."

"What about Deja? You takin' her?"

I looked at Cassandra with incredulity. Did this woman just say what I *think* she said?

Cassandra said, "But your lawyers have filed a—" Before she finished her sentence, Mrs. Smith took some papers from a drawer and, raising them up in a show of solidarity, she ripped it all down the middle—much like a strong man would rip a phone book.

"Forget the lawyers. I was made to think you all took Deja from me. But now that I find out she lied . . ." She looked over at her daughter, admonishing her, eyes only. "And that you all are on the up-and-up, I'd like to see her fulfill her dream."

I watched Deja's smile form. Deja's smile and her mother's tears. I almost wanted to cry with them, I was so happy.

"Maybe you'd like to talk it over with Deja, Mrs. Smith. I mean, we wouldn't want you to make any hasty decisions. Take a few days . . . let Deja tell you her experiences with us so far. Do that mother-daughter bit, and then, if you still allow it, we'll need your consent, and—"

I cut in on Cassandra. I said, "What about *Mister Smith*?"

"Him? Trust me, he'll do as I say, otherwise he better be lookin' for a place with y'all."

Cassandra and I held in the big laugh. I said, "You think you can call off the pitbulls, Mrs. Smith?"

"The lawyers? Those white mens better *not* come back around here with their sales pitch."

"No. I mean, what's his name? Squirm?"

"Oh. Him. That boy done lost his marbles goin' out there like that. Did he threaten y'all?"

"Well . . . I . . ."

"He does that 'round here, too. Got himself in trouble with the police more times than I brush my teeth. Don't mind him; he's just blowin' hot air."

I thought about her brushing her teeth, knowing that as big and as many as there were, this Squirm cat had to be as lawless as they come.

"Just the same, could you have a talk with him?"

"Will do, Mr. Lewis. Soon as I see him, I'll tell that boy to stop his foolishness. Not like he'll listen to me, but maybe him seein' Deja's at home will change his mind." Mrs. Smith leaned into the conversation as if the following was a secret. "He has a thing for her, ya know. Swears she's his wife." Mrs. Smith backed off and looked up to the cracked ceiling. She said, "Lord Jesus, help us all."

[F I F T E E N]

"JUST LIKE THAT?" Troy said on the way home. Cassandra was cuddled up against me, all happy about the outcome, evoking envy from my brother all the while. "She ripped up the papers?"

"I'm telling' you. We laid it on her thick, dog. And you're not gonna believe what she said next."

"I'll believe anything at this rate," said Troy.

"Cassandra, tell him what she said," and I looked out at the Meadowlands Arena as we neared the merge onto I-95.

"She wants Deja to stay with us."

"You're shittin' me."

"I shit you not," Cassandra replied. "It messed us up, too. Trust me. I still can't believe the words came from her lips."

"Her big lips, too," I said. Cassandra punched me in the arm.

"That's not nice, Spence," she said.

I looked at her as if to say, *It ain't my fault.*

"So why's Deja not with us now?"

"We figured they needed some time to talk this over, but

actually, I'm gonna call this lawyer we deal with. Have him draw up some papers so Mrs. and *Mr.* Smith can give their consent."

"So this was all a big waste of nerves and stress," Troy suggested.

"Actually, it was more like a wake-up call. Now we know that we have to doublecheck our girls, seeing as how they're so desperate they'd lie to be down with us."

"Wait . . . what's with that Squirm cat?"

"I'm tellin' you . . . Mrs Smith said she'd handle everybody: Mister Smith, Squirm, the lawyers. We have a new friend, bro, and it's Deja's mom."

"Man. Just when I was getting used to seeing all of that—"

"Troy!"

"I digress. Can you blame a single man?"

"Yes."

"So now what? I'm out of a job?"

"Cut the shit, Troy. You know you got a job at KFC."

"Right, but can I at least visit? Maybe go on trips with you from time to time?"

"Cassandra, remind me to help my brother find a wife."

"You think he'd like Charisma?"

"She's too good for him. Besides, she's one of the best we got. I can't—"

"The best?"

"Okay, the second best," I said, provoking Cassandra to grin.

"You both make me sick," Troy said. Then he knocked on the glass partition to get the driver's attention. The glass lowered and Troy said, "Stop over on Dakota Street, would ya?"

"*Yessiree,*" the driver responded.

At the same time, Cassandra whispered in my ear. I answered, telling her, "As *soon* as we get home," with as much emphasis as I could muster on the SOON.

Troy made a face, raised the level some on the car stereo, and closed his eyes to escape inside of Anita Baker's sultry voice. It was like this until we got to Dakota Street.

Even before Troy shut the car door, Cassandra and I were attacking one another. Tongue-kissing and groping like we were students that just passed the SAT tests. I'm sure the limousine rocked some and that Troy said something like *Lucky stiff* as he stepped in the house. Without getting too sloppy in the back, or going too far, Cassandra and I muttered the rest of the way home, feeling that exhilaration, that relief, and the satisfaction of winning our first battle against Murphy and his law.

It was getting late after so much driving, so much talking, and we were restless from having sat in the back of the limo for, it seemed, forever. The only practical end to the night was roughhouse sex. I asked the driver to kill the headlights before pulling into the driveway, and to take the car as close to the garage as he could, the less for us to have to sneak around. I didn't want to alert Tia. Cassandra and I got out, I closed the door as quietly as I could, and we virtually tiptoed up to the studio over the garage.

We wasted no time.

Cassandra lit a candle, incense, and we began to fuck like it was a fight to stay alive.

Somewhere between the long strokes and soft cries, there was a draft in the studio. Cassandra was on her hands and knees at the time, too absorbed in the thrusts I gave. My hands held her breasts as I pushed and pulled in and out of her. The draft was but a tickle against my skin and its film of perspiration. That's when the candle's glow disappeared. That's when I felt the sole of someone's boot against my butt. That's when I was thrusted myself, my whole body reacting to the force of being pushed forward, deeper than I ever expected, into Cassandra, provoking her final scream, and leaving me with a painful erection. I swore it was broken, sprained . . . or some kind of fracture. I yelled at the top of my lungs while my body rolled off of Cassandra, writhing in agony. That's when the lights were turned on.

"Just what I thought. You the mafucka that snatched my Deja, then chased me outta Connecticut . . ."

My eyes had to adjust to the circumstances, these four, no, five figures standing around Cassandra's bed. The one who spoke, caught my eye first. *Deja? He said "my Deja"?* This was Squirm, and did we chase him outta Connecticut? Or was he exaggerating for his friends? Making it seemed as though I attacked him.

Cassandra had bunched up a sheet to herself, with her knees folded into her chest. I never saw her so afraid.

"Look at this freak-ass dude. He be luring them chicks down here to his mafuckin' attic in the garage . . . prob'ly keep all the rest of 'em in the main house and take 'em out here one at a time. What? To do an *audition?*"

Now I had a grip, even with my hurt ass and throbbing penis. Squirm was the closest, with his booted foot up on the bed. Two others had on baseball caps, like Squirm. The beady-eyed one had his hat to the side; the darker cat had big bulging eyes, a big-toothed chipmunk grill, and his hat was turned to the back. The one on the other side of the bed had a diamond stud in his left ear, and his afro head bent down some, as tall as he was, to avoid bumping into the eaves of the roof. The last guy was the biggest of the five. Shoulder and chest muscles bulged through his shirt, his brown skin was pockmarked, he had a short crew cut, and a front tooth was missing. Not to mention that he was grinning at what he saw of Cassandra's naked body, and pounding a fist in his palm. Not to mention that the four others all had wooden bats ready.

So this was it. This is how my dream would fold. I went and got so relaxed, so comfortable inside of my temple of black beauties and of undiscovered wealth, so deeply submerged into the norm of raw, uninhibited sex, that I ultimately had to be the most vulnerable fool alive.

"Come on, Squirm. Let's get this shit ova with. You said in and out."

"Get what over with?" I asked.

"The beat-down, asshole. That's what we're here for. To beat your mothafuckin' pervert ass and teach you a lesson. Now where's my girl?!"

I had managed to pull on my boxers and tried to console Cassandra with a pat on her thigh. But when he said beat-down, and considering that there were four guys with bats looking me at me from head to toe, I had to object. I negotiated to my feet in a way that would seem threatening. And now my hands were up, the traffic cop again, pleading for some cooperation in here.

"Squirm. Hold up. First of all, Deja's not here. She's home. Second of all, this ain't how you do shit, just bustin' up in somebody's spot—"

"The fuck it ain't. That's how we do shit, mafucka. Just when you thought it was safe to live like a king . . ."

As Squirm said that, before it had a chance to go out of my other ear, the door eased open.

"Cassandra?" It was Tia, peeking her head in the wrong place at the wrong goddamned time.

"Who you?" asked Squirm as Tia stepped inside.

"I beg your pardon, young man. Who are you? And what are you all doing on my property . . . with *bats* nonetheless." Eventually Tia's gaze found Cassandra and me.

The gold-toothed, pretty-boy thug said, "Oh shit! That's that actress bitch, be on all them reruns!"

Now the bug-eyed chipmunk added, "Oh yeah! Yo, Squirm."

While the vapors of fame got acquainted with the threat of violence, Tia was beside herself. So much happening all at once.

"Young man, you need a lesson in manners."

Squirm sucked his teeth and said, "What the fuck? You done lost your minds? We got business here. Whoever that ho is, actress, singer, or hooker, grab her cuz she about to see a *show*."

"Hey! Get your hands off of her!" I yelled and charged into the team of intruders.

The first strike was a thud to my back. Then there was the one to my head. Someone screamed. As I blacked out, I felt something, then another something, but they felt like heartbeats instead of blows, and then there was the feeling of nothing at all.

[SIXTEEN]

I NEVER THOUGHT I'd go to heaven and see this: all of them: Denise, Qianna, Elise, Valerie, Lia, Trina, and Sugar. Egypt was fully nude, bent over backwards in the midst of a freakish upside down walkover. Charisma was doing cheers: "Gimme an S! Gimme a P!—" And she went on until she shouted "What's that spell?"

"Spencer!" they all responded.

"What's that spell?" she repeated.

They repeated, "Spencer!!"

Then everybody shouted, "Goooooooo, *Spencer*!"

I wondered if I was dead, and they were cheering for the hell of a job I did while living, or if I was still alive, barely hanging on, with the chorus cheering me back to life. Probably that.

"Mmm . . . they all love you," said a sexy voice into my ear. And that's when I realized I was laying against Cassandra, right there in her lap, with my body slumped back onto hers. And then I looked out into the billowing clouds where all of them, all of my angels were floating, meandering, drifting in some kind of aimless pursuit, with Deja standing larger and more brilliantly than the rest. Deja was glowing. She was smiling. In one hand was a framed photo, three feet in height, of Squirm. In her other hand was a poster with black block letters that read:

ALMOST LEGAL!

Most everyone in my dreamy projectile was wearing a see-thru negligee, huge feathery wings, and moving about with a choreographed, theatrical fluidity. Nipples were slightly visible, showing like darkened coins underneath the sheer white linens. And then, as if by a dimmer dial control, the brilliant heavenly images grew darker, until it all went black.

It felt like years had passed by, as heavy as the pain was in my head, at my sides, somewhere along my arm, but I was certain just moments passed. I must've been sleeping, or falling in and out of consciousness. I could see things in real time now, abstract images to go with the confusion of sounds. Somebody was sobbing—maybe Tia or Cassandra—I couldn't quite make out who, but the sounds were familiar.

Then I recognized Mimi's sultry smile directed toward the chipmunk thug as she dabbed my head and face with something cold—unbearably cold like a hundred frozen sewing needles all pricking at my senses. In the foggy vision, I could make out Trina, Sugar, and Denise over on the sectional couch. Trina was caressing the temple and cheek of the pretty-boy thug, the one with the gold tooth and his hat to the side, while Sugar and Denise were sandwiching the big one, the one with the cheesy smile and missing tooth up front, under those blubber lips. Why was Charisma blowing kisses at the one with the diamond stud? Why was she playing with his bat as though it was a golf club, then a witch's broom, then a paddle—everything but the weapon it was intended to be?

There she was. Tia. She was the one crying, to me putting on an act, I guessed, while Squirm was poking the handle end of the bat at her cleavage, saying, *It didn't matter* if she was famous. She was *probably a freak, too, settin' all these young girls up to turn them out one by one.* Squirm said, "You already done turned *that* one out. I caught her all butt-naked with that pimp in the garage." Squirm was talking about Cassandra, who I soon realized was sobbing also, caressing and stroking my head while Mimi applied hot and cold packs. "We should beat his ass again!"

"Why don't you call Deja's house?! Then you'd know that she was home, jerk!" That was Cassandra's voice.

"Hey, girl . . . lemme tell you somethin' . . . I'm sure you were nice at one time, but watch your mouth. Cuz I wouldn't mind stickin' a bat between your jaws. And anyway, everybody knows Deja ain't *got* no phone. That's why you prob'ly said that, knowin' she ain't have no phone and thinkin' I'd just up and leave . . . thinkin' I'd *believe* yo' ass."

I could see but so much, as swollen as my eye was. Swollen shut, it felt big like a football. All I had was the one eye, slowly regaining its ability to show me the world, to show me Mimi—what a beautiful sight she was to see! It was a confirmation that I *was* alive, but dammit! Ouch!! Everywhere she touched me, my sores and concussions throbbed.

Somehow, I was lying upright against something—it was her voice in my ear, and that had to be her leg to my left and one to the right, like arms of a lounge chair. So, then, this part of my dream *was* real.

"It's gonna be okay, baby. You just rest. This won't last long," Cassandra purred in my ear. She said this inside of her whimpering, while other conversations were ongoing in the vicinity.

The last thing I remembered seeing was Mimi leading the chipmunk from the room. The group on the couch was pretending this was *The Dating Game*, and Squirm was highly upset that he couldn't get what he wanted from Tia, because Tia didn't know what was going on in the first place. The last thing that I heard was the phone ringing. But nothing mattered anymore, not what I managed to see or hear. I was losing it again . . . or perhaps I was floating away, until it all went black and silent again.

[SEVENTEEN]

AS I SLIPPED in and out of consciousness, a lot of my drug-induced sleep got me recalling the past. All of those faces of people I once knew, or now knew, all of them crossing through my mind's backyard for deeper reflection. At times I'd be in the midst of some activity, whether it was doing business or doing the nasty—since that was all that I did anyhow—and I'd actually experience the movements, and every sound or conversation connected with people, places, and things. It was an experience that I had to remain submerged in—like an actor assuming his or her character's state of mind—to realize the full impact. Otherwise I'd awake in a daze, upset that I couldn't fulfill the experience or live it out until its inevitable end.

Someone was turning up the volume in my head. There were murmurs, then garbled sounds, and then the voices, some ongoing conversation. That sterile smell.

". . . See, you're very protective, Charisma, but that's how the Taurus is. You've gotta let go of some mental chains so that you may pursue your dream. Because you don't take risks, you're holding back on your creative inspiration and imagination."

"How would I do that?"

"Same as you did with that guy yesterday. You rose to the occasion."

A third voice said, "It's more like *he* rose to the occasion, as excited as she had him. What'd you do with him, anyways?"

"The main thing is she did the job, we all worked together as a team, and—Spencer! You're awake!"

"Where am I?" I asked Valerie. I had to ask the question twice before the girls all simmered down to answer me. Stamford General Hospital.

"Tia was here earlier. We've been watching over you in shifts," Valerie said.

"Mimi and Cassandra went down to the café for a bite to eat," said Charisma.

Then Egypt said, "Wait 'til Cassandra finds out you're awake. She's gonna do cartwheels."

"I feel like Rip van Winkle."

"Who's that?" asked Elise.

"Never mind, Elise . . . it's just a fairy tale—an American fairy tale," I said. "Does anyone know what happened?"

"You don't remember? Deja's boyfriend? The morons with him?"

"Oh. The bats." It hurt just thinking about it.

"Yeah," said Egypt. "They hurt you pretty bad, but the doctors say you'll be good as new—everything in working order."

"Everything?"

Valerie chuckled and said, "Yes . . . *everything.*" I could swear I caught her winking at me.

"Jesus. My head is *killing* me. What day is it?"

"It's July seventh," Valerie replied. "The day after, Mr. Lewis."

"Do me a favor, Valerie."

I had her complete attention, as if sex might be an option.

"Call me Spencer from now on, okay? I feel like we've all been through enough to be on a first-name basis."

Valerie smiled, expressing that she would be okay with that, but also that she didn't mind being let down easy.

"What were you all talking about while I was in never-never land?"

"Egypt was going over some astrology with us. Tellin' us what to expect of our futures 'n stuff."

With a light chuckle underneath my words, I said, "Well, I guess if anybody knows that stuff, it's her." They couldn't possibly know I'd be snooping.

"Tell 'em what you told Cassandra, Egypt. Remember Miss Gemini? And check this out, Spencer, how the things she's sayin' applies to both of them, Cassandra and Egypt. Go on, Egypt," urged Valerie.

"Well . . . I told her that she was full of passion, entrapped with the sheer beauty of ideas and expressions . . ."

Charisma was perched there on the hospital bed, next to my bandaged leg, her face expressing awe in response to Egypt's words. "Wow. Entrapped in the ways of passion," Charisma said.

"Cassandra tends to get caught up in perfection," continued Egypt. "But she's gonna have to be willing to break more than a few rules in the quest to use her special abilities . . ."

"See, Mr. Lewis? That's just *like* Egypt."

"You, too, Elise. Call me Spencer, please."

"Guess I gotta get used to it. Spencer. Well, that stuff she said about breaking rules? That's definitely Egypt. You shoulda seen her in San Diego, how she tipped the bartender."

"What's so bad about that?" I asked.

"You had to be there," Charisma said. "She just grabbed his collar, like this." Charisma pretended someone was in front of her and put her two hands out as if to grab that imaginary person's shirt collar. "Then she just pulled him in and kissed him. I mean a full-blown, wet-your-whistle *kiss*." Charisma with the sound effects, I looked at Egypt, knowing that the girl was a little extreme in how she did things. In that instant I calculated that on a scale from one to ten, ten being the least extreme, the kiss rated a nine. As far as I was concerned, Egypt's act during our interview (her eye-opening, butt-naked dance) was as close to a number-one rating as could be.

"Can I finish?" Egypt asked.

The girls were snickering, but they let her go on.

"Anyway . . . It was just that Cassandra has a strong, competitive spirit and always manages to find energy as she reaches for her star."

"Like I said . . . the girl *is* deep," I noted.

"Relief is *here*. Oh my *God*. You're up! You're *awake!*" exclaimed Cassandra as she and Mimi stepped into the room. Both of them had flowers in hand.

I put a hand up to hopefully stop Cassandra as she lunged for me.

"No, Cassandra. I'm still in pain, baby."

"How about my supersoft and sensitive hug, and maybe a bigger kiss," she haggled.

The ooohs and awws filled the hospital room. Five women sounded like ten.

"Just take it easy, girl . . . everything feels broken, lips included."

Mimi asked, "You feeling better, Mr. Lewis?"

"A little bit, Mimi. How's Tia? Did those dudes hurt anybody? I still don't know what happened."

"You should've seen us . . . it was like *Mission: Impossible*, how we handled those guys . . ."

Cassandra said, "They took us like prisoners, Spencer. Had all of us in the house, interrogating us about where Deja was being hidden . . ."

"Deja's boyfriend wouldn't believe us. We told him you all took her home, but Deja doesn't have a phone at home, so there was no way for him to call. But why take it out on us? Why hold us captive?"

"In the meantime we were schemin' on them dudes," said Valerie. "Trina was seducing one guy. Sugar and Denise were working on the big guy . . . the one with the missin' tooth."

"And I had the exclusive attention of the tall one with the diamond earring," said Charisma. "Got him to leave the room with me and everything."

"What'd you do with that guy anyway, Charisma? How'd you get him tied up like that? Shoulda seen how she had that man, Spencer. Tied up like a Bronco at a rodeo."

"It's a secret," Charisma said.

"Are you tellin' me that you all overpowered those cats?" An inquiring mind, me, wanted to know.

"Sorta. We had them all seduced . . . open like you wouldn't believe. In the end, they turned out to be weak."

"We had his buddies tied up, locked in rooms, or half asleep—Mimi put some sleeping pills in the coffee—all of us tackled Squirm. What could he do?"

"I bet he never had so many women on him at once."

"I bit his cheek!" exclaimed Elise.

"Well, I kneed him in the dick!" said Egypt with pride.

I was laughing so hard it hurt. The big bad boys with bats, outsmarted by amateur models.

"They're in a lot of trouble, last I heard. Mrs. Tia called the cops . . . I think one of the neighbors did, too. Must've been the motorcycles they parked on the street. Suspicious."

"Mmm . . . so they're in jail? That only means they'll be back on the street after bail," I suggested.

"I doubt it," said Valerie. "Mrs. Tia said something about a judge she knew down in Stamford. Stern, is it? I understand that they're gonna be locked up long enough to supply all of Connecticut with new license plates."

Cassandra added, "Trespassing, kidnapping, assault with intent to kill. Trust me, babe, somebody's gonna pay something, somehow, after all of this mess. And, oooh, my boobie is all bandaged up and in pain . . ." Cassandra's lips were pursed as she said this, all sympathetic as she zeroed in another peck on the lips.

I WAS well enough to go home just a few days later. They rolled me out of the hospital in a wheelchair because of the sore ribs and the dizzy spells, but I was determined to live again, to be a normal being again. I intended to be up and about within days, maybe sooner.

It felt a lot different going back to the house, as if the whole world knew me inside out. No stone was left unturned. They knew my pains and my anguish. They knew that I was victimized and that I received a major beat-down. They watched me bleed. And one more thing . . . By now, everyone had to know that Cassandra and I were up there butt-naked, doin' the *damned thing*, when Squirm and his crew busted in. Everyone including Tia, who was an even bigger problem. Bigger, almost, than the royal ass-whuppin' I took.

There was no acting, or performing, or lying my way out of this situation. In San Diego, my going to bed with Cassandra could be taken as a one-time-only affair. Something that just happened. Tia could accept that as a sort of punishment for dissing me, *the black man*, and then marching off and leaving San Diego in a huff. She believed what I told her, that I was faking so that we might engross ourselves in some hot and angry sex. She believed every word. But the other day was nothing isolated like in San Diego; we'd been caught with the smoking gun, so to speak. Clothes off and too shocked and afraid to be embarrassed. That was then; this is now.

"Egypt . . . before we get home, can you give me a lecture about *my* future? Something to lift my spirits?"

"What's your birthday?"

"February. February second."

Egypt put her hand on her knee, closed her eyes, and took a deep breath. My eyes shifted over to Cassandra, who was at my side in the back of the limousine, all of us heading up I-95.

Cassandra rolled her eyes, then Egypt said, "You sometimes feel the need to please everyone, but you will have to avoid the traps of popularity and take a stand for what you truly believe . . ."

I'm listening to her and trying to absorb the heavy meaning in the words, but somehow I just couldn't get those past images out of my head—Egypt with the stiff breasts and pointed nipples. Egypt with the slim line of pubic hair that disappeared once it reached . . . right . . . there. Still her words went on.

"You fall for trends, fads, and beliefs, but aside of that, you must keep your challenges and dig deeper beneath your own surface. Discover your true nature and innermost needs. You are destined for real success, Spencer. Personal satisfaction will be yours. Except, there is a trap that you must avoid: that space between the need to please others and the need to please yourself. If you get stuck there in that space, you may somehow fail at both."

When Egypt finished, I swear that I could've drifted off to sleep again, as spellbound as I was. But sleep was so far away from how my body felt, filled with anxiety, the want to move around, to be active despite the pains. Lying down in the hospital bed for days had me stiff and restless. Those statements got me: *I had to take a stand for what I truly believed. I was destined for success.* And the thing that was hitting me hardest: *I had to choose between the need to please others and the need to please myself. If I didn't, I'd fail.*

I tried to apply some of the things that Egypt said to some of the issues that I had to address. I *did take a stand* for what I truly believed. I didn't think that it was right for those thugs to put their hands on Tia, and *because* of my stand, I got my ass kicked. Was I destined for success? I always *imagined* I was. True, I never quite knew how it would happen, but I somehow assumed it would.

And this thing about choosing: Was I pleasing others by keeping a physical relationship with Tia *and* Cassandra, when I really only wanted someone who was right for me? Wasn't Cassandra right for me? Didn't she mirror everything that I am about? Didn't she complement my peanut butter with her jelly? Didn't she feed my hunger with her abundant spirit, and inevitably satisfy me from head to toe? Wasn't Cassandra devoted and dutified, honorable and committed? Didn't she believe in me?

Egypt was right. Tia was the "others" that I felt I needed to please, while Cassandra was all I needed to please myself. It was time to take another stand—and make that big choice in life. This was a time to tie up loose ends . . . a time to face the music.

[E I G H T E E N]

"DO ME A favor?"

Cassandra sucked her teeth and put her hands on her hips. A salty expression across her face.

"I am just so tired of doing you favors, *mister.*" Cassandra's sudden change in attitude shook me and I froze in my tracks, looking at her with wild eyes. That's when her sneer melted into a saucy grin. "How you like *my* acting," she said, with her hands still on her hips and her leg cocked out front in a pose.

I wagged my head, tricked again, wondering who among us *didn't* act or pretend.

"You know I'd do anything for you, baby," Cassandra said, now slithering up to me out in front of the house. The rest of the girls had just gone inside and I had waved the limo off. It was just me and the braided, beautiful one now. "Just say the word, and it's yours." Cassandra said that with eyes that dug into my own, promising me the world if I asked for it. Mmm-mmm-mmm, that felt so good to see and hear. Just the devotion was like a slam dunk that sent shivers through me.

"Let me go and have a word with Tia before I come up with you. There are a couple of things that I need to straighten out with her."

"Well, hurry, I'll be upstairs . . ." She kissed me. "Keepin' warm . . ." She kissed me again. "For you." There was another kiss before I nodded to Mr. Kim, who had been standing in the doorway, waiting to assist me.

He hurried up and helped me into the wheelchair and pushed me into the house. Cassandra went her own way into the garage, where I'm sure she had a little cleanup to engage in. It's not every day that a band of thugs bust into a girl's home.

"Take me to her, Kim."

"Miss Tia in back, inside porch."

Since my right arm was in a sling, I pointed with my left, as if I were a general leading the troops into battle.

I put my finger to my lips as we approached her, indicating that Mr. Kim should ease me up to her side. Tia was lying there, relaxing in a lounge chair, the indoor lights off, a few candles burning on the table, her sunglasses on despite it being close to dusk.

I waved Mr. Kim off and I sat watching Tia for some time. I imagined that she had to be asleep, having not been obvious about my presence. She had a robe on, a pink silk with fur lining and fringes. Lord only knew what she had on underneath, but I didn't venture to speculate. What I had to do had nothing to do with sex and everything to do with me. Still, I couldn't help but to know this woman's body; her sculpted calves and legs peeking out past the end of the robe.

Her hands were clasped there on her waist weathered by
experience and some age, with fingernails that were
picturesque, painted with the detail of a masterpiece. Her
face showed her remaining youth and at the same time the
promise of old age. Even though the eyes were shaded, I
knew the importance in them. I knew their depth and
meaning, even if they were idle and inattentive toward me. I
knew every inch of this woman. *Every centimeter.* And I
suddenly felt crazy to want to throw this all away. Insane for
not keeping the pleasures that she awarded me.

"You're having a hard time doing it, aren't you?" I was
startled. How long did she know that I was sitting there?
What, do I stink? The woman was forever filled with
surprises.

"Hard time doing what?"

"You think that I don't know? You think that I am blind?
That I somehow forgot you and her . . . naked there in her
studio?"

"I . . ." My mouth let out an exhaustive *phew,* her having
covered so much with so few words. "Wow . . ."

"So San Diego was more than just a one-time love
affair . . . Tell me, Spencer, when exactly did you start
fuckin' Cassandra? Was it the day that she started working
here? Or was it at the Marriott, sometime during the
interviews . . . a quickie perhaps?"

"Tia. You're blowing this up much bigger than it is . . .
San Diego was when it started. Just like I said."

"And then?"

"Tia, I came in here to tell you the truth. The whole
truth. Cassandra and I are in love. I love her *and* she loves
me. Not an inch less than that."

"Oh." Tia still looking up at the indoor plants in the massive atrium around us.

"Yes, we've been together since San Diego. A number of times."

"That so?"

"Come on, Tia, what'd you expect? I'm not a *bad*-lookin' guy. And every day I am around these young voluptuous women. Seen them half-naked, fully naked, I duck and dodge their advances. When it comes down to it, I'm just a man. I'm not *Superman*."

"I guess you're right," said Tia, hardly budging the whole time that we spoke. "A man's gotta do what a man's gotta do, right?"

"Uh . . . right," I hesitated to say.

"So then tell me, Spencer. Are you man enough to take us both on?"

"Huh?"

"Just what I said." Tia lifted up out of her relaxed position and sat facing me. "Are you man enough to take both of us? Two relationships, you know, sharing."

"Tia . . . I . . ."

"You don't know what to say? You never thought that I'd go for that?" Tia stood up. "I have news for you, lover. I've invested a lot of money in . . . uh . . . with you, and I *don't* intend on losing out to some young, wet-behind-the-ears bitch trying to steal my man from under my nose. So how about it? I don't want for much. A little here, a little there. You don't even have to take me out, how's that? Very, very little maintenance. And . . . how about this; we can keep it our little secret. And in the meantime, everything continues to go on smoothly. Just like we always said."

I was suffocated and speechless. What could I say? How could I turn down a woman who was willing to allow me to have my cake and eat it, too? I felt subservient again, with Tia standing over me. Now she put her finger under my chin and lifted it. "Having a hard time saying yes? Let me help you decide."

Tia undid the belt of her robe and had it fall to the floor by her feet; again with the striptease. She put her hands on her hips—the pose of a mannequin in the window of a clothing boutique. *Check this out, shopper!* Only Tia was virtually saying, *Turn this down Spencer!*

"Take a good look at me, Spencer. From head to toe. Look at *all this woman*. Rich, brown, soft, flexible, sexy . . . every part of it touched by you . . . kissed by you. This woman is familiar. She's safe. She'll not only satisfy your body, but she'll enrich *your mind*. She'll do wonders for your soul. Take a good look at me and tell me you want to turn this down."

Tia's eyes were daring and promising at once. As much as I'd been familiar with Tia, just like she said, I still couldn't turn her down. I just couldn't get myself to say no. Just like the very first time, I was just as excited now. Where was Cassandra when I needed her?! My silence indicated my agreement, and Tia bent over. She supported herself on the armrests of the wheelchair and gave me the most sensual kiss, busy with her tongue inside of my lips.

"If I didn't see it myself I wouldn't have believed it." The voice came from behind me. It was *certainly* Cassandra's voice. My face changed to that of one who had just swallowed a rat; a rat still alive and scratching at my larynx as it struggled to survive.

Tia stopped the kissing and the fondling at my zipper.

She showed no surprise as she dipped down to pick up her robe. I squeezed my eyes closed, not knowing what to say. *Caught again.*

"What did you think, darling? That your mother was a dried-up hag? Did you think I'd be living with Spencer just to do business? Because if *that's* what you thought, then you're as naïve as a newborn."

My mouth was open from the word *mother*. I couldn't believe it. *I didn't want to believe it.* Then I thought back to that photo: a young Cassandra in a classroom at her desk. The lie about her being the *daughter of a friend at the tennis center.* Of course! Tia was Cassandra's mother! From who, though? From the judge? Or the music producer, Ken? And now that I thought of it, what were they *thinking* matching Cassandra and me up for the Premium Fudge venture? My *assistant* . . . why didn't they just tell the truth? I swiveled the wheelchair around, the inexperienced wheeler that I was, to look at Cassandra. There was anger in her eyes, directed toward Tia, but once I set my eyes on her, those eyes of a man betrayed, Cassandra looked away. Her arms were folded. She was shaking, like a turkey on Thanksgiving Eve, just before they met with the oven.

Sure, I was a cheater in Tia's eyes, a two-timer in Cassandra's eyes—but what was Tia but a liar and a con artist? And if Cassandra was somehow a part of this con, what was she but a pretender, a liar, a con herself?

"I was gonna tell you, Spencer. Tonight, I was gonna tell you. But *never* did I think you'd be—*oh my God!* She's more than twice your age! She's old enough to be *your* mother . . . I mean, God, Spencer! She *is* a mother!! MY MOTHER!! Who knew that you were *lovers?*"

In tears, Cassandra ran off until I heard the front door close, but not before she flashed a fiery gaze at her mom.

I turned back to Tia. She shrugged.

"So now you know. At least we don't have to hide anymore."

"Where are you taking me?" I asked as my wheelchair lurched forward.

"You need some TLC. We're gonna get you a nice bath . . . GIRLS!"

"But . . . shit, Tia, look at how fucked up things are! How the fuck could you bring your daughter in here, have her work with me, and not say anything? What, was that suppose to be slick? A trick?"

"We'll talk about it later. Right now, you need to simmer down. We need to get you some attention."

WHAT COULD I do?

Recuperating would certainly be a priority. And once I was all healed up, I figured I had to get away from these crazy women. Tia and Cassandra, both. I couldn't believe that I was fucking *mother and daughter*.

I had enough money saved to get my own crib, and if things didn't work out business-wise, where I could operate Premium Fudge from, say, an office in downtown Stamford, then I could always start from scratch. How hard could it be since I'd already done it once? Since I knew all there was to know about the business? And it was probably best that all of the skeletons came out of the closet earlier than later. Before anything more than emotions and money were at stake. *Shit*, I grew immediately callous from their sudden revelations. As far as my emotions were concerned, I was numb. And as far as money goes, much of the money invested in Premium Fudge was Tia's to begin with, so no sweat off my back. That is, except for the experience and hard work. But I imagine that could be chalked up to establishing good habits. Patterns of success.

"You need to sit down and learn something from this here gentleman. He might be young, but he's got it on the ball."

Those proclamations by Mrs. Smith, Deja's mother, were still fresh on my mind. Only now they just had begun to have an impact. Whether it was how I carried myself, how I communicated with others, or how I managed to make the best of my resources to pull myself up and out of the 'hood, and the limitations which the 'hood baked into the souls of those who lived there, I was doing *something* right. If I was left on the street with nothing but my mind and body to carry me, I could still accomplish some things; make my mark in the world.

But first things first; I couldn't let these two—whatever they were up to—get in my way.

SOMETHING WAS slowing this process. I was as alert as a bright morning sun the day that I returned from the hospital. I was shocked and amazed by what I had learned, and then, finally, I was determined to bail out the first chance that I got. But it was that evening, after a bath, some tea, painkillers, and a nap, that I had felt heavy. My eyelids would barely open. I felt sounds drumming at my mind's walls instead of merely hearing them. Something was warm and tingling in my arms, fingers, legs, and toes. I didn't feel the pain that I had left the hospital with, although I was conscious of the bandage still on my head, the cast on my arm, and the padding around my ribs and torso. The only desire that I had was to accumulate some more sleep. That seemed to be the only answer.

Later, it felt like I woke up again. Only now the room changed. I wasn't in my bedroom, with the modern conveniences and effects that I had grown so accustomed to seeing. Instead there was the dark red and green upholstered furniture. There was that gaudy feel about the room—dark and moody like in the corner of a candlelit café—that played on my brain like a bloody aftermath in a horror flick. Some jazzy music—was it Miles? Coltrane?—was filtering into my ears, louder than a pulse, but softer than a whisper.

Before I could think of what to say, I felt a hand at the back of my neck, propping my head up for the warm tea that streamed along my tongue. My throat muscles acted on their own to swallow the tea, because that's how throat muscles have been trained to respond. It's liquid, it's sweet, and it's familiar, so swallow. There were words. A woman's voice. My lips, stimulated by the warm tea cup, managed to form a word, a response, a plea.

"Tia . . ." Two painkillers were placed in my mouth, then more tea. And my head was laid back again, my body sensing a touch, fingers, hands, sliding along my bare chest. Something slick being basted onto me. Oil? Lotion?

Again, I murmured, "Tia . . . ," and then all went black again.

I was rocking back and forth. My eyes were closed and I was drowsy as I last remembered, but I could still feel my body in motion. Side to side. Back and forth. Hands suddenly buried themselves at my sides, making impressions in the mattress where I laid. I managed to open my lids enough to see Tia there on top of me, fitted onto me, and in deep concentration. She pursed her lips, she gritted her teeth, and her eyes were shut.

Her head bobbed up and down and back so that she was facing the sheer canopy over the bed, even if she wasn't looking at it. Even though I was not a participant in her freakish act, I was indeed cooperating. Or, at least my body was. What was it they said? Something about it having a mind of its own.

In the meantime, as I served as the perfect saddle, a saddle with a joystick, I watched Tia carry on with her hootin' and hollerin'. Nothing new here. Only I had to be the closest thing to a corpse, there for her very personal enjoyment.

There was a finale she went through. A manly grunt, and then some panting, as though she needed air, and then the ultimate scream. Her screaming always had two effects on me: It either embarrassed the hell out of me, making me happy that the room was soundproofed, or it got me off, because I had somehow given this woman pleasure from out of this world.

In my helpless state, now, I was feeling neither. I just hoped her screaming was loud enough for somebody to come and *get her off of me*.

Sounds were clearer since the scream. Her voice . . . "Oooh, yes—yes—yesyesyesyesyes . . . yes! Spencer! I could never let you go. I could *never* let another woman take you from me. No matter who it is . . ." Tia seemed so talkative, so exhilarated from the high, the nirvana, and then the climax. She let out her own body fluids, drowning me, making things icky down there.

I continued to watch her with unfeeling eyes, knowing this sight from times before; our history together. Tia didn't know what to do with herself. She grabbed her hair, her breasts, her face, and she bit down on the fingers in her mouth. There was, it seemed to me, so much energy locked up inside of this woman, even after the fact.

Then, in a rush toward her objective, Tia climbed off of me, and just as soon, took me into her mouth. Maybe at some other place and time this would be heaven, but for me, more than less a captive of hers, this was absolute hell. If I had the urge, I would toss up what was in my stomach. Painkillers, tea, whatever.

THERE WAS knocking. I had heard this sound a few times before—I wouldn't possibly know how many—and again, Tia's voice sung out, "*Who?*"

And just as before, I couldn't make out who answered Tia. Although, at least now, I realized the knocking was at the bedroom door. There was the muffled voice, then Tia chirped, "*Hold on . . . be right with you.*"

This time I could make out Mimi's Norwegian accent. "Ms. Tia, there are all kinds of messages . . . calls regarding Premium Fudge. Calls from San Diego. Calls from the photographers. Somebody from a lawyers' convention—"

"*Quiet.* Mimi, I told you two days ago, take a message."

"But Ms.—"

"Don't talk back to me, Mimi, or I'll let you go. Now run along. You and the girls go out and play in the pool. Stay out of my hair. I'm busy."

Mimi managed to say, "Cassandra left, Ms. Tia. We don't know—"

Mimi's sentence was never completed.

Tia had slammed the door shut. Bolted it, too.

"Why can't these nuisance bitches leave us alone, Spencer? Can't they see that we're on our honeymoon?"

That word raised enough of a red flag for me to muster enough strength. I felt my face tense up into a question mark.

"Yes, darling. You and I are now Mr. and Mrs. Spencer Lewis . . ." Tia let out a rejoicing sigh. "It was an expensive deal, paying a preacher to come in here and fix things up so we could make it official. I had to lie to him, you know . . . tell him you were on your deathbed. But . . ." Tia raised up her hand where on her finger was a big glistening ring. A wedding ring fit for a queen. "You'd be surprised what ten thousand dollars could buy these days."

I used all of my might to look down at my hand: A wedding band. OH SHIT! SHE CAN'T BE SERIOUS!

I yelled. I screamed. I hollered and I made the call-of-the-wild like some broken Tarzan. But every sound remained unheard, welled up in my throat with literally no energy with which to push them out. All that I could manage was a whimper.

"Oh, I know, baby. I know. I could just see the happiness in your eyes. It's calling out to me. And . . . yes, I can hear your mind. I can feel your joy. And I love you right back, Spencer. I love you right back . . ."

The tear that rolled down my cheek was not so as to correspond with Tia's tears. It was not a happy tear. It was my unheard cry for help.

"I WANNA go home!" a girl's voice screamed. It woke me more than the preceding knock, the "Who?" and the muffled voice thereafter. I got my lids open enough to see a watery image of a woman. She had very short hair. I immediately guessed that it was Elise by the accent and the hair combined. And then the image cleared some. I had energy to rise.

"You can *go* home. Take your shit and *go!*"

And again, Tia slammed and bolted the door.

"These children! Arrrgh! Why did I even let them in my house?!" She stood there with folded arms, back to me.

"Tia," I said. "What are you doing?"

Tia spun around with the quickness. The surprise was evident on her face, in her eyes.

"What are *you* doing out of bed?" Tia was a couple of feet from me now.

"I . . . I'm better. I wanna go out . . . talk to the—"

Girls, I wanted to talk to the girls, but *girls* was smacked right out of my mouth. Tia's blow half-spun me and I fell to the floor, writhing in pain. *My arm. My head. My ribs.*

"Ohhhhh . . ." My volume was low, like a hum, but it didn't make the pain any less extreme.

"Did I TELL you you could go out? That you could talk to the girls? Did I, husband? Now look at what you've gone and made me do." Tia made the tsk-tsk-tsk sound with her tongue against her guns. Pity on me. "You have *got to* be more careful. Now you're gonna have to be bedridden for another few weeks. Maybe a month or two. That means more Valium, more of my special tea . . . Oh, Spencer, what am I gonna do with you?"

I couldn't remember ever sobbing, sobbing like a two-year-old, like I was sobbing now. Minutes later, Tia was back at me. Painkillers and water.

"Here, baby, take these. Come on, open wide," she said. But I kept the pressure. My lips wouldn't part.

"Oh, come—come," Tia said, and she put her hand on my leg and squeezed.

My mouth opened with a harrowing, agony-filled cry. I wanted to die, but what I *didn't* wanna do was disobey Tia again.

"Now that's a perfect husband. A husband who listens and does *as he's told*. Now, for being belligerent, you get to lay there for an hour. Mmm-mmm-mmm . . . you really must be more careful, Spencer."

As I lay there on the floor, my body in shambles and as weak as an ant in a mudslide, I begged for the painkillers to set in and take me away. I just wanted to disappear.

[N I N E T E E N]

THIS WAS A much bigger knock than the ones before. In
fact, it was more of a smash. It seemed like so much time
had passed since the last interaction at the door. Time
that found me so lost in pill-popping, sleep, and being
semiconscious for whatever pleasure-seeking that Tia called
for.

"Spencer!" a man's voice called out. "Spencer, it's Troy!
Can you hear me?" The voice was accompanied by a touch,
a woman's touch to my cheek.

"Spencer, it's me, Cassandra. Are you okay? Can you
hear me, baby?"

"So . . . brother dear to the rescue," said Tia. I couldn't
see her, but I could sure feel her presence.

"Ms. Tia, please. We don't want any trouble. I'm just
gonna take my brother home."

"You can't do that."

"Sorry, lady, but if you get in my way, I'm—"

"Let me handle this, Troy," Cassandra said. "It's over,
Mother. Your little game is over. You got me to go along

with your scheme in the beginning, all that talk about wanting to keep our personal lives out of the way. And now, come to think of it, it really is true . . . I mean our personal lives are indeed screwed up . . . too screwed up to understand. You might have been right to want to keep our little family problems quiet, but not anymore. Not since I fell in love. Not since I found out that I'm *pregnant*. The game is over, Mother."

"So you think," said Tia with a deep gritty laughter under her words. Troy was helping me from the bed as I listened to this. "I'll just have you know that you are speaking to a newlywed, Miss Thang. I am now *Mrs. Lewis*, something that you'll never be." Tia held up that ring again, admiring it with that awesomely wicked smile of hers.

"Huh. You must be kidding," Cassandra said, and then Cassandra came over, worked the band off of my finger, and approached Tia. Cassandra fitted the band over the tip of her middle finger and, using her thumb and finger together, flicked it at Tia. She then said, "You can take your wedding ring and stick it up your ass. You know, it's actually a good thing that you left us to live with Dad. I was better off with him. Imagine if I grew up to be like you. Yuck!" Cassandra backstepped and helped Troy. "Come on, dude . . . we got some healing to do. You *and* me."

As Troy and Cassandra helped me to the door, Tia scurried over in front of us.

"Miss . . . I already warned you. I will hit a woman if I have to," Troy said.

"Stupid youngsters," she said, closing the broken double doors as best she could. "Don't you know how these situations end up? Haven't you all seen the movies? Do you *believe* that you all get to just walk out of here? Leave with *my* prize? Huh? I made Spencer what he is. Groomed him. Trained him. You see . . . how this is supposed to end is that the scorned woman—"

As Tia spoke, she also presented a palm-sized pistol, her hand emerging from beneath her silk robe. "—wins in the end."

All of us sucked in air.

"You see, back in the day, I always got my man. Whether it was on TV or in real life, Tia is not to be denied her pleasures. Isn't that right, Spencer . . . and you, Cassandra . . . you sure are cast from your father's mold. Ken was always so bold . . . he always tried to challenge me, but as with all things, I shall win in the end . . . like now." Tia shifted the pistol toward Troy. She said, "No sense playing hero, Mister Kentucky Fried Ghetto. I'm a good shot, I promise you. Now where was I? Oh yes . . . Cassandra . . . my beautiful daughter. My only child. Did you know that you were unwanted? That I went to a doctor to get rid of you? But that damned Ken, he crashed my party. He saved your life. I bet he didn't tell you that, did he? Bet he didn't tell you that that's why we broke up, did he?"

"You scandalous bitch. How dare you try and crush my existence? Your spiteful ways. I can't even believe that I came out of you. I hope it was the worst pain that you ever experienced. I hope that you felt yourself ripping when I came out." Cassandra spit on Tia. I *know* Troy had to be as dumbfounded as I was. *Cassandra, what are you doing? She has a gun!!*

Tia was calm, however. She said, "So I made a mistake trying to work you back into my life. It's much too late anyway. After all of these years, I understand your pain, darling. I do, but hell if you're gonna take my family jewels. That boy is bought and paid for. Let him go. Now, or I start shooting. And I'll start with you, bitch!"

Just then, the doors were pushed in behind Tia, knocking her forward. The gun went off. Troy spun away from me unharmed. All that I could hear was *Oh God!* All I could see was pandemonium. Cassandra hurried me away from the melee as fast as she could, while as many as three, four, or five of our models rushed Tia. Qianna had a leg, Denise had another; Sugar grabbed Tia from behind, and Valerie struggled to take the gun away from her. Shots went off. Again and again and again, until the pistol was empty. Everyone with near deaf hearing.

Cassandra got up and charged toward the others, as if she wasn't satisfied with how this was going.

Close enough now, Cassandra said, "Let her go. Let her go!" A face-off.

Cassandra slapped Tia. Tia put her hand to her cheek and turned back with an enraged look at her daughter.

Cassandra said, "You never were my mother. Just a place to stay until I was born." Cassandra followed her words with a left hook that caught the side of Tia's face. Tia hit the floor with a rippling thud.

"You were right. A scorned woman does win in the end."

[CONCLUSION]

SO MUCH HAS changed in two years.

Most important, Cassandra just had our second child, also a girl. Of course, I've been wanting a boy, somebody to look like and grow up like me—but I guess we can't always have what we want, especially if it's nature's rules that control things. I don't mind that Cassandra and I keep on trying. Often.

We have plenty of hope taking care of Hope and Dream. One of the girls is always at home with us, glad to sit, feed, and even change diapers. I still get a big laugh out of that, supermodels changing the babies' shitty diapers. The stereotype is so much the opposite, where these girls are pampered dawn to dusk and that they party dusk to dawn.

Well, *our* Premium Fudge—our models—are not your everyday average or ordinary celebrity chicks. Like *Egypt*, for instance. She's been in constant demand, just like the others, but never did the phone calls and inquiries come in more—from fashion designers, video producers, and movie directors—than after Egypt showed up at the VH1 Fashion Show Awards on a media mogul's arm as his date for the evening. She basically outshined him. Egypt in the super-tight knee-length Dolce & Gabbana skirt, the polka dot blouse tied off at the navel and the very high-heeled lizard sandals. All that and the sexy smile have gotten her two-page spreads in *W, Vogue,* and *Mademoiselle* magazines.

Denise has been making us proud with her face and sensual dancing in six rock music videos so far. One rock icon wants her to join him for his movie debut as sort of lady-next-to-the-leading-man. No matter; the more expo-sure, the better.

Qianna isn't working as much as the other girls. Her image is constant, however, since Cassandra got her on the package of Dark & Lovely, seen on probably every super-market shelf in America.

Deja was put to work the moment she returned with consent from her parents. Cassandra has her likeness on the cover of three paperback romance novels. She's been the leading lady in three R&B music videos—exclusive to those songs that are of the smoothed-out, candlelit-incense-and-furry-rug theme.

Valerie is more of a devotee and soldier to our purpose at Premium Fudge Unlimited. She not only answers phones, does light office work, and looks after the children now and then, but she also serves as a knowledgeable spokesperson for the company. When we go out to further the P.F. brand, such as conventions, trade shows, and whatnot, Valerie is right there at your service.

Sadly, *Sugar* died in a plane crash. She had been away on a photo shoot for the swimsuit issue of a popular men's magazine. By her own choice, she chose to take a flight with one of the magazine's photographers on a chartered plane instead of the commercial flight and its first-class seat. The pursuit of the photographer ultimately added an additional 100-plus pounds to a flight that was already overburdened. And, so, Sugar went down with the plane.

All of the girls made appropriate cancellations to come together for Sugar's funeral. Even *Lia*, who was scheduled to costar in her first movie, a movie with a fourteen-million-dollar budget.

The funeral ultimately brought us all closer together, where the girls affirmed all sorts of vows. One being that they wouldn't waver from the overall purpose, the success of Premium Fudge, and every individual in the family.

Trina and *Elise* could be seen in clothing catalogs wearing the outfits of Calvin Klein, Versace, and Victoria's Secret. They also get constant calls to walk the runways for these designers, earning as much as $5,000 to $10,000 a day.

Charisma is winning, now touring the world for her second year as a cover girl.

ON FEBRUARY 2, my twenty-second birthday, I was pleasantly surprised. Everyone gathered at the house in Stamford. They trickled in on the first, so it wasn't as big of a surprise as it should have been, but I was over-whelmed nonetheless. Cassandra was fixing my bow tie, getting me all ready for the formal dinner that three cooks prepared.

"Big night, huh?" I said, looking over Cassandra, into the mirror.

"Big night, for our big man. You know all of those girls downstairs owe their success to you, Spencer."

"No you don't. Don't go laying all the blame on me, Cassandra. You had a lot to do with it, too. A lot."

"But it was *your* dream. I just helped you push things a little."

"True," I smiled proudly, welcoming the boost to my ego. "You know, Cassandra . . . I really miss everybody here all at once, but at the same time, I'm happy to see them out there growing . . . doing their—"

Cassandra put her hand over my lips.

"Spencer? Save it for the girls. Tell *them* how you feel." Another good idea.

THEY ALL raised their glasses. All of them with the most glamorous dresses, the most sparkling jewelry, and the most impeccable overall appearances, enough to take my breath away . . .

". . . And that's what you all do for me . . . you take my breath away. Not a day passes that I don't see your faces on TV, in magazines, in the movies . . . here at the house, and I just can't put in words how proud you all make me . . . yes, I've heard it time and time again . . . my dream. Right— well, guess what? Making my dreams come true is the result of my dream. So, as good as this feels, to contribute to your lives, I hope that you turn around and do the same for others. In some way I hope that you take what you've learned from me and become leaders in your own right. I don't want you

to merely exist out there . . . out there in that cruel, cruel
world . . . the world that hardly promises tomorrow. No . . .
I want you to be leaders in your own circles, large and
small. A lot of you will be living lives and building families
of your own—some sooner than most—and you'll marry
some jet-setter, some movie star or rock star, ahem,
Denise . . ."

The mention got a lot of laughter along with Denise.

"But no matter where life takes you, help to encourage
those in your circle—your children, your lover, your
parents. Make that contribution stick more than just
becoming another pretty face."

"So now that the godfather has spoken . . . I want to say
something. And really, I'm trying not to cry, seeing
Charisma—our cover girl standing right there in my face . . .
you are so beautiful, Carrie . . . you're representing all of us
out there on the front line. You make us all so proud. Truly,
truly proud . . ."

Cassandra pulled away a tear with the back of her wrist,
and then she went on to say, "Now . . . if I could just
straighten out here . . . I want to turn the attention . . . *all*
of the attention to *this* man. My man. The father of my two
daughters. Daddy to all of us. We . . . are truly blessed to
know you, Mr. Spencer Lewis. And it's been quite a time
we've gone through together, with the early struggles;
well . . . you know the story. Anyway. Uhm . . . we . . . you
and I never quite got around to this, just something
small . . ."

Cassandra passed me a flat jewelry box.

"This is a bracelet I got for you—just a little something
to commemorate the occasion . . . could you sit down for a

minute? I know it's not ladylike to do this—so against the grain and all—but I felt I wanted to . . . to show you how much I love you . . ."

Cassandra went down on one knee. A whoosh of expressions and responses swept through the dining hall.

"Spencer Lewis . . . would you marry me?"

I felt incredible and guilty all at once. The love of my life kneeling to ask for my hand in marriage. Something I should've done, and which after two children was long overdue.

I always had one excuse after another. Always busy with building these careers, when I really should've been making the ultimate commitment to Cassandra.

"Get up, Cassandra; *of course* I'll marry you. And not a day past February fourteenth!"

Applause filled the room. Oohs and awws.

"Febru—"

I cut her words off with a deep-throat kiss. When I stopped, she started to talk again. And I cut her off again. I finally gave her a chance to speak, embarrassment washing over her face.

"That's twelve days away."

"But look at all of the help that we have—right, ladies?"

Everyone agreed and we ate better than ever.

LATER THAT night, Cassandra and I were up in what once was her mother's room, since Tia was still a long-term resident at the Reedmore Psychiatric Center. I was the first to admit that this was crazy, Cassandra and I occupying the same room . . . *the same bed* that her mother and I once frolicked in. But Cassandra took this very personal. She called it therapy for her, to mate and create with me in this room, in this particular bed. I started to think it was some ol' freak nasty idea she had. But soon I realized it as an affirmation of what and who was hers. It empowered her to know that she won me over her mom, and somehow she wouldn't fear her now. Now that she could lie here and not be ashamed, guilty, or afraid.

"Did I get to say happy birthday to you tonight?"

"I forgot. There was so much going on. I feel like I ate a cow."

"Forget what you feel like. You *look* like you walked into a kissing factory. All of this lipstick on your cheeks and whatnot. Smellin' like every third woman's fragrance. You oughtta be ashamed of yourself."

"I was gonna run off for the bathroom . . . tidy up a little."

"Wait a minute, mister," Cassandra said, her grips on the lapels of my tuxedo.

"Oooh . . . a little aggressive, are we? I *like* aggressive."

Cassandra smiled as we stood there and enjoyed one another. She said, "I don't want you out of my sight for the rest of the night—you've been with every other woman to-night, Mister Big."

"For the rest of the night, huh?"

"And until the morning."

"Well, *Miss-Gotta-Have-It*. I was just heading to the shower. Care to join me?"

"I do. And afterwards, I want you to help me with something."

"And what would that be?"

"I need your help to make another baby."

"I can do my best."

"And that's all that I ever want from you. Your best."

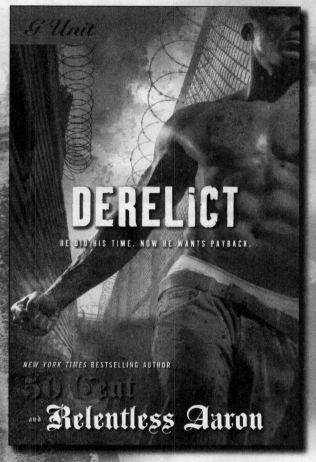